Escape from Texas

A Novel of Slavery
and the
Texas War of Independence

James W. Russell

2012
Sloan Publishing
Cornwall-on-Hudson, NY
12520

Library of Congress Cataloging-in-Publication Data

Russell, James W., 1944-
Escape from Texas : a novel / by James W. Russell.
p. cm.
ISBN 978-1-59738-035-5
1. Slaves--Texas--Fiction. 2. Texas--History--19th century--Fiction. I.
Title.
PS3618.U74926E83 2012
813'.6--dc23
2011047770

Sloan Publishing
220 Maple Road
Cornwall-on-Hudson, NY 12520

ISBN 978-1-59738-035-5

1

By the side of a horse trail in the Mexican state of Coahuila y Tejas a slumped-over black man, his hands tied around a tree, was regaining consciousness. It was still dark, the morning light an hour away. The first thing he felt was the burning pain on his back. The whiplashes had come down feeling like liquid fire. They had been so sudden that they had left him stunned, separating him momentarily from the pain, leaving him an instant to think that it was better to have pain on the back than around the neck. This consolation did little to salve the pain when it came full force or to prepare him for when lash after lash came down and cut through him like a scythe. His only respite had come from passing out, but that had not been altogether at first. It had not put his mind at rest. For the longest time his thoughts had swum from place to place and image to image. And then finally he had felt his mind begin to lose all activity. This he had thought was death coming. Instead of lynching him they were whipping him to death for being a runaway. But he had not died, he knew, because he was awakening from the pain in his back.

Because his hands were still tied around the tree, there was little he could do but bear the pain. After a while he willed a separation once again of the pain from his body and put it in a box. For a time he observed the pain. It was not his pain, he told himself, but a pain. He analyzed the pain. It pulsated, it burned, it jumped from part to part of the back. Then he tried another separation. The pain was in one box, his body in another. With pain and body so distanced, he tried to see if he could make his mind operate independently and he thought back when he had first stepped foot in Texas.

He had actually set foot *on* Texas the year before in 1828 from the sea—or rather the Gulf of Mexico. He was not sure whether there was a difference between a sea and a gulf. He had been sitting in a skiff headed for shore. High above the crashing surf a gull had been circling looking for prey, alternately sailing with the wind and then flapping its wings madly to regain momentum. Her screeches had broken through the lingering morning mist onto him and three others on board—his owner, Samuel Bingham, the wife of his owner, Sarah Bingham, and a sailor who was pulling hard at the oars.

With a bump the boat hit sand. The sailor jumped out into the surf, grabbed the bow, and began to pull. James—that was his name—also jumped out to push from the stern. When the boat scrapped up onto the sand he cupped his hand over his eyes to shade them from the now brightening morning sun and surveyed what lay before him. To his left, down the beach, water rushed out through the mouth of a river and into the Gulf, creating a swirl of foamy turbulence at the point of meeting. Beyond, low-lying grasslands stretched, interrupted at distinct points by piney woods.

"That's the Colorado River over there, sir, where that building is," the sailor said to Bingham. "They're building the port of Matagorda there."

"I know," Bingham replied, taking a coin out of his pocket. "This is for you."

"Thank you and best of luck to you, sir."

James watched the sailor push the skiff back into the surf to begin his trip back to the schooner that lay anchored a hundred yards out. He stood watching until the skiff was in deep enough water that the sailor had begun rowing against the incoming waves. Then he heard his owner say, "Come along now, James. They're supposed to meet us at the river."

He turned and picked up the luggage so that there were two valises under both of his arms and two larger suitcases hanging from both of his hands. His own possessions were in a bag slung over his shoulder. He fell in behind the Binghams as they began walking down the beach.

They had walked about halfway to the mouth of the river when he looked up and saw two men on horseback approaching from the other direction. It was probably the people who were to meet his owners, he thought. But maybe not. Bingham looked nervous. He saw him reach under the tails of his coat to the pistol that rested against his waist.

The riders stopped and Bingham looked straight up at them. "Good morning, gentlemen."

The two riders heard but did not understand the salutation and said something in Spanish to each other. Then they nodded at Bingham as men sometimes do when they can only acknowledge each other's presence in an encounter.

Bingham took his hand off the pistol as the riders rode off and said, "Mexicans. Can't understand English."

But James had recognized the words of the Mexicans. They were words he had learned from his mother. He'd grown up on the Bingham plantation in Tennessee. His mother, though, had grown up on a plantation in Cuba and then, somehow, been transported to New Orleans and from there up the Mississippi River to Tennessee and the Bingham plantation.

They resumed their walk. As they drew closer to the river and a couple of half-constructed buildings, he began to make out the figure of a black man who was leaning against the side of a wagon.

"You Master Bingham?" the black man said with a big smile when they arrived.

"Yes, I am," Bingham responded. "And who might you be?"

"Ezekiel, sir. Master Holmes send me for you. I'm to take you back to his house."

"Well now Ezekiel, that was mighty kind of your master to send you to fetch us." Bingham looked over at James and motioned for him to put the luggage in the wagon.

After depositing the bags James put his hands squarely on the backboard and sprang aboard making a half twist in the air so that he came down squarely seated with his feet dangling off the rear. He liked sitting on the back of the wagon so he didn't have to look at the Binghams. He could concentrate on this new scenery even if he was moving through it backward. He thought to himself that he could easily turn to look at what lay ahead without his master seeing him, but through habit of custom he had become comfortable with facing backward.

"Okay, let's go," Bingham said, passing him and going to the front of the wagon.

They were now rolling down the road, first through grassland and then through cottonwood and oak trees. Ezekiel did his best to steer the wagon around the most offending holes, bumps, and ruts from other wagons. James kept his eyes looking out to the rear. He gazed out to the right and left of the road, trying to get a sense of what this country was like. Part of the land, he thought, looked like it did back in Tennessee because they were going through freshly plowed land. But the rest of it, beyond the furrowed rows, looked wild and desolate.

He was normally a field slave but for the purposes of this trip he was a manservant. He was in his early twenties, had a thin build, and a look of seriousness to him. He rarely smiled. It was not the look of sullenness that many slaves projected and the whites hated. It was rather a look that puzzled and sometimes worried them. They feared what might be behind it. A Negro who thought too much was a Negro not to be trusted, although there was though also a grudging respect for the seriousness since they took it as a sign of intelligence.

James understood these mixed perceptions of him and he tried to use them to his advantage. If for nothing else, they kept people guessing because he fit neither of the polar personality types that whites were used to among their slaves. He was neither like Ezekiel—the smiling, seemingly eager-to-please Negro that whites felt comfortable around—nor the sullen-looking Negro who put them in a bad humor. Nor did he seem to be somewhere in between these personality types. He had once overheard Bingham's father refer to him as an oddity.

2

A couple of hours later the wagon cleared a small hill and then passed by two small log cabins. A black woman stood in the door of one nursing a baby. Ezekiel nodded at her. He continued driving the wagon beyond the cabins and through a small grove of trees until coming to a much larger log-built house with a roof that sloped down over a front porch. He drove the wagon around to the front of the porch and pulled the horse to a stop.

The house fit in with its rustic surroundings. The logs that made up the outside walls matched the grove of trees that the house was set in, as if its builder had been attempting to make the transition from outside to inside as seamless as possible. A person would go from being among trees to being within an arranged clump of cut trees. The only initial hint that the builders had done anything more than arrange what they found already existing in the forest to make their dwelling lay in the unpainted but planed boards which stuck out from this front-facing wall of horizontal logs.

It was on these boards that a man and a woman stood waiting to welcome their guests. The fine cuts of their respective clothing contrasted sharply with the rustic surroundings.

James and Ezekiel waited until the whites were in the house before unloading the luggage onto the porch.

"You come with me," Ezekiel said once the wagon was emptied.

James climbed back onto the wagon, this time into the seat his owner had occupied minutes earlier. For the first time on the trip he felt relaxed, even if the seat under him was hard and wooden.

"What they call you?" Ezekiel said after he had driven the wagon out of the clearing.

"James. I'm from Tennessee."

"Tennessee?"

"Up river from New Orleans."

"Right, I know that. Why you coming here?"

"Because he came."

Ezekiel let out a long slow laugh. "Ain't no other reason why a nigger would want to come here. But now it ain't a question of wanting, now is it? Your master going do what mine did and build himself a nice new plantation here which means you going to build it for him."

"You been here long?"

"Six years since we come from Louisiana."

"How is it?"

"Ain't much to like. There ain't nothing here so you have to break your back to clear the land, move all them rocks and trees and bushes out of the way before you can plant. The master, he real enthusiastic because he think he building something new. But the nigger just have to work so much harder to make his master's dream." Ezekiel paused and took a deep breath as if to emphasize that he had just said a mouthful. Then he remembered something else. "Another difference between working here and working there is that we are isolated here. Not many black folks here."

Ezekiel stopped the wagon when they reached the first of the two shacks they had passed on the way in. "You stay with us till you leave. Over there." He pointed to the second of the shacks. "There ain't nothing in it now but some sacks of seed. But first you going to come in and meet my wife and baby."

The two unhitched the horse and tied it to a tree and then Ezekiel pushed open the rough-hewn split log door to his cabin. Across the dirt floor in a corner a woman sat sewing. In the other corner a baby lay sleeping in a wooden box.

"Rachel, this is Mr. James. He come all the way from Tennessee. Look like he come here to stay."

The woman looked up from her sewing at James and then motioned for him to sit down on the floor. "We have to be quiet," she said. "The baby, he take a long time to sleep. Don't you dare wake him up."

She took an iron pot from the fireplace. With a heavy wooden spoon she first stirred the broth and then dipped enough out to fill two bowls that she brought over to the men. "Take this Mr. James. You must be hungry."

"James, I'm just James," he said to her.

"You look pretty scrawny," Ezekiel said. "Don't they feed niggers enough in Tennessee?"

"Don't pay him no mind," Rachel said. She was taking down a large loaf of cornbread covered by muslin cloth from a shelf by the fire. She broke off two pieces and handed them to the men.

James ate slowly and deliberately, dipping each piece of bread into the broth and placing it in his mouth. It was a little too salty for his taste but there was enough of a turnip taste to make it feel good in his stomach. He had not eaten since the night before on board the ship and what he had eaten then with the pitching back and forth in the rough waters had made him want to throw up. So he was breaking fast and he wanted to chew slowly anyway. But beyond that reason he had somewhere learned to eat slowly and chew thoroughly.

Ezekiel devoured his food and then leaned back against the wall and watched with a certain fascination as James worked little by little at finishing his. Finally, he could not stand the silence any longer. "This man look like he afraid he never get another bite to eat."

"No, I'm just slow. Food tastes better if you chew it a lot."

"I just thought of something you might like to know. There's one advantage to being here if you got a mind to escape. It's much easier here than back there."

"I'm not looking to escape," James said.

"I tell you why anyway. There are very few of them out here. It ain't like back there where they got sheriffs and all that to go after you."

"Why are you here then, if it's so easy to run away?" James said.

"Because he all talk," Rachel said from the corner where she had returned to her sewing.

"No, that ain't it. I figure it ain't no better down there. Besides, they don't speak like we do."

"You just lazy," Rachel said.

"We saw Mexicans on the beach—"

"They're around. But they keep to themselves. Don't have much to do with us. Besides, can't speak the language."

"Ever seen them owning one of us?"

"How could they if they can't speak the language?"

"That don't make no sense Ezekiel," Rachel said, looking up once again. "Master and slave don't have to speak the same language. Slave here to work, not to have no parlor conversation with the whites. But no, in answer to your question James, we ain't never seen the Mexicans with slaves."

"That's not the way they do things," Ezekiel said.

"Well," Rachel said, standing up, "the way they do things here is that I got to go up to the master's house now and help the lady fix dinner for that master of yours."

"One more thing," Ezekiel said. "Watch out for Indians around here. It's not like back there. You got to be more careful. Most of them okay, but they some real bad ones too."

It was mid afternoon with the sun still shining brightly when James stepped out of the small cabin. Across the yard a chicken pecked about searching for something to eat. He smiled at Rachel as she left the cabin with her baby wrapped in cloth. The truth was that he had always had a fantasy about escaping. But he wasn't ready yet, maybe for lack of nerve. He wasn't going to tell them that, at least not yet. You never knew who you could trust, even among Negroes.

3

At twenty-four years of age Samuel Bingham was striking out to start a farming operation in a foreign country still unsettled and unstable from a revolution. It was risky what he was doing, leaving an established family plantation in Tennessee to work up entirely new land in Mexico. He could have stayed in Tennessee and inherited part of his father's plantation and lived well. That was the safe course. Even with three brothers, all with families, there would be enough to go around, though of course none would have as much as the father. That was what his wife and parents had wanted him to do. But to do that he would be living on the basis of what his father had built, not his own labor. He would not even be able to increase the size of the family plantation. Others had already claimed all the nearby land.

As he thought about the verdant land empty of people that he had passed through that afternoon, he felt reassured that he had made the right decision. There was a lot of land and very few people—the opposite of where he came from. The Mexicans and their ways would be a problem but not an insurmountable one. With enough talk and bribery, he had been told, they would not get in the way. All that was needed was a lot of work and it would look like Tennessee. New Tennessee, he thought.

The last thing his father had said to him after expressing his disappointment that he was leaving was that at least he wasn't going up north. Southerners actually had more in common with Mexicans than they did with Yankees. The Mexicans knew what it meant to appreciate life and live well. They weren't always thinking about business and how to make money like Northern businessmen. The North was one big, cold business operation. That was why abolitionism that wanted to turn slaves into paid labor came from there. They didn't understand that the slave received as much out of the Southern system as did his master. If the slave worked very hard—and not all of them did—that was because he was doing his part. The master did his part too, insuring that the slave had a place to live and food to eat even in the worst of times. It had taken generations to develop this civilization that was now entering an age of refinement. Leave it to the Yankees to want to come and tear it all down just so that they could pay the Negroes a miserly wage. The black man would not be any better off under that. He would be worse off because the Yankee would not hesitate to fire him without any means of support if he did not work well or his business was in hard times. That didn't happen on the plantation. The black man always had his place no matter what the market for cash crops. No one ever fired a slave. The

Mexicans were like that too. True, most of them did not have slaves. But they did have peasants who were almost like slaves. The peasants—Indians and mixed bloods—were a laboring race like the Negroes. And like the Negroes, they appreciated having white men see after them. These señores made sure that the peasants had a place to live and food to eat. They appreciated too that life was about living well, not how much money you made. It was much better to exchange a service with your servant than to pay him cold cash.

He had said nothing after his father's long discourse because he did not fully agree. He was going to Mexico to build a modern plantation that would take advantage of new conditions in the world market, not preserve a style of life.

Bingham had a ready smile for his hosts, Jonathan and Lily Holmes, a smile that showed his boyish good looks and friendliness. He always treated encounters with strangers the same: outwardly treat the other with friendliness; inwardly be prepared for the worst. He had smiled at the Mexicans on the beach while keeping his hand under his coat firmly on the handle of his pistol. Here with Holmes there was no need to be so prepared for any possible physical threat, but there was always need to be prepared for the kind of person his host might be.

Holmes seemed knowledgeable and that was what was important. He looked to be in his late thirties, forty at the most, older than him, younger than his parents—old enough to have the advantage of experience but not so old as to be able to dismiss him as a kid.

Jonathan Holmes stood up in the now darkening room and lit a candle. Then he turned. "Another whisky, Samuel?" "Yes, please. You were starting to say something about what grows well here in Mexico."

"Texas," Holmes corrected.

"But is not Texas a part of Mexico?"

Holmes handed Bingham his drink. "Well I suppose that technically it is. Mexico likes to think that this is the state of Coahuila and Texas. But your original question, Samuel, was about the business of planting. Here you have two major crops and some minor ones."

"Cotton and corn." Bingham leaned forward in his seat.

"Yes, cotton and corn. You grow the cotton to sell and the corn is for you and your animals to eat. It's really very simple that way. The soil couldn't be a better for growing and, as far as the cotton goes, the market couldn't be any better. The English can't buy enough of it and I can't clear enough land to keep up with the demand. The only thing holding me back is labor."

"How many niggers do you have?"

"Just the one you saw plus his woman." Holmes motioned toward the kitchen. "She helps Lily with the house. But that's permanent ones. When I need more I can always lease some. There are several large planters like Jared Groce who have more than they can use all the time. They're not too close by, but then again they're not so far away that I can't get some of their men when I need them. The cost is higher than it is back there in Louisiana or Tennessee. But it stands to reason that it would be. Back there you have lots of slaves. When a man needs one for harvesting or whatever he can talk to lots of different planters. If the price that one planter demands for leasing seems too high, he can simply say, 'Thank you so much, I'll think about it' and then go to another planter till he gets the right price. But it's different here—"

"You don't have that many planters to go to," Bingham interjected.

"That's right, so the price is going to be higher. But it's still within reason."

Bingham had not been so naïve as to think that he could get along with only James as labor. He had assumed that from time to time, especially during harvests, he would need to lease more slaves. He had come with enough spare capital to cover those costs. He had not counted on the leasing cost being higher than it was in Tennessee, though, and he did not want to be at the mercy of what another man might charge for the use of his labor.

"This is only a temporary solution," Bingham said. "Eventually you will have to buy more slaves if you are to stabilize your labor supply and your farm is to grow."

"I'd buy more now," Holmes said, "but nobody wants to sell here and if they did, the price would be too high. Have to go to Louisiana to get a good price."

"The Mexicans don't object?"

"Don't object to what?"

"Buying slaves if you can find 'em to buy," Bingham answered.

Holmes frowned. "Even if they did, it wouldn't count for much. This may be politically Mexico but economically it's still the South, and economics in the end counts more than politics. There's some talk in Mexico like in the United States about abolishing slavery. It won't happen though. There's too much at stake economically."

4

Pedro Gomez Quintero found overly religious names to be a curiosity and a curse. He was crossing the Rio de los Brazos de Dios on horseback. What possibly could los brazos de Dios—the arms of God—mean and why would anyone want to name a river after them? It must have been a friar from one of the missions who had come across the river decades ago in the midst of his own agonizing personal meditations. What had possibly gone through his mind? Did he think up that imposing name on the spot or did he spend days pounding his head to come up with it? Was the idea the answer to a prayer for inspiration? The more he thought about it, the more ridiculous it seemed. The Anglo Americans were right to just call it the Rio Brazos. All that religious superstition and fanaticism, Gomez now thought, was weighing the country down and holding it back. Progress would come only from a scientific approach. God gave minds to men so that they could perfect their world, the French said, and perfection of the world did not mean intensifying devotion to superstitious ideas in religious clothing.

He was now firmly back in Texas and he wondered whether he had made the wrong decision in returning.

Four years earlier he had left Texas to go forward, to become educated and to become a priest. Now he was coming back without having become a priest. That he would never become a priest, that he had not made that elevated position in life, did not bother him now. It was of no importance because now he believed other things. When he had set off from Texas he was much younger, maybe not in years, but in how he thought. He was no longer interested in the elementary soul of man and the afterlife. He was interested in what would become of man in this life.

He had thought that he perhaps made the wrong decision because he would be isolated here. There would be no one he could really talk to about much beyond the occurrences and struggles of everyday ordinary life except for the priests, and they could talk only of religious meaning. What he needed would be people or at least someone to replace those he knew in Mexico City who passionately thought and argued about the future of Mexico itself now that it was free from Spain.

He would miss Mexico City if not the life of a seminary student—the streets that he could wander down at will, the faces of people going in all directions, the snow-capped volcanoes on the eastern landscape, the thin mountain air, the moderate temperature year round. All of that was so different from where he was returning now, where in the eyes of his family and the people they knew he would be ignominiously returning after dropping out of the seminary.

In Mexico City after leaving the seminary he had met a general, Manuel de Mier y Terán, at the house of a friend. Terán, as everyone called him, took a special interest in him when he learned that he was from Texas because he would soon be going there to investigate conditions in the area bordering the United States. According to Terán, the border had been demarcated in the 1819 Treaty between Spain and the United States. It followed the course of the Sabine River from the Gulf of Mexico to the Thirty-second Latitude and from there ran due north until it struck the Red River. But now that Mexico was independent, a new treaty needed to be signed to guarantee these limits and the government needed to place physical markers on the line. The government was especially anxious, Terán told him, to establish its authority over its side of the border now that large numbers of Anglo-Americans, with and without permission, were beginning to stream across it.

It had taken him some time to agree to the general's request to accompany him to Texas as an aide and guide, but in the end he assented. It would be good to see his family again, of course. And Terán had told him that he would be serving his country by acting as his aide and guide all the way to Nacogdoches in the northeast corner of Texas, just short of the border with the United States. Further, once they parted company in Nacogdoches—he to return home on the other side of the Colorado River and Terán to remain investigating conditions—Terán would count on him to be a source of information about conditions in his part of the department, especially those regarding the Anglo-American colonists. He would form part of a network of loyal contacts that Terán was eager to build.

Sprinkled among the two hundred or so Anglo Americans living in haphazardly placed wooden structures along this unfortunately-named river were ten Mexicans and a couple of Europeans. Two stores served this town. One, for indulgences, sold whiskey, rum, sugar, and coffee; the other, for basics, had rice, lard, flour, and cloth. Outside of the town many more colonists lived—some two thousand in all—on small farms scattered about the low rolling hills, woods, and fields.

Word of the general's official visit had been sent ahead, and the town authorities had set aside a house for him to use. There he would stay for at least ten days, and while necessary repairs were being made to the wagons, he would catch up on correspondence and journal entries and cast about for information on all matters from climatic, to soil, to economic, social, and political conditions. Terán, who Pedro observed seemed to be in worsening health, also needed this time to gather strength for the trip that lay ahead through the wilderness on to Nacogdoches.

This was the general's first contact with an actual Anglo-American settlement of significant size and he was anxious to observe all that he could of their way of life. That it was Stephen Austin's original colony gave it more importance since it was the center of gravity of the Anglo-American enterprise in Coahuila y Tejas—and Mexico as a whole, for that matter.

The name of the town, San Felipe de Austin, like that of its river, sent Pedro Gomez's mind racing with its ironies. Some friar, maybe the same one who named the river, had named the place for a saint—San Felipe. Then an Anglo American had come along with the arrogance to claim the place as his personal property along with immortalizing his name by adding de Austin—signifying property of Austin. But could a mortal, even an Anglo-American one, own a saint?

On the third day in the town, while Pedro was talking with the general, there was a loud, persistent knock at the door and the mortal who presumed to own the saint presented himself. Stephen Austin extended his hand, introduced himself with enthusiasm, and excused himself for having been away when the general and his party had arrived.

So this was the famous Austin, the most important Anglo American in Texas. Terán returned the greeting correctly and allowed Austin to guide the two of them over to his house. Austin spoke Spanish very well for an Anglo American and he had a certain grace to his actions that inspired confidence, Pedro thought. No wonder he had been able to get so much out of the authorities.

Austin's house consisted of just two simple rooms. If all his efforts to build up Anglo-American colonization were going to make him rich, it had not come yet. Terán took the rum offered by his host and listened to what he had to say.

"Right now," Austin said, "we're just scratching the surface of what Texas could be."

"Coahuila y Tejas," the general corrected.

"Of course, Coahuila y Tejas," Austin acknowledged as if it were indisputable. Then he quickly moved on. "We're at a very primitive stage, barely beyond the Indians. We plant mostly for subsistence and a little for export. The future that I see is one in which all of Coahuila and Texas are producing agricultural surpluses that can be sold throughout the country and abroad."

"And just what crops do you have in mind?" Terán asked.

"For Coahuila, wheat, tobacco, olives, wine; for Texas, corn, tobacco also, possibly sugar, some vegetables. Now, I'm saving the best for last."

"Cotton."

"Yes, cotton," Austin said. "This is the situation as I see it. The English want all the cotton they can get. They buy it from the United States, but they don't like the United States much because of the 1812 War. They also don't like the fact that the United States has high tariffs that are prejudicial to their own exports. The way the English see it, they buy all the U.S. exports of cotton with no prejudicial tariffs, and then the U.S. slaps tariffs on the goods that England wants to sell there. This is where Mexico, our country"—Austin said with emphasis—"comes in. We make a reciprocal trading relationship with England where the English buy our cotton and we let them sell their goods here duty-free."

"To the advantage of both."

"Yes, definitely. Once this is clear, the English will shift their buying of cotton to Mexico and that will greatly stimulate our whole economic development. Texas, that is, this part of Coahuila and Texas, would be the lead in all of this because we have the best climatic and soil conditions for cotton. We also have men who know cotton and a lot more who would be willing to come here."

"I note the conditional way in which you are speaking," Terán said. "There are men who would be willing to come here, except for—"

"The uncertainty of the labor situation."

"Slavery, you mean."

"Yes, slavery," Austin acknowledged. "No one knows whether it is exactly legal or, even if it is, whether that will last."

"And just why is that so important?"

"Because it will take black labor to clear all these forests if we want to truly get a cotton economy up and running. Also, if we want to attract planters with experience in cotton from the United States, we must make it clear to them that they can operate here as they are accustomed to with slave labor. It is as plainly simple as that, General."

"Our country is opposed to slavery," Terán responded. "The ambiguity regarding it here is a thorn in the side of the national body politic."

"Look," Austin said, "I am personally opposed to it too."

"I note that you own slaves." This he and Pedro had learned inadvertently from a comment by Samuel Williams, another colonist.

If Terán's bringing up of the contradiction bothered him, Austin did not show it. He continued on without breaking stride. "I am opposed to it in theory, in the long run. But I am not a utopian. The conditions that we live in now demand slavery. At some point in the future it will no longer be necessary. But that is not now. If we wish to develop Texas to its potential, it is absolutely necessary that black labor be employed to the task."

"That is a point, Señor Austin, on which we must agree to disagree. Slavery cannot last much longer in any part of the republic."

Austin leaned back. "Let me put it another way. We're at a very early state in the development of our economy, generations behind what exists in the rest of the country or in the country to the northeast. To catch up will take more than having more farmers come here just trying to make a subsistence living. They come and plant and are happy if it yields enough to feed their families. That's all fine and good for them. It's better than what they had. But if we really want this area to be prosperous, we will have to have products to trade on the international market so that they yield profits that come back here and are turned into capital—"

"And that's where cotton comes in."

"Yes, precisely," Austin said. "The future of Coahuila and Texas rests with cotton because it will bring back new capital. And once it is here, everyone benefits. The rub is that to export cotton right away to take advantage of favorable conditions on the world market, land has to be cleared in a much larger scale than most farmers who are only interested in feeding their families want to do. Hence, the necessity of black labor."

Austin ended his second attempt to convince with the look of someone who was pleased with himself for having at last found the right words to articulate the truth that he knew. Then there was a long silence, as if the words were sinking in on their intended target.

Finally Terán responded, but slowly. "Your economic logic is impeccable, Señor Austin—"

"I knew you would understand, General," Austin said, eagerly. "You are a man of much experience and learning."

"But, Señor Austin, I have not finished. Your economic argument is indeed impeccable but it is also politically fallible. As I told you, we cannot, indeed we will not allow slavery to expand in the republic."

5

Samuel Bingham's eyes squinted under the two o'clock sun. He was growing sleepy to the sound of the horse's clip clops on the beaten road, and there was still a good two hours to go before reaching Brazoria where he needed to sign papers to legalize his ownership of the land he was now occupying. Jonathan Holmes was riding beside him. From time to time he saw lakes of water in the road ahead only to have them dissolve into the mirages that they were. He felt himself fall into a languid stupor as he was studying one of them, waiting for it to dissolve.

Suddenly long-haired riders galloped out of the mirage.

"Oh my god, Indians," Holmes said.

Bingham shook his head and the lake disappeared but not the riders. "What'll we do?" he said, now fully awake.

Holmes was looking wildly in all directions for an escape route. But they were coming up too fast and there were too many of them. "Nothing we can do," he said, settling back in his saddle and pulling up the reins, "except hope for the best."

An Indian, his face covered with ochre streaks, motioned with his rifle for them to dismount.

"Do what he says," Holmes said quietly. "Whatever you do, don't provoke them."

As they stood on the side of the road, two Indians searched through the saddlebags but didn't find anything of interest.

"Americanos?" one of the Indians asked.

"Yes," Holmes said.

The Indian's expression did not change. Then he made a motion with his hand, "Vayan."

Bingham was puzzled.

"It means to go," Holmes said.

They rode forward, each one dealing with the fright alone. After fifteen minutes Holmes pulled up his reins and dismounted. Bingham could see him trembling. "What was that all about?" he asked.

"Horse thieves," Holmes answered. "Comanches. They're the worst of the lot here. They rob horses from the Mexicans and then trade them for guns across the border in Louisiana. They didn't take ours because they don't want to lose the market there."

"How many of them are there?" Bingham had gotten off his horse too.

"They say that altogether there are some fifteen hundred families. Supposedly the Mexicans have a peace agreement with them. The problem is that not all of them abide by it. That's why it's never safe to farm out west near Bexar, no matter what general agreement the Mexicans have."

"And what is the solution to this?"

Holmes shrugged. "They'll have to be physically eliminated as soon as there are enough troops to do the job. But it won't be easy. They're fierce fighters. Well enough of that," Holmes started to remount his horse. "We need to keep moving if we want to get to town in time to get things done."

At times Bingham thought he heard horses on the road and feared the worst. They always turned out to be nothing and he was careful not to share the false alarms with Holmes. It was best that he not show the other man the depths to which the fright had affected him.

"It's not much of a town yet," Holmes said as they reached the edge of a group of log cabins in late afternoon, "but in time you'll see Brazoria rise to rival the best of where we come from."

Bingham, who was still looking over his shoulder for Indians, was glad to see the town, any town. He counted twenty-seven cabins stretched in an irregular pattern back from an embarcadero on the Brazos River. There were also three brick houses, indicating a step up in town possibilities. All of the houses had wooden shutters rather than glass windows.

"First things first, Samuel, we'll make a little courtesy call on the authorities. This is where the land commissioner works." Holmes pointed to a cabin by the embarcadero.

The land commissioner was seated at his desk when the two entered. "What can I do for you gentlemen?" he asked in English.

"George Baker," Holmes said by way of an introduction, "this is Mr. Samuel Bingham from Tennessee. He is coming to register himself as a member of our colony. He has a letter from Stephen Austin granting him permission to move onto the land just east of my holding."

Baker stood up and leaned over the desk to shake hands. Then he sat back down and opened a side drawer to his desk and took out a sheaf of papers. "Stephen was in here last month and said to expect you. I took the liberty to draw up the papers."

"I thought you would be Mexican," Bingham said.

"I am Mexican."

"But your English is a good as that of any American I have met."

"That's because I used to be an American. Came down to Mexico fifteen years ago from Ohio."

"George hasn't yet become thoroughly Mexicanized," Holmes said, smiling.

Baker ignored the comment and turned toward Bingham. "Now, Mr. Bingham, do you understand Spanish?"

"No," Bingham answered. Then he looked toward Holmes. "Is that a requirement?"

"I certainly don't think so, is it George?" Holmes said. "I can't speak it yet either, though I wish I could."

Baker shook his head. "It's not a requirement, but it will be to your advantage to learn it as soon as you can since all legal business is conducted in Spanish and what you're about to sign is, too."

"What do those papers say?" Bingham said, realizing the quandary that he was in.

"What these papers say," Baker said, "is that you will be allotted one square league of land for grazing and farming."

"That's over 4,000 acres," Holmes said. "Should be enough Samuel, no?"

"In return you agree," George said, "to become a Mexican citizen and Roman Catholic. After six years of continuous residence on and working of the land, you will get the title. Your first payment for it will be due in the fourth year."

Bingham listened to Baker's summary translation of the terms and heard what he had been led to expect, first by a cousin of his in Tennessee who had first sold him on the idea of setting out for Texas, and then by Holmes the night before. He didn't like the idea much of becoming a Mexican citizen and even less the idea of becoming a Catholic. But he had known ahead of time that those were the conditions and he was prepared to accept them. Besides, Holmes the night before had told him not to take them very seriously. No priest, way out where they were, would be calling on him any time soon.

6

The few streets of Nacogdoches ran at right angles to each other, unusual for a town in Texas where they usually crosscut each other at whatever angle that had made sense at the moment of making. Here there had either been some planning or a tacit unspoken agreement to keep to an orderly pattern as new buildings sprang up.

Pedro Gomez had known some of what to expect in the town. Among the problems confronting General Terán would be what to do about the Indians now crossing the border from the United States. They were occupying lands without legal authorization. So too were Anglo-American squatters. But the Indians were a different matter. They came as peoples, not as individuals and families. Among them the Cherokees were the most advanced and they were eager to win favor with General Terán, most certainly because they wanted to have their claims to land recognized. But they had miscalculated a year back when they allowed themselves to be misled by Anglo-American fanatics. The Anglos attempted to take control of this part of Texas, secede it from Mexico, and then call the rump republic Fredonia. In return for Cherokee support they promised recognition of their land claims. The rebellion collapsed when the army approached and the Anglos fled. The Cherokees would have to answer for this.

On their third day in Nacogdoches he and Terán had just reached the inn where they were staying after having returned from an interview with the comandante of the presidio. Waiting anxiously on the porch for them was a man. He wore a ruddy red turban around his head, and a blue cloth tunic for a coat that came down to his knees, leather leggings with red garters just below the knees, and moccasins. He announced himself as Dutokeh, a Cherokee. He was here to invite General Terán, the great representative of the Mexican people, to visit and see for himself their lands, how they lived, and to talk. Terán politely accepted the invitation but without any show of enthusiasm as if to say that he would attend only because of the obligations of his office. Dutokeh bowed ceremoniously, said he would return in the morning to escort them to the village, and left as quickly as he had unexpectedly appeared.

Pedro and Terán watched him go and then stamped the dust off their boots on the porch of the inn and walked through the front door. Marcos, the loquacious innkeeper, was puttering about the parlor as if waiting for a chance to talk. This was a job, Pedro thought, he would never want for himself. He did not mind talking to strangers when he had a direct purpose for talking with them. An innkeeper though had to be always ready to make conversation with all manner of men or women regardless of whether they had anything useful or interesting to say. Such a use of his time would drive him crazy.

"Well, Señores," Marcos said in Spanish, "I trust that you have had a productive time so far in Nacogdoches."

"Señor," Terán said, addressing him formally and ignoring the pleasantry, "I would like to ask you some questions about the Indian situation here."

Marcos warmed quickly to the opportunity to communicate with a high officer from the capital. "There are few problems with the Indians here. It is not like with the Comanches. Most of the Indians in this part of Texas have drifted in from the United States looking to get away from the pressures that the Anglo Americans are putting on them."

"And the cruel joke is that the Anglo Americans are coming here too," Pedro said.

"That is quite right young man. But from the Indians' point of view, there are still fewer of them here than there. So they are trying to settle here as their best option. Now of course the first of the immigrant Cherokees came here earlier than any of the Anglo Americans. That is why they think that it is unjust that the government recognizes the Anglo-American land claims but not theirs."

Terán acknowledged with a nod that that was at the heart of the Cherokees' grievances.

"They believe that they even had permission to settle," Marcos continued. "Twenty or so of the first Cherokees to come went to Bexar back in 1822 and spoke with Governor José Feliz Trepalacios. According to them, the governor gave them permission to settle. He granted it along with agreeing that the Cherokees would form a militia to patrol the frontier with the United States. However, they were not to trade arms with the Comanche or other nomadic tribes."

"What happened to the militia?" Pedro asked.

Marcos shrugged as if to say that neither side had made the idea into a reality.

"They joined the insurrection here," Terán said.

"That is true," Marcos acknowledged, speaking slowly for the first time. "So did others here. Well, really, it was only a small number and they are not here now. They all fled."

"It is still a matter of concern," Terán said sternly to Marcos who seemed less than eager to talk about it. "And the indigenous Indians, the ones who were already here, where do they stand?"

"Right close by those would be the Caddos. They are one of the oldest peoples in Texas, about three hundred families in all. They strattle the border with the United States." Marcos was now talking freely again.

"Yes, but the question is—how do the immigrant Indians get along with the indigenous ones?"

"There are tensions, but I have not heard of any fighting. The fighting goes on with the ones west of here."

"The Wacos?"

"Yes and also the Tawakonis. You will find that the immigrant Indians that live near here are a lot different than the nomads from the west."

"In what ways?" Terán asked.

"They look different physically. Their skin is fairer, perhaps the result of some mixing with Anglo-American blood. They are definitely more civilized than the nomads since they farm. Some can even read and write."

"Is your last statement really true?" Pedro asked.

"It is among the Cherokees. They even have their own alphabet. But for the most part the immigrant Indians cannot read or write. But they recognize its value and want to learn."

"And their vices?" Terán said.

"Drunkenness is the worst. They have a taste for liquor and do not know when or how to stop."

"This is curious," Terán said. "According to what I have been told in Béxar, the Comanches and other nomads completely avoid alcohol."

"I have heard that too. So, the more civilized the Indian, the more likely he is to succumb to liquor. It is ironic, is it not General?"

"One more question, Señor," Terán said before ending the conversation.

"What is that, General?"

"You see the Anglo Americans pass through here on their way to the interior. About how many slaves accompany them?"

"I would say that it is about one in three."

"One Negro for every three whites?"

"That is right General. It depends on the party. For some there are no slaves, for others the proportion is higher. That is my overall estimate."

In the morning the red turbaned Dutokeh returned to the inn to take them on a two-hour ride north to the Cherokee village. Before leaving Nacogodoches they stopped at the presidio to pick up an escort of twelve soldiers both as a precaution and as a display to show that Terán was on official business.

"We, like you, came on a long journey to be here," Black Leg said. They were now sitting in a long house in the village around a fire, he and Terán with Dutokeh and six other Cherokees, two of them chiefs. The smoke of the fire trailed up and out a hole in the thatched roof. Outside the soldiers waited. "We started in what the whites call North Carolina in 1810. That was a long time ago and we are still weary from the trip."

"There were many whites moving in to our lands then as there are now," one of the two chiefs, Duwali, said.

Dutokeh, who was sitting immediately to his left whispered to Pedro: "He is Duwali, the chief who settles tribal disputes. Tell that to your chief."

"They forced us to live in smaller and smaller spaces. We could not hunt as widely as we did before and there was less game to hunt because the whites were hunting it too. That was when I decided that it was time to move. Not all the Cherokees were in agreement. Many are still there but their life is poorer. We traveled to what the whites call Arkansas, almost as far as we are now. The mountains of Arkansas were like those of where we had left and there we made our home for ten years."

"It is there that I grew up," Dutokeh whispered to Pedro.

Pedro wondered why the Cherokee seemed eager to be especially friendly toward him. Perhaps it was because both of them had something in common in being aides to powerful men. More likely it was because the Cherokee thought that if he could get his ear, whatever he wished to convey would make its way to the general's ear. He was making an investment in a relationship for a calculated purpose. He was not just being friendly. This was something that would have to be handled carefully. He would respond in kind and then report what he learned to Terán.

"But then whites began moving into the lands of Arkansas." Now the other chief, Gatunwali, was speaking. He, as Dutokeh whispered once again, concerned himself with Cherokee relations with outsiders—Mexicans, Anglo-Americans, other Indian peoples. "It became time to move again and that is how we have come to Mexico."

Gatunwali looked in the direction of Black Leg, who continued the story. "The hunting was very good when we first came here because there were few other people. But because of all the whites and other Indian peoples coming in now, the deer and all other game around the camp are becoming scarce. It has become necessary that we give our attention to the planting of corn and the raising of cattle so that our children may not go hungry, that we build up our village, and that the old give good advice to the young."

"We do not want," Duwali said, "to go on wandering through the woods like the other tribes; we want to raise cattle, to plant corn, and to teach our children to be good men."

Pedro glanced over at Terán. He was listening with inscrutable attention as speaker after speaker added to the points made. Occasionally he would write down something in his journal that he kept open in front of him.

"That is good," Terán said, "but last year your people disobeyed the law."

The words shattered the easygoing cordiality. Gatunwali looked at Duwali. Duwali looked back at him.

"It was the whites," Gatunwali said.

"I have it on the best of reports that Cherokees were involved," Terán responded sharply.

"A few," Gatunwali acknowledged. "They acted on their own and they have been punished."

Dutokeh whispered to Pedro: "Their leaders were all killed on orders from the chiefs."

"The Mexicans are our fathers," Duwali said. "We have shaken hands with them not for temporary but for permanent peace. We are old and will soon be dead and forgotten, but we want our children to follow in our footsteps without breaking the peace with our fathers, the Mexicans, because we know your sincerity."

After still further professations of full loyalty, Black Leg said what was on everyone's mind. "We accept the Mexicans as our fathers. We have been a part of Mexico for longer than the whites but we still do not have full possession of the land on which we plant, live, and stand ready to defend Mexico always. We ask you to take this message back to the supreme government so that we may get our land."

Terán continued listening impassively and then said that he would look into the issue of legalizing the land that they were occupying. Later, on the ride back to Nacogdoches, he said that he thought that the Cherokees were a major factor in the whole equation of protecting the border. They could either be a big problem that, added to the problem of so many Anglo Americans moving in, would completely throw the area out of control, or, if the government was skillful enough, they could be used as a buffer against any move by the Anglo Americans to take over. They could be a third force to parry both the Anglo Americans and the Comanches. This latter option would require satisfying their land claims. It was an option worth thinking about but not to be moved upon immediately. The Cherokees still needed to be reminded that disloyalty, even if it was only for a temporary period and even only a part of them, carried with it consequences.

Pedro thought back about Dutokeh, who seemed so eager to ingratiate himself to him. After the meeting he had said that he could be of special use to the Mexicans.

"Can he be trusted?" Terán said.

"I do not know him well enough to know."

"I will make inquiries. If he is trustable, I will add him to the network of contacts."

7

During his first weeks and months in Texas, James worked harder than he ever had in his life. Bingham ordered him to get to work immediately on planting. In the mornings and afternoons he plowed to break up the ground and turn under the wild grasses of this new homestead. In the late afternoons he joined Bingham in building the latter's house. Late at night he would collapse into sleep in the shed next to the cabin inhabited by Holmes's slaves, Ezekiel and Rachel.

James knew cotton. He had grown up around it and had worked long and hard with it. Bingham knew this, which was why he had chosen him to bring along. Unlike other slaves who needed constant supervision to keep them working, James was independent. Even when left alone, James did the work. As long as Bingham provided seeds, a few tools, and a draft animal—he bought a mule from Holmes a few days after arriving—James could be trusted to go out and develop fields of cotton and corn. He was also good at putting in the garden of black-eyed peas and sweet potatoes for house consumption and taking care of the pigs that he bought from another colonist.

This trust and confidence gave James an edge that he liked. He set his own hours, always being careful though to look like he was busy when either one of the Binghams appeared. He raised the pigs so that the Binghams could have their meat. For himself, he trapped rabbits out in the forest.

He was checking the rabbit traps one late afternoon when he heard the crashing of horse hooves on the forest floor. He froze momentarily, worried that hostile Indians were approaching. Slowly he stood up, turned, and looked up to see a Mexican holding a rifle.

"What are you doing here?" the Mexican said in Spanish.

James heard the words and recognized them. He could not find the right words to say that he was checking traps so he pointed to them instead.

"You are a slave from over there?" The Mexican pointed toward the other side of the woods.

He recognized well the word for slave and nodded his head and found the words in Spanish to say, "Am I not supposed to be here?"

The Mexican looked down at him and then shook his head. "No, this is nobody's land. You can trap here." He swung his leg over the saddle and dismounted and came over and looked at the trap. "Your trap is empty. You have no rabbit. Try the other side of the hill."

"I will take your advice," James said awkwardly in Spanish. "And you, where do you live?"

The Mexican pointed with a sweeping hand toward the other side of woods. "Over there. Come."

James understood the meaning of the words, but he asked anyway. "Me, go?"

"Yes, you come." The Mexican patted the flank of the horse behind him.

He was not sure whether this was an invitation or an order since the man was armed and he'd had no direct experience with Mexicans before. He followed the instructions, placing his foot on the stirrup and letting the rider help him swing up and behind him.

The horseman guided the horse deeper into the forest than James had explored before and then out onto a trail on the other side. Once on the trail he let the horse break into a little trot which the horse gladly did since it was once again on familiar ground and on its way home.

Home turned out to be a corral next to a low wood-built house.

James looked around past the shoulders of the man. There were chickens scurrying around the yard.

"¡Ya!" the man in front of him said. "Get down."

James grabbed the back of the saddle, slid his right leg up and over the horse's rump, and dropped to the ground.

The man then dismounted and with a slap on the horse's flanks sent it into the corral. "Come inside," he said, motioning James to follow him into the house.

Inside the house a middle-aged woman and a girl who appeared to be eighteen or nineteen were crouched over a fireplace. The woman glanced around and, seeing the guest, stood and bid him to sit on the dirt floor. From the comal over the fire she scooped off three corn tortillas, placed them in a straw basket one by one, covered the basket with a cloth, and then gave them to the girl to take over and place in front of him and the man who had brought him. Then she took a wooden spoon and scooped beans out of a clay pot that sat in the corner of the fireplace and filled two wooden bowls that she placed in front of the men.

James watched the man take a tortilla from the basket and then use it to scoop up beans from the wooden bowl and push them into his mouth.

"Eat," the man said, motioning at his mouth.

The smell of warm corn tortillas and beans reminded him that he was in fact quite hungry and so he copied the motions of the man and ate, as always, slowly and deliberately as if the food would have to last him for a very long time. Eventually he neared completion, long after the man next to him. As he was sopping up the last of the beans on the bottom of the bowl with the last of his tortilla, he heard another man enter.

"Who is he?"

"A slave, papa."

James started to stand up.

"Sit down." The father gestured with his hand for him to stay seated. "Who is your owner?"

"Who is he?"

"Yes. Who is he?"

"He owns land over there on the other side of the woods and he owns me."

"No one should own a man," the father said.

James nodded his head. "I agree." The Spanish words were coming easier now.

"What is your name?"

"James."

The father heard the name and struggled to pronounce it but could not and spoke once again to his son.

"It is a hard name," the son said. "It would be good if you could write it so that I can see it. Can you write it?"

James nodded and with his finger scratched out J-A-M-E-S in the dirt in front of him.

The son leaned over and studied the letters for some time. Then he said, using a Spanish J and two syllables for it, "Ha-mes."

"Ha-mes it is." James said. "And your names?"

"Pedro Gómez Quintero, and my father, he is don Alfredo. My mother," he pointed to the woman who smiled in return, "she is doña Luisa. And she," he pointed to the girl, "is my sister, Pilar."

James hesitated and then reached out his hand and both men shook it. He tried to find something to say. All he could think of was, "Your family has been here for a long time?"

"My father," Alfredo said, "first came to what was then called La Bahia—"

"Goliad now," Pedro said.

"Yes, Goliad."

"They just changed the name to honor the great leader of our revolution, Father Hidalgo. Goliad has the same letters as Hidalgo, only rearranged."

James shrugged. About this revolution or its leader he knew nothing.

"My father," Alfredo continued, "first came as a soldier for the presidio many years ago. He liked it so much that he stayed and it was there that I was born. Two years ago, when the Indian problem became less, I moved out to here."

"I and my sister grew up in La Bahia," Pedro added. "It was there that I learned to read from a priest."

It was late afternoon now and James remembered that he had to be back and be about the Bingham place. If he waited much longer, one of them might go looking for him. In any event, it was best to avoid problems. He looked out the door to see how late it was and Pedro noticed.

"You have to go back now?" Pedro said.

"Yes, it is time."

"Here you have your house," Alfredo said.

James furrowed his brow.

"It is just an expression," Pedro said. "You will always be welcome here. I will take you back to where I found you."

"I will come to visit. You cannot visit me though."

"No," Alfredo said. "That would not be prudent."

"You do not need to take me back," James said to Pedro. "I will walk back so that I know the way for sure."

As James walked he thought about the encounter and felt very good about it. It was the first good thing that had happened in a long time. Bingham had been pushing him far beyond what even a slave could be expected to do and he resented it and had been thinking about it a lot. Bingham controlled from a distance what his body did but he could not control at all what went on in his mind. His inner thoughts were his own and he kept it that way. Bingham did not even know that he had secretly learned to read and write in Tennessee. It had happened years earlier. He had found out that Bingham's father had engaged Joseph Robinson, the area's only schoolteacher and Quaker, to give his son extra lessons at the plantation itself. Robinson had been new to the town, taking a position of schoolteacher that no one else either wanted or was capable of performing. One Sunday afternoon as he had been walking on the road to the plantation, the schoolteacher had stopped to give him a ride. He had known that he was the schoolteacher and directly asked him if he could learn too. That of course was against all of the rules and Robinson told him so. Then he had asked whether God made those rules. No, Joseph Robinson had answered. They were but rules made by fallible men and he could not in good conscience as a Quaker obey them in this case. Then Robinson had worked out an arrangement. When James came to town to bring in cotton or was sent there to pick up supplies, he would let him come by his house for a quick lesson. He proved to a quick learner and Robinson soon arranged it so that he could take spare primers with him so long as this was kept secret even from the other slaves. When it was for certain that he would be going to Texas, the Quaker teacher gave him a Spanish primer to take with him to perfect the language of his mother.

Now he knew some Mexicans. He could talk with them in a language Bingham did not understand. This gave him more independence. He remembered the Spanish primer that Joseph Robinson had given him and vowed to open it up when he returned.

8

Pedro Gomez thought about how things had been going since he had left General Terán some months back in Nacogdoches and returned home. It had not been terribly difficult to readjust to the routine chores of rural life after having lived in Mexico City. The hardships on the trail of the four-month trip back had proved to be a good transition, a period of readjustment to living so close to the land. He had not become so spoiled by city life as to never be able to return to the life he had grown up in. What was difficult, though, was the sudden cutoff of contact with men like General Terán who knew about the whole country and the world surrounding it.

He had come back to his family filled with information and concerns about the wider world. They listened respectfully at first and they never acted like what he had to say was uninteresting, but he had the sense that they were not nearly as interested in it as he was. And so as the weeks went on he found himself keeping more things that he wanted to talk about to himself so as not to upset the easy flow of family interactions. When he had met the Negro in the woods and decided to bring him home, he had wondered how his family would react. To his pleasant surprise they had not only found what he had done acceptable but had actually been enthusiastic about it. Afterward his father had said that he hoped that the Negro would return often. All of them found it intriguing that the Negro seemed to understand enough Spanish that they could communicate.

He had not thought of making contact with one of the Anglos' slaves before. But now that it had happened, it presented interesting possibilities. What could he learn from this Negro about the Anglos? For sure the Negro's perspective would be limited, but at least there would be something and that would be useful. When he had left General Terán there had been an agreement that he would act as a correspondent for him and find out what he could. In his first letter he had reported on the attitudes of the local Mexicans to the increase of Anglo-American colonists. Most had a passive attitude toward them—as long as they did not interfere, they were welcome to develop their own farms in their own areas. Very few voiced any active concern about any threat that the Anglos might pose. Pedro thought that this complacency was dangerous and noted it in his reports. It was rare to find others who were as concerned as he was about the Anglo invasion. If they did not see Anglos right around them—and most did not because the Anglo colonies were more than a day's horse ride away—they did not think there was a danger.

Now he had something new to report. He had met and befriended one of the slaves of the Anglos. He would be a useful source of two types of information—on how he was treated and what he observed about his owner and the others with whom his owner associated. Pedro thought for a minute on this last point. If he could win enough of the confidence of this slave, then he could work on him also to become an active informant. That he would have to do with caution. For now he would get whatever information he could from him without letting on to its ultimate purpose.

He would have composed a new letter with this information for the general except for the fact that three days earlier he had received a letter from him indicating that he was leaving Nacogdoches. His inspection tour was being cut short by orders to go to Matamoros. Violent conflicts had broken out over the results of the election for the presidency. Both Manuel Gómez Pedraza and Vicente Guerrero claimed victory. Near anarchy prevailed in the capital and elsewhere in the republic. The general's military skills to reestablish order now in the rest of the republic were needed more than his scientific and diplomatic abilities to ensure future order on the border.

Terán was reluctant to leave Texas after having been able to spend only ten months. There was still so much work to be done. He felt that he was just beginning to get a grasp of the Indian situation. It was more and more clear to him that ties needed to be cemented with the Cherokees. They were the natural leaders of the immigrant tribes. As they went, so would go the others. The price of their loyalty was title to the land they occupied, and it was time to move ahead on that. He had talked for a long time with Dutokeh, the Cherokee who had come to see him in his first days in Nacogdoches, about these matters and now counted him as among his contacts. He had made inquiries about him and felt reasonably sure that he was trustable. He, along with a local Mexican, Vicente Cordova, promised to keep him informed about developments in Nacogdoches, especially any renewed separatist movements among the Anglo Americans that sought Cherokee support. He wanted Pedro to know this because there was now a network of loyalist agents in Texas that he wanted to survive should something happen to him later on.

He felt that he needed to know more about the issue of the Anglo Americans and their slavery. It was clear that it was growing in Texas while the winds in the republic as a whole were blowing in the other direction. There would soon be an open clash and it would be best for him to have gathered as much information about it as possible. He had seen it from a distance at San Felipe de Austin and he had seen it much closer up here around Nacogdoches. Brazoria and the Colorado River were other centers of it and he would take advantage of the trip south to Matamoros to see it there as well.

9

Samuel Bingham was standing in the front room of the Holmes house with a whiskey glass in hand. They had just finished a midday meal and were getting ready to go out onto the front porch where Lily was when they heard her shout, "Jonathan, come quickly. Mexican soldiers are riding in."

Holmes looked at Bingham and then reached for his rifle. "You never know," he said. Then he rested the rifle against the wall by the door and peered out.

Fifteen or so soldiers sat mounted around a wagon.

"They look official to me," Bingham said.

"They're here on some kind of business. We better present ourselves."

Bingham had not encountered so many Mexican soldiers at close hand before. He found himself feeling strangely apprehensive about them now. They were less threatening than the Comanches but a far from welcome sight. No question that they had the upper hand and no question that he and Holmes would have to submit in any disagreement. His eyes swept across the brown faces of the soldiers until they rested on the one climbing down from the carriage. This one's face was whiter than the others. Then a scraggly little man he had not noticed before jumped down from a horse and walked straight up to the porch. He was not in uniform and his face was as white as that of the officer.

"This is General Terán," the scraggly one said with an Irish brogue. "He wishes to buy some provisions from you if you have any to sell."

Holmes looked at his wife and then said, "Tell the general that we have none to sell. He should go further south to Victoria. He will find goods to buy there."

The scraggly man said this in Spanish to Terán who said words back. "The general appreciates your advice. He would now like to ask you some questions about your farm."

Bingham grabbed Holmes's arm and drew him back. "What right does he have to do that?"

Holmes pulled away quickly and addressed the Irish man. "Tell him that I will be most happy to discuss anything he wishes to know about my farm."

Bingham watched as the words were being translated and then saw the general looking in his direction.

"He wants to know who you are," the Irishman said.

"I own another farm over there." Bingham swept his arm toward the east.

"He also wants to know whether you own any slaves."

Bingham felt perspiration beginning to form under his shirt despite the weather being not at all warm. Why this question should make him anxious he did not know, for he was perfectly within his rights to bring a slave in with him. Then he regretted having been drinking the whiskey. It was putting him at a disadvantage in dealing with a perfectly sober man. Finally, he said, trying to form the words as clearly as possible, "Yes, I own a slave."

The Irishman translated this and Bingham saw Terán's brows furrow and his gaze harden.

"He wants to know," the Irishman said, translating, "why you don't speak Spanish since you are in Mexico."

"More people speak English than Spanish in Texas," Bingham said.

"Don't tell him that," Holmes said. "Say that you're learning as fast as you can but that it is difficult."

The Irishman translated and listened to the response. "The general says that it is useful to understand languages."

"Our main problem here, General," Holmes said, "is that we are connected to Coahuila when Texas ought to be its own state. We really don't have anything in common with Coahuila."

Terán nodded in understanding as he heard the translation and then responded on another matter.

"The general wants to know," the Irishman said, "if you could operate your farms without slave labor."

"What does he mean by that?" Bingham said.

"Don't worry," the Irishman said with a wry smile, "He's not going to take them away from you."

"I am sure he won't," Holmes said with his own smile.

"They don't understand the question," the Irishman said in Spanish to Terán.

The general looked annoyed and spoke in sharp tones.

"He says that the question was clear enough."

Holmes looked at the general and then to the Irishman. "Tell him that there is no other way to get labor and that the crops are doing well."

"Tell him also," Bingham added, "that they aren't really slaves because they want to work for us."

Terán listened to their responses inscrutably. Then he looked at Bingham and asked, through the Irishman, if his worker was happy because he treated him well.

"Definitely," Bingham said.

Had he ever had to use a whip? Terán asked.

Bingham turned toward Holmes. "What should I tell him?"

Holmes counseled. "You never have personally."

"No," Bingham said to the general.

That is very good, the general said, because it is an abuse to whip a man who works for you.

Holmes listened to the Irishman's translation and then said. "Tell him that we are in complete agreement."

Neither he nor his government, the general continued, wanted to hear of cases of abuses. Slavery was legal for now, but they would not tolerate the abusing of slaves.

After the translation, the general looked directly at Holmes and Bingham and said, "¿Me entienden bien?"

"He wants to make sure you understand him clearly," the Irishman said.

Holmes and Bingham nodded.

Terán turned to leave.

"That's it," the Irishman said. "We'll be leaving now."

"What do you think?" Bingham said after they left.

"Hard to tell." Holmes said. "I would not underestimate him. I've heard of him before. They say that he's here from Mexico City to investigate Texas and has a lot of power. I just didn't expect to see him on my doorstep."

10

James was plowing alongside the common trail that led away from the Bingham and Holmes properties when he saw the military entourage coming out. He watched them pass, then stop and double back to where he was. A man out of uniform motioned for him to come over.

"General Terán wants to speak to you," the man said.

"To me?" James said in puzzlement. There was no way in which he could have done anything wrong.

"I don't see anybody else here," the man said. "The general just wants to talk to you."

General Terán took a step forward and said in accented English, "What is your opinion of the slave system?"

This is a dangerous question, James thought. It was not like talking to Joseph Robinson about slavery. This man is wearing a uniform. "I don't know what you mean," he answered after some deliberation.

"Do you want to continue being a slave?" Terán said.

James pondered the more direct question and again evaded it. "I want to do a good job, make these crops grow."

Terán looked exasperated and then said, "Thank you for your information. You can go back to work now."

When they had left, James slowly walked back across the deep furrows to the mule and plow. He had handled the unexpected questioning well, he thought to himself. There was no chance that he could get in trouble for those answers. He remembered that Joseph Robinson was always telling him that a virtuous man was always forthright and truthful. If that was true, then no virtuous man could ever be a slave and survive.

11

"I've heard the general is going to be President," one man said. The room in Victoria was filled to capacity by men awaiting the arrival of the representative of a distant authority that in anyone's memory had never presented itself so directly.

"Is he that powerful?"

"That's what they say. He's making a plan for what to do about the Anglos and Indians. Whatever he says will be the policy."

"If he is a national figure, let us hope that he understands our situation."

Pedro Gomez stood among them nodding his head from time to time. He had set up the meeting and most of the men present knew that he had been an aide to the general, but he preferred to not overly display this personal connection. He wanted the others to think of it as being like an old acquaintance who turns up in one's life as he is passing through on a trip. He did not want the others to know that he maintained a current relationship as Terán's informer for the area.

The back door of the room swung open and Terán and two aides entered. He wore a ceremonial uniform with a sword. "Señores," Terán said, "I am at your disposal for questions."

"General," one man said, "you have been in Texas for over one year. What is your opinion?"

"Opinion of what, Señor?"

"Our problems."

"You must tell me your problems."

"We are worried," Pedro cut in, "about all of the Anglos. There are now more Anglos than Mexicans in Texas. That is dangerous." The question had not been set up in advance. He was just anxious that it would not be asked if he did not.

Terán nodded at the question. "It is a serious issue. I have been charged with making policy recommendations. This I will do when I get to Matamoros."

"What will you recommend?" someone said.

Terán looked annoyed at being pushed. He began slowly. "It is a very complex question that has military, political, economic, and perhaps cultural dimensions. From a military point of view one cannot discount the possibility of insurrectional threats from the Anglo-American population. Three years ago in Nacogdoches there was a small rebellion. Only a few Anglo-Americans and some confused Indians supported it. But there is no guarantee that future insurrectional attempts, with more solid support, will not come. There is also the threat of an invasion from the United States. That country has already proven that it has a voracious appetite for land expansion."

Terán pulled his sword out and began to make a rough map of Coahuila y Tejas on the dirt floor. "Right now we are too lightly defended. The existing garrisons at Béxar, Goliad, and Nacogdoches need to be strengthened with more soldiers." Terán poked with his sword point at the rough locations. "New presidios are also needed. These I will recommend be placed at the entrance to Galveston Bay at Anahuac, the mouth of the Brazos River, at the mouth of the Nueces River, the border between Coahuila y Tejas, and where the road from Nacogdoches to Béxar crosses the Brazos River." He poked more locations in the dirt map.

"An expanded military preparation, necessary as it is, will not be sufficient to provide a long-term solution to the instability of Texas. It will do no good to have Texas made up of resentful Anglo Americans surrounded by well-armed Mexican troops. There were only two logical solutions. Either the Anglo Americans have to become sufficiently assimilated to identify the troops as representing their interests, or Mexicans have to become once again the majority of the population."

Pedro looked into the faces of the men listening. They seemed to be following. You could not tell, though, whether these were men who were genuinely interested in what Terán was laying out before them or men who had, through courtesy or being accustomed to showing deference to authority, were feigning facial gestures of respectful interest.

"It is not likely that the Anglo Americans will become sufficiently assimilated," the general continued. "From all of my contacts with the Anglo Americans and despite their great claims of loyalty to Mexico, I am convinced that they will not shed their cultural affinities with their country of origin. At any moment of serious conflagration with the United States, they could not be trusted. The only logical solution, then, is to decrease their proportion of the population. We must entice with offers of free land more Mexicans from the south to migrate here. We must also encourage Europeans to settle here."

"Why not offer land also to Negroes from the United States?" Pedro interrupted. It was a provocative intervention that he knew no other man in the room would make. It was also a way to raise a question that was unlikely to be on the minds of the others.

Terán paused. "I will think about that. It is an interesting proposal. It would of course make a difference as to whether the offer was to free Negroes or to slaves. The former has possibilities, the latter would provoke the United States and that we cannot afford to do. In any event, these measures will help but they will not be enough to reestablish a secure population balance." Then Terán shifted to another thought, one that his face showed was really on his mind once the interruption had been handled. "The stream of Anglo Americans coming into Texas will have to be slowed down. Stopping it altogether will be impossible. But if the Anglo Americans can be reduced to one out of every four new immigrants, then in short time they will lose their majority position. And with that, the threat of Texas separation or annexation by the United States will dissipate. There is no way to avoid it then. The government will have to severely restrict future immigration from the United States."

Pedro looked around the room. The men were nodding their assent. It was hard to know whether these were only obligatory nods. Most of what he said made sense to him. The part about encouraging European immigrants he had heard before in Mexico City for different reasons. There were men urging more European immigration to the country as a whole to diminish the Indian majority, to whiten the population so to speak. Terán was white and he could not be entirely sure that he did not share the same motives.

There was a lull now and Pedro decided to bring back the slave issue. "What about slavery?" he asked. "There are not just more Anglos here, they are also bringing in slaves."

Terán turned toward Pedro. "That is a question that I have thought about for a long time. Slavery is a vile institution that no civilized country should tolerate." This was being said for the benefit of the others since Terán had said this many times to Pedro before. "We had our share of it in the colonial past and there is still a little of it being practiced in Veracruz. You are quite right that it is growing here in the Anglo-American communities. I have seen that with my own eyes.

"I had a big argument with Stephen Austin, their leader. He thinks that the cotton industry is what needs to be developed in Texas and that black slaves are necessary for it. I told him that no amount of economic wealth was worth having slavery." This also was being said for the benefit of the others since Pedro had witnessed the argument. "I can assure you though that the words of Austin carry no weight with the national government. In fact, I can predict with confidence that slavery is about to be completely abolished in the whole country."

"When?" someone asked.

Pedro felt a sense of relief that finally someone else was responding.

"Soon," Terán answered. "Very soon. All of the leaders of the revolution opposed it and none more than the man who is now president. There are a lot of issues that I disagree with Vicente Guerrero about, but that is not one of them. In very short time, I predict, you will receive a proclamation announcing its abolition."

The Anglos will not like that, Pedro thought. Abolishing slavery will not have much effect elsewhere in Mexico where it is no longer significant. But not here. This was news that he was anxious to share with the slave he knew and curious to find out his reaction.

12

"You remind me of my teacher," James said to Pedro later that week when they met in the forest. "He was very opposed to slavery. For a man who wasn't a slave, he sure was opposed to it. He said it was because of his religion. What is your reason?"

Pedro thought for a moment. It had nothing to do with his religion. "It is because all men are equal—"

"I know. Before God."

"No. They are just equal. It is not reasonable that they should be treated unequally." This was not the answer he would have given in the seminary. He looked at James for any expression of what he thought.

"I never did believe," James said, "that men would start or end slavery for religion. The way I see it, it all has to do with money. The slave is like a cow that produces money instead of milk. Of course the white man wants to own a cow like that. Otherwise he would have to do all the work himself."

"It is economic," Pedro said. "But it is not all economic. It is political too. It depends also on what the men who have power believe and want. They can make laws that either keep or get rid of slavery."

"Not if the slave can keep making money for the master."

"I disagree. They can prohibit it if they want to."

"That I would like to see."

"You will very soon. No one in Mexico City likes slavery. They will end it very soon."

"Here too?"

"Of course. This is a part of Mexico too even if it does not seem like it with so many Anglos."

"What happens to slaves who escape and go further south? Do they hunt them down and send them back here?"

Pedro shook his head. "I have never heard of anything like that. Sometimes you hear of Anglos going to Matamoros to look for their escaped slaves. But they never come back with them. They say that escaped slaves live openly there."

"Maybe that is where I will go one day."

"You will not have to. I tell you, slavery will end soon here. Then you will be as free as I am."

"To get land?"

"To get land too. I will help you. I know people. It is all a question of knowing people and how to do things."

"You?" James said. "Why are you so interested in me and what happens to me?"

Pedro shrugged. "I like people who think."

"Everyone thinks."

"That is true. But not everyone thinks beyond their immediate lives. You think about your problems as a slave as any slave would. But you also think about slavery itself."

"And you? What do you think about?"

"Mexico."

"Mexico?"

"About what will come of this new country of ours. I was too young to be in the revolution that made it. But I am a child of that revolution."

"Do you know anything about the revolution in Haiti? I heard about it from a teacher of mine."

"A little. It was like our revolution, except against the French instead of the Spanish."

"They were also slaves."

Pedro nodded.

"And now there are no more slaves or slavery there."

Pedro nodded again and smiled. "Don't get any ideas. The slaves were the vast majority there, not like here."

"I don't want to start a revolution?"

"Nobody wants to start a revolution," Pedro said. "They are forced to."

13

James reported to work later that week and found the Binghams getting ready to eat breakfast. He had thought a little about what Pedro had told him about slavery ending soon but did not put much credence in it. How could Pedro know that? It was true that he had never heard that in Tennessee. The closest he had heard to it, and it was not very close, was when his teacher, Joseph Robinson, had said that one day slavery would end. He had replied that one day we would all go to heaven too.

Sarah was lifting a heavy black skillet off of the iron rack in the fireplace. Pig fat danced on the skillet around the frying eggs. With both hands grasped to the rag around the handle, she carried it over to the table and placed it on top. Then she scooped out two eggs each for her and her husband. "What are you working on today, James?" she asked after sitting down.

"This door, ma'am." He pointed at the back door. "It don't close right. Then I'm going to try finishing putting down the floor boards if you can get me some nails."

"If you need more nails," Bingham said, "take the mare into town. I can't get them today." Then as an afterthought, he added, "Watch out for Indians. There are reports of marauding bands."

By the afternoon James had the door fixed and the boards cut and placed on the floor joists he had laid across the rock foundation to the unfinished west side of the house. He had now reached the limit of what he could do without nails. The Binghams were gone, so he took the money that Bingham had left on the table and rode to Matagorda. It was fine with him that Bingham did not have time to get the nails because he liked getting away from the work and being able to spend the day on the road and in town even if there was some Indian danger.

Not too many black men came into town unaccompanied and he was aware of the looks as he rode down the center of the road through the length of the town until he reached the only store where nails were likely to be found. He tied the mare to the railing and walked into the store.

The owner looked up. "What's your business?"

"Nails. Do you have any?"

"You're lucky. We've been out for a long time, but a shipment just came in this morning. How many?"

"Twenty pounds."

The owner took a weighing tray and scooped nails out of a wooden box and into it. Then he placed the tray on the balance scale. The tray was not heavy enough yet to lift the twenty pound weight, so he reached back into the box and grabbed a handful of nails and then dropped them a few at a time onto the tray until it began to lower.

"That should do it," he said. "Two dollars."

James gave him the two one dollar coins and then held out a cloth bag into which the owner poured the nails.

"What are you building? Barn or a house?"

"House. It's the house of Mr. Samuel Bingham on the other side of the Colorado River. I'm nailing down floor boards."

"It's good to see more houses here with wooden floors now. Sign of progress."

It was far into the afternoon now and he did not look forward to riding all the way back in darkness with what Bingham had said about Indians and so he asked the storeowner, "Is there a place where I can sleep the night?"

The storeowner looked annoyed at the question but then assented. "Go around the back. There's a stable. But be sure to be gone first thing in the morning."

James thanked him, grabbed his bedroll, and walked around the side of the building and back through an alley that separated it from a blacksmith shop. To his surprise, he found that a white man had already claimed a place to sleep for himself in the stable.

"You going to sleep here too?" the white man said. He was tall and thin with a red beard.

"They said that I could."

"Don't bother me none." The man smiled. "I just work here. Just don't leave no mess."

"You know where I can get something to eat?"

"I'm going to cook a chicken. You're welcome to share it."

This surprised James and he hesitated to answer. Except for Joseph Robinson, no white man had ever offered to share a meal with him before.

"It's really okay," the white man said. "It's a mighty big chicken, more than I can eat."

"That is good of you."

The man nodded and extended his hand. "Jake Smith's my name."

"They call me James."

"I already got a fire going outside. Let's go out there and get this chicken going."

When they were outside, Smith stuck a stick through the chicken to make a spit and then carefully laid it on two rocks that sat on opposite sides of his fire.

"Where you headed for James?" Smith said after being satisfied that the side of the chicken was the right height above the fire.

"My boss has land south and west of here, so that's where I'm headed. Here to buy some things for him."

"Where you from, originally?"

"Tennessee."

"Me too." Smith slapped him on the shoulder. "Us and half of Tennessee are here. Everybody wants to come here with things so bad there."

"What do you mean bad? It all seemed the same to me."

"That's because, if you don't mind me saying it, you're a slave. Don't matter whether times are good or bad, you always work like a horse and you always get the same. But it's different for people like me. The economy has been real bad there. I had me a farm in east Tennessee back near the mountains. Then it got so bad that I couldn't make payments on what I owed and the bank one day just up and took it."

"So, that's why you came here?"

"Well, that's part of it, but not all of it. There was also a woman. I'll tell you this cause I'll probably never ever see you again. There was this woman named Mary who I was seeing. And as things tend to happen, she got to be with baby. Her father didn't like that at all. Didn't like me either. So he sent her away to have the baby. Sent her to Memphis to live with some family members who had a boarding house. So when I lost the farm I went to Memphis to try and find her and our baby." Smith lowered his head. "They told me that the baby had died and that she then got married to someone else. Can't say I blame her, but it hit me real hard. Everybody was talking about Texas and how cheap land is here, less than half of what it is there, so I decided to keep going and here I am. But when you ain't got no money, it don't matter how cheap the land is and I ain't got no money." Jake Smith leaned over and blew on the fire and a piece of chicken fat lit up and cackled.

"You trying to get up a grubstake of money to buy?"

"That's it. If I can find work here, I'll be able to get up enough to make a down payment."

"What kind of work you do?"

"Carpentry. Been working on houses here. But that's not what I want to do forever. I want to go back to farming if I can get me some land. By the way you don't know how that owner of yours got his land, do you?"

James shook his head.

"I don't suppose you would," Smith said. "Don't matter none. There's lots of land here all right. I'll find a way to get some of it. Then they tell me that you can pay for it on easy credit."

"Well, that's one thing I don't have to worry about," James said, inspecting the chicken that looked like it was done.

"No, I suppose not," Smith said. "That chicken look ready to you?"

"Ready enough," James said. Even if it wasn't, he was.

Smith pulled one of the legs off, handed it to James, and then pulled the other one off for himself. They ate the chicken rapidly and James felt much better afterwards. It was the first he'd had to eat all day. Then they talked some more until it was dark and time to sleep.

The next morning he was starting to bid farewell to Smith and thank him again for sharing the chicken. It was the best chicken he had ever eaten, he would say. That would be an exaggeration but he had been so hungry that his palate had welcomed it about as much as any previous one.

Before he could say that though, Smith said, "I see you got some nails there. You building something?"

"My owner's house." James felt free to scowl when he said it.

"Maybe he'd hire me. I'm a carpenter you know."

"Well I'm not going to recommend you," James said, "cause that's a sure way you wouldn't get the job. But I think he would hire you because there's no way that I'm going to finish that house and a barn as well before plowing season and his lady is real anxious to get that house finished."

"So how do I find this master of yours? Does he ever come into town?"

"Yeah, he comes here. But you best go out to the house and ask him directly. No telling how long before he come in here."

"Why don't you take me with you?"

James wasn't quite sure of what he was getting himself into. He hardly knew this man and he was a white at that. But he was the only white man except for Joseph Robinson who had ever sat down to eat with him. He would have to take precautions around the Binghams though, and act as though he had never seen him before. That way if it did not work out well, he could not be blamed for it. At the same time, having him around for a while would both make the work go easier and make things more interesting.

14

"I don't think you can lose," Holmes said to Bingham. "You'll get your house built a whole lot faster if this man has the experience he says he has. James is a field slave, not a carpenter."

"The only question is whether I can afford to pay him."

"You do have to pay him. That's true. But look at it this way. Once he's done the work you hired him for, you can let him go and never pay him again. You pay for exactly what you get and nothing more."

"That's what some Yankee once told me. Said it was better than having slaves."

"They have a point." And then Holmes paused and smiled. "Well, up to a point. Fieldwork is different. You need to have labor on your property ready to work all the time. It's not like hiring a carpenter to build a house. That is a fixed, cut and dried operation. There it makes sense to pay a man by the job or hour. But with farm work, there are always details to be done at all hours of the day and night that will never really be done once and for all, like the building of your house will be."

Bingham rode back home later convinced by what Holmes had said. It would be an expense he had not counted on that would cut into his already dwindling capital. But it would take care of the house once and for all, assuming that the man really was as skilled as he said he was. They would also end up with a better house. James's work was competent but lacking in finesse. In addition—and this might be the biggest advantage— he would be able to spare himself the nagging pressure from Sarah, who never failed to remind him how primitive their living conditions were. The last thing Jake Smith had said was that he would make it into a very comfortable place for the master and missus to live in. If this man came anywhere near to living up to his promise, that would make the whole expense worthwhile.

15

The work on the Bingham house now was going a lot faster with Jake Smith sharing it. It went faster, James could see, because so much of building requires having an extra set of hands always available; and also, he had to admit, because Smith was skilled at carpentry and could get jobs done faster. At the same time though he began to feel resentment toward Smith, who was now directing his work. Before, when he was working alone, he just had to answer to Bingham who was there infrequently. Now he was no longer in control of how he worked. He kept his growing resentment to himself until he could not stand it any longer.

"Jake," he said one morning, "I consider you a friend—"

Smith looked up from the board he was sawing. "When a man starts to say something like that, it means he has something very good or very bad to say."

"I'm going to say it to you because I think you'll understand."

"Okay, out with it."

"You're a white man and I'm black and the white man is always the boss—"

Jake Smith looked at him incredulously. "What kind of bull crap is that?"

"Let me finish. You're not a slave driver but you act like a boss and I don't like it."

"You mean because I tell you what to do?"

"Yes."

"The only reason I tell you what to do is because, God dammit, I know more about carpentry than you do, so it makes sense for me to direct the work. In everything else we're equal."

James took in the response and thought about it. Maybe he was too sensitive. Maybe he should just shut his mouth and learn what he could about carpentry from Jake Smith. It had been risky to directly confront Smith with what he was feeling, even if maybe he had been wrong. He for sure would never do anything like that with Bingham. Maybe there were different types of white men like Joseph Robinson had said, but he had never taken that very seriously. Joseph Robinson was as white as they came, but he didn't really count because he was so unusual. Jake Smith, he had to admit, came closer to being a usual type of white man. But then again he was unusual for a white man though not as unusual as Joseph Robinson. He would have to just take them as they came.

16

Matagorda was taking shape as a respectable looking town as boatload after boatload of new immigrants from the United States landed. For most it was a temporary stop on the way to moving on to one or another of the farming colonies. For others, including men who wished to open up shops and at least one saloonkeeper, it was their final destination. And over the summer more cotton plants pushed their way to the surface of Samuel Bingham's land than James would be capable of single-handedly picking. Bingham had expected this and was in Matagorda to lease three extra slaves for the harvest.

He tied his horse to the rail in front of its new saloon and walked in. Three men sat drinking together at a corner table. Bingham ordered a whisky at the bar and then joined them.

"What brings you into town?" one of them said.

"Looking for three slaves to lease," Bingham answered.

The men looked at each other.

"What's so strange about that?"

"Nothing, except there might not be any to lease. There's a rumor that the government in Mexico City has abolished slavery."

"What?" Bingham cried. "Surely you must be joking."

"Don't get so upset, son," one of the men said.

"I'm not your son."

The abruptness of the response shattered the easygoing calm of the table. "Easy now," the patronizer said. "No offense meant."

"I've got a right to be mad. I came all the way here from Tennessee with my slave to plant cotton and now they say that they won't allow slavery anymore. I don't even know if I can lease slaves to pick this crop."

The other men looked at each other and then one said, "At least you didn't get swindled out of land. Man in here yesterday said he paid two thousand dollars in New York for some land and got here and found the claim was worthless."

"Mine might just as well be," Bingham said. "How can you possibly make cotton profitable without slaves?"

"I don't know how you could either. I know I couldn't plant mine alone."

One of the men began to laugh. "Imagine. Doing all that picking ourselves."

"Sir," Bingham said, his face reddening, "I don't know why you think this is a laughing matter. Our livelihoods are at stake and you're making jokes."

"That's only because we've been here a little longer than you have and know a little more about how things work in this country. There's ways to get around any law here. If they came down with a law against slavery— and we still don't know if they did—that's only the start of it. That law can be reversed, suspended, amended, or thrown out entirely."

"Then you're not worried?" Bingham asked incredulously.

"Do I look worried?" the man said mockingly. Then he became more serious. "Yes, there's reason for some worry. But I'm going to carry on as I always do. We'll get through this if it's true."

"It's more of an annoyance," the man to his left at the table said. "Could cause problems if it reaches the niggers."

"That's right," Bingham acknowledged. "It would not be a good idea for them to get the wrong idea." Then his mind shifted to the principal reason for his trip to town. "You men know where I can lease three niggers to harvest my cotton?"

"I can help you out," one of them said. "But it will cost more than last year. But then again, you weren't leasing last year, were you?"

Bingham shook his head. "Why's the price higher anyway?"

"More people need labor and it's driving the price up."

Bingham nodded matter-of-factly. He had expected the answer. After some dickering over the price, he lined up the three extra slaves. They were working on someone else's harvest now, but would be available in a week.

He calmed a bit more as he continued to drink and listen to the others. He left the saloon feeling more at ease from when he had entered it with the shock of the rumor of abolition. His drinking companions were right. You couldn't assume that everything was as it appeared in this country. Laws here didn't have the same finality that they did back home. But it was disturbing nonetheless. How could you plan for the future when there was the possibility that the rules of something so basic as how you got your labor done might radically change?

"You're so tense," Sarah said to him when he returned home later that afternoon.

"There are problems with the farm."

"The cotton is starting to grow good, isn't it?"

"Yes, but I don't know if we're going to have anyone to grow it for long."

"You mean all this fool talk about ending slavery?" she asked. "That's got you worried, hasn't it?"

"How did you hear that?" he cried.

"Oh, from Lily. Who else could I hear anything from, stuck out here all the time?"

"And you didn't tell me?"

"I thought you already knew."

"You act as if it's not important," he accused. "Doesn't it distress you in the slightest or do you just not care?"

"If they end slavery here, we will just go back to Tennessee," she said. "Besides I have news for you." Her face brightened. "If we're still here in the winter we're going to be one more."

"You're with baby?"

"It sure looks that way," she said with the relief of someone able to finally release held good news. She patted her stomach. "This is going to get mighty big before you know it."

"It's a damn inconvenient time for that to happen," he said, standing up.

Her face froze and then tears began to well in her eyes. "Is that all you can say?"

"We're not ready for children."

"Children come when they come." Her voice was breaking.

"Don't you care about the farm?"

"The farm can go to hell. I'm going to have a baby to take care of."

"You won't be able to take care of any baby if we don't have anybody to work the fields."

She looked up at him and did her best to glare through the tears. "You deserve to fail, Samuel."

17

A long low whistle cut through the air unlike any bird James had ever heard. He was out in the field picking cotton with the three leased slaves who had arrived the day before. He turned his head in the direction the whistle and saw Pedro among the forest trees at the edge of the field waving for him to come. He dropped his hoe and walked to the woods, acting as if he were going to relieve himself. It would not be good for the others to see him talking with a Mexican. No telling who they might tell.

"I have important news for you, mister Ha-mes," Pedro said. "You are no longer a slave."

James stared back at him. "What are you talking about?"

"Slavery is abolished in all of the republic."

"Where did you hear that?"

"It is true. I can prove it." Pedro took a paper out from under his shirt and handed it to James.

James took the paper and studied the words in Spanish. "I can't read this."

"It says that slavery can no longer be practiced in all of the republic."

"Are you sure?"

"I have no reason to lie to you. You are my friend."

"Is it over now or is it going to be over?"

"The proclamation is dated September 16, 1829."

"That was one month ago."

"Yes, you are free. I thought you would want to know. I leave now." Pedro remounted his horse. "Come and see us." Then he turned and rode into the woods.

James stared at the announcement and then refolded it and put it in his shirt and went back to picking cotton. He thought about telling the others but then decided against it. He had better make sure for himself that the announcement said what Pedro said it had.

That night in his cabin under the light of a candle he took out his Spanish grammar and worked at translating the proclamation. It was not that he did not believe Pedro. It was that this was something too important to not make doubly sure of. After two hours of tortuous reading, cross checking with the grammar, rereading, translating, and retranslating, he convinced himself that the proclamation had said what Pedro told him it had.

Then it hit him and he stood up and walked around the cabin. He was actually free to do whatever he pleased. This was too much news to hold in and he lit out the door and trotted under the full moon for thirty minutes.

He arrived at Ezekiel's cabin out of breath.

"Did you hear the news?" he said to Ezekiel who was very surprised to see him.

"What news?"

"There's no more slavery. We are free."

"How do you know?"

"Mexicans gave me this." James took out the proclamation and handed it to Ezekiel. "It says that slavery was abolished officially last month."

Ezekiel took the paper and looked at it. "It look real official but you know I can't read, besides master Holmes ain't never told me nothing like that."

"He knows but he doesn't want you to know."

"What you going to do?"

"Don't know yet. All I know is I'm free to do what I want. You? What are you going to do?"

"Me?" Ezekiel said. "First thing I'm going to do is find out whether what you say is true or you is just dreaming. Then, if what you say is true, I'm going to wait and see. What the Mexicans say and what our masters do ain't necessarily the same thing."

"I'm not waiting for nothing. I'm clearing out."

"Where you going to go?"

"I'll figure that out."

The next morning was Sunday, and James rolled off of the hay in the corner of his cabin where he had been sleeping with it figured out. He quickly pulled on his clothes and headed for Pedro's house.

He found himself unable to contain his excitement and this caused him to break out in a trot. Then he would get out of breath and have to slow down until he had regained enough energy to trot again.

All of the family was out in front of their house when he came trotting over the ridge.

"Why the hurry?" Alfredo said.

"Since I no longer am the property of Mr. Bingham," James said, catching his breath, "I have decided to leave there and I want to work for you."

Alfredo stepped back and thought. Then he said, "I could use someone to work but I have no money to pay. I can only give you food and let you stay in the old cabin across the way. Maybe in the future if I get some money I can pay you something."

"I can live with that. I never had money anyway."

"I have heard that you are a very good worker."

"I will work harder for you than I did my former owner."

James did not wish to spend too much more time there. He was anxious to get back so that he could clear out his things and get moved. Pedro offered to help him but James declined. Having him with him would complicate his exit from the Bingham farm. Besides, he did not want Bingham to know where he was headed.

Walking back to his old cabin, he thought about whether he should say anything to the Binghams or simply leave. After much deliberation in his mind, he decided that the latter was the best course. If he said anything to them, it could get complicated.

In his cabin he gathered up his possessions in a sack. These consisted of a bowl, three candles, the Spanish grammar that Joseph Robinson had given him, his other shirt, a wool blanket, and the coat he wore in winter. He then took one look around, spat on the dirt floor, and left.

He decided to take a route that would take him past the Bingham house because he could think of no reason not to and it was shorter that way. They would be inside and not see him pass.

As he came up upon the house that he with some help from Jake Smith had built for them, he thought that it was not quite as big as they wanted, but big enough to live in. They would have to make it bigger themselves if they wanted to. He was thinking this when he saw Sarah come rushing out the front door toward him, holding her skirts up to avoid the dust.

"James," she said, catching her breath, "we need you at the house this evening after you finish your work in the field."

This caught him by surprise. He had not wanted to actually see them. He felt fear coming up in him. For the first time he would have to say something to one of them that was dramatically different from what they were expecting to hear. He let out a breath and said as calmly as he could, as if to make it easier for her to take. "Ma'am, I am no longer working here. I've got a place of my own now."

Sarah looked perplexed. "You've what?"

"Surely you've heard the news, Mrs. Bingham. Slavery is over."

Sarah's expression turned stern. "James! Somebody has played a terrible joke on you."

"No, ma'am, it's no joke. I've seen the official announcement myself."

"You can't even read, James. Now get back to work before you get into bad trouble."

"No ma'am, I'm leaving. In fact, you can tell my cousin that I'm leaving the family."

"Your cousin? What are you talking about?"

He wasn't sure why he had said that to her. Maybe just out of spite. Now that he had, he had to explain. "Didn't he ever tell you ma'am? He and I have the same granddaddy." With that James picked up his sack again, slung it over his shoulder and said, "You have a nice day Mrs. Bingham. I've got to go now."

"James! Stop this foolishness. You will surely regret this."

"No ma'am, not at all."

18

"That nigger!" Samuel Bingham said when he heard what had happened from Sarah, especially the insolence. "Where the hell does he think he can go? Did he say where?"

"No. He was just headed toward the road."

"You just let him go?"

"I tried to stop him but my words had no effect on him."

"I know what will have an effect on him." Bingham slapped the back of his right fist into the palm of his left hand.

"This is so ugly." Sarah began to cry.

"He'll pay. He'll pay. I swear it."

Bingham left his wife crying for the only place he knew to share this alarming information. He had to tell them of his misfortune. But he wouldn't just be running to them for help. He would also be doing them a favor by putting them on guard against their own slaves escaping. It would be an even trade.

Jonathan and Lily had just sat down for dinner and Rachel was in the kitchen when Bingham arrived.

"I'm sorry to spoil your dinner, but James just escaped."

"Are you sure?" Jonathan said.

"Oh, I'm sure. The rumor got to him, too, and he thinks that there's no more slavery here."

"This is serious. Where'd he go?"

"I have no idea."

"There are only two possibilities worth talking about. South, further into Mexico or back to the United States. Either one is possible."

"He can't get very far because he doesn't have a horse."

"Unless he steals one."

"He won't steal. We never had any problems like that with this one."

Holmes cocked his head and said with a slight sardonic grin, "He never escaped before, either."

"I'm not thinking straight. You're right. Anything is possible. Are you sure Ezekiel hasn't left too?"

Lily lowered her voice. "He won't leave without his woman and baby and, as you can see, she's here."

Now it was Bingham's turn to use what little advantage this unfortunate experience had given him and speak as if he had earned the right to give advice on the question of escaping slaves. "You must realize that when one slave escapes, no one's slaves are safe. His example can become contagious. Even the trustworthiest of slaves will secretly hope that he gets away. And if he gets away, then any slave begins to entertain the idea that maybe, just maybe, he too can run away from all this hard work."

"What they think they're going to find when they run away has always been a mystery to me," Holmes said.

"I hear," Lily said, "that most runaways starve within three months if they're not caught. They find 'em by the sides of roads all shriveled up."

"That's what they deserve," Bingham said, "but it's no comfort to the owner who has lost his investment and has had to suffer the disruption to his work."

"Samuel," Jonathan Holmes said, "you might as well report this to George, not that you're going to get a whole lot of help from him. But he does represent the law in a manner of speaking, or what exists of it, around here."

It was too late now to ride on to Matagorda to share his distress, so Bingham went home. He found Sarah looking fidgety in the front room rubbing her hands on her stomach.

"There's something wrong," she said. "I don't feel right."

"Now don't you dare get sick tonight," he said. "I can't handle two emergencies at once."

She put her hands down and icily stared at him for a few seconds and then said, "I'm going to bed."

"Yes, do go to bed. You'll feel better in the morning."

After she was out of the room, Bingham poured himself a drink of rum and paced back and forth, trying to calculate what he would do now. The leased slaves were still on the property harvesting the cotton crop. At least that was taken care of. Good thing James had gotten it and them started before leaving. Not everything would be a loss. This realization calmed him enough so that he felt that he could sleep now.

When he woke in the morning he heard Sarah in the front room moving about. He got up out of bed and pulled his pants on. There was no time to lose. He had to get into Matagorda with the news.

"It's real bad now," Sarah said grimacing, when he came rushing into the front room on his way out.

"There's nothing I can do about it. I've got to get to Matagorda."

"You're not going to leave me alone here, are you?"

"What choice do I have? An escaped slave is serious business."

"At least take me to Lily's," she cried.

"Okay, I'm going to saddle the horse and you can ride behind me."

"You know I can't do that in this condition. Take the wagon."

Bingham looked at her in frustration and then acceded. Hitching his horse up to the wagon would cause him to lose time but he had to do it so he rushed out the door to get it done, shouting back as he left, "You be sure to be ready when I get the wagon to the front."

Twenty minutes later he left Sarah on the front porch of the Holmes house. Holmes was gone somewhere but Lily was there. She looked concerned and took Sarah inside. It was probably no more than one of those small sicknesses that women get when they're with child, he told himself. Then he unhitched his horse from the wagon, took the saddle from the back of the wagon and put it on the horse, and started the ride to Matagorda.

Two hours later, covered with dust, he rushed into the land commissioner's office to find George Baker from Brazoria sitting there. "I've come to report an escaped slave."

Baker looked up from a mountain of papers on the wooden desk. "There is no such thing."

"C'mon man. This is no time for jokes. I have crops to be tended."

"Slavery was abolished over a month ago in the Republic."

"Are you sure? What's your proof?"

"Just found out about it myself." Baker picked up a paper from the corner of the desk. "You can read it here if you want." He put the decree down on the side of the desk where Bingham stood and turned it so that he could read it.

Bingham looked at the words in Spanish and then back at Baker. "You sure it says that slavery is abolished?"

"I can read Spanish and that's what it says. And that seal," he pointed to the corner of the paper, "makes it official."

"You can't enforce that here."

"Perhaps not. But I can't spend any time going to a presidio to try to get troops to go after your runaway either."

Bingham felt the anger coming up in him. But he knew better than to show it here where it could cost him, so he did his best to effect a civil retreat. "I appreciate your time, George."

Out on the street now, Bingham took the reins of his horse and walked him up the street past two new storefronts that were going up. He tied the horse again, this time to the rail in front of the saloon.

Bingham saw Adrian Johnson standing at the bar and went up to him.

"You don't look too good," Johnson said.

"My slave just escaped. He thinks he's free."

Johnson took a drink and put the glass down on the bar. "All of us are having problems now, but this is the first actual runaway I've heard about. You know where he went?"

"No. He could be anywhere."

"Maybe he's lit out and is putting as much distance as possible from here. But maybe also if he thinks he's free, he's around here somewhere. Let me make some inquiries. He won't be among the whites. None of them would harbor him. He could've gone with Indians. It'd be hard to find him there. Then there are the Mexicans. There's one of them I know who'd tell me if he was with them."

"And if we find him?"

"There's nothing to be done about it for the moment."

"For the moment?"

"There's some chance that the Mexicans will reconsider and let Texas keep slavery."

"Some chance?" Bingham said, "I can't do business on the basis of 'some chance.' How am I supposed to finish with this crop with my only slave gone?"

"Don't know what to tell you."

Bingham left the saloon not much impressed by the slim hope that slavery would be relegalized. He mounted his horse and headed for home. Not much had been accomplished in town. He let the horse slow down to a walk. There was no real reason to hurry now and he had options to consider. With James gone there was no possibility to build up the business. He had no extra money to hire anyone. Every bit of money brought from Tennessee had either been spent on starting up or was already budgeted for expenses down the road. He had been here for a year and a half now, which was not that much time. It would all be a loss but it would be better to cut his losses now.

By the time he reached the Holmes house he had decided what had to be done. First he told Holmes that he had confirmed that it was true that the Mexican president had issued a decree abolishing slavery.

Holmes shook his head and spat into the dirt. "They'll regret this."

"This country is just not stable enough to do business in. And that's why I have to tell you that Sarah and I will be going back to Tennessee."

"Not so fast, Samuel. It's not as bleak as you think, certainly not enough to give up on Texas. The one thing that you are right on is that the government is none too stable. Decrees can be reversed. I am sure that Stephen Austin's already on his way to Mexico City and he has influence there. But you better deal with your wife now." Holmes nodded toward the stairs that led up to the bedrooms. "She's hurting a lot."

It was probably nothing, Bingham thought to himself. That woman was always complaining. But he went up anyway to see what was the matter.

At the top of the stairs he saw the door of the bedroom open and Lily Holmes come out.

"How is she?" he asked.

"Not good. She lost the baby. I'm sorry."

Bingham heard the words and nodded. It was just as well. It was not a good time to have a baby with all the problems with the farm now that James was gone. "I'll talk to her," he said. He started for the bedroom door only to be stopped by Lily whose eyes told him that he would not be welcome inside.

19

Most of the late November morning was gone. The sky was clear and a cool breeze blew across his face. It had been two weeks since he had walked away from the Bingham farm and now he was fixing up the outside of the cabin for winter on the Gómez land where they were letting him stay. There was not a lot of work to be done with the land because most of the crops had already been harvested and prepared for storage. He had talked to them about preparing the land for cotton but they did not seem interested so he did not pursue it. They seemed more interested in growing what they could directly eat or use. They understood that cotton would bring them cash that would also be useful, but it would mean having to work through the Anglos and this they did not want to do.

He still did not feel completely safe. He was just five miles away from the Bingham and Holmes farms. Even though the Mexicans kept assuring him that slavery was over and that he was free to do as he pleased, "para hacer lo que te da la gana," they said, he was not so sure. It had never occurred to him that slavery would just end like that. It had in fact never occurred to him that slavery would end at all. He had always thought that the only way he would be free would be to run away from it. He was really free, they kept telling him, but he did not feel completely free. He was not far enough away from Bingham and the others. This thought gnawed at him and kept him nervous. Apprehension had replaced the exhilaration he had felt back in his old cabin on the Bingham farm when he concluded that the Mexicans really had abolished slavery. Denied to him was the feeling of rapture he thought he would have when in the past he had dreamed of no longer being a slave.

"In time," Pedro said to him later that day, "you will have your own land and then you will not work for us." He and his sister had come over to the cabin to tell him that the midday comida was ready.

"You forget that I am a Negro and a Negro can't own land."

"You could get land here," Pedro responded. "There is plenty and the government could grant some of it to you."

"Is that really possible here?"

"Not right away," Pedro said. "But if you work well here, my father will help you. As I told you, he knows people."

"Tell your father that I will work extra hard for him and not just because I would like to have my own land some day."

"He knows that. He knows that by working for free for him that you are doing him a big favor and so that is how he would repay the favor."

"Mi papa will be your patrón," Pilar said.

"But only for a little time," Pedro added.

James looked puzzled. "I'm not following."

"My father is not don Santiago," Pedro said with a knowing look at his sister.

"Don Santiago?"

"He is the patrón of a lot of peasants who work for him. The difference is that he wants to keep them working for him forever. My father does not have that intention. He only wants to exchange favors with you."

"I think I understand," James said. "I will work for him for a few years and then he will help me to get my own land."

Pedro and Pilar nodded.

"My father also told me that don Santiago asked him why you were living here."

"And what did he tell him?"

"That you were a friend who didn't want to continue working where he was and since slavery was abolished he let you come to work for us. Don Santiago said that it would cause problems with the Anglos. When my father said that it was not against the law, don Santiago said that the issue of slavery was still not resolved."

"And what did he mean by that?"

"That the Anglos are appealing it."

"Appealing it?"

"They will try to get the government in Mexico City to make an exception so that Texas can continue with slavery."

James heard this and he felt his heart sink. "Will they succeed?"

"I do not think so. It is only the Anglos who want slavery and they are a very small part of the population of Mexico."

He did not know what to make of this for he really did not know what the situation was in the rest of the country. You would think, he thought, that if something like slavery were abolished, it would be ended forever. You could not temporarily abolish something. You might be able to suspend it but not temporarily abolish it for by abolishing something it meant that it had been so completely eliminated that there would be nothing left of it to enable it to start up again. Slavery obviously had not been abolished enough here if they were talking about the possibility of it starting up again. It would be like a corpse coming back to life; or maybe it wasn't really a corpse in the first place. Where that left him and his situation and what he should do was unclear. What was clear was that his situation was uncertain. He might be free or he might be living a very dangerous illusion.

20

Samuel Bingham was at the saloon in Matagorda with Zachariah Nettles in the late afternoon nursing his fourth drink and making plans to return to Tennessee. They were discussing James, who had been reported seen to the south living with some Mexicans, when Adrian Johnson came bursting through the doors.

"Well, men, it's official. Our slaves are still slaves."

Bingham turned his head. "Where did you hear that?"

"I heard it from Stephen Austin himself. He just got a letter from that big shot general Terán who came through here earlier." Adrian Johnson now had the attention of everyone in the saloon. "According to Austin, the general found out that the decree now does not apply to Texas."

"That must mean that Stephen did some real good work on convincing down in Mexico City," Nettles said.

"It also means that I have some business to take care of," Bingham said, suddenly realizing that he didn't have to go back to Tennessee after all.

"You mean your runaway," Johnson said, nodding in a knowing way.

"Yeah, him." Then Bingham added. "Not that it'll do me much good. He's ruined even if I get him back."

"You mean just because he ran away, you think he might want to run away again." Nettles paused and then said, "I wouldn't look at it that way. I have some experience with runaways and it is possible to teach them a lesson so that they'll never try it again. You whup the hell out of 'em and they'll think a thousand times before they try it again."

"If he's with the Mexicans," Bingham said, now getting excited, "how do we get him away from them?"

"That won't be hard," Johnson cut in. "There's one of them named Don something-or-other who'll help us."

"They all have Don for a first name," Nettles said. "Take that Don Juan for example, "watch out for your wife."

Bingham smiled faintly at the attempted joke. His mind was more occupied though with this sudden change of events. He knew that he had to take charge of the situation and it excited him. "What about the Mexican soldiers? Can't we now demand that they go and get him?"

Adrian Johnson shook his head. "I don't trust 'em. They're going to let us keep our slaves, but that doesn't mean that they're going to help us. It's our business and we have to take care of it."

Nettles nodded agreement and Bingham acknowledged that they were right.

Pedro was reading a just-arrived letter from General Terán and shaking his head. He was reading what he did not want to read. Terán was in Tampico where he had met up with General Lopez de Santa Anna coming up from the south to repel a Spanish attack on the coast. Some thought the attack was a half-hearted attempt at reconquest that failed miserably. More likely, because it was coming from the Spanish fleet stationed in Cuba, its purpose was to serve as a warning against any plans that Mexico might have on attempting a takeover of Cuba. Pedro remembered hearing speculation that Cuba could be liberated and added to the Mexican republic. Apparently the Spanish had too. In any event the danger was over with the Spanish defeated. But there was another enormous problem confronting Terán. Despite being away from Texas and having no plans on returning, he wrote in the letter, he was still regarded by the Anglo Americans in that department to be the key representative of national authority. It was to him that Stephen Austin had addressed an urgent plea that he intercede on their behalf and work to rescind the President's decree abolishing slavery for Texas, if not the whole country. He had had no intention of reducing himself to being the advocate for Anglo-American slaveholders. He responded to Austin's plea for help by simply stating that he would obtain clarification of the decree, especially, as Austin requested, whether it covered Texas. His great hope had been that it indeed covered Texas, and then he would have been able to report that as such. The response from President Guerrero had not been what he had expected or hoped for. The President wrote him that Texas was exempt from the decree and that it was his duty to relay this information to Austin and the Anglo Americans there. He felt terrible when he received the news and doubly terrible that it was he who had to communicate to the slaveholders what they would be overjoyed to hear. Guerrero backed down, he believed, because there was a centralist campaign underway to depose him. With his hold on power tenuous, it was logical that he had wanted to avoid any danger of setting off an Anglo-American insurrection in Texas to add to his troubles. Terán knew this sudden change of affairs would cause huge disappointment to any slaves who had heard the earlier news of abolition. He asked Pedro to monitor the situation.

Pedro thought quickly. There was only one solution. He must get James out of there and to Matamoros. He grabbed his coat and started for the door when he heard the sound of galloping horse hooves approaching. He stuck his head out the door to find rifles aimed at it.

"He's in the cabin over there," a voice he recognized as belonging to don Santiago said. "You stay here and make sure this one does not interfere."

21

Bingham was the first to see James running out the door. He spurred his horse. Someone fired a shot. "Wait," he said, "don't shoot him."

"Just trying to scare him into stopping."

They were closing in on James when Bingham saw a rope go over him and pull him to the ground.

"That's some fancy rope work, don Santiago."

He felt his heart race as he saw James being pulled to his feet. Better that he stay in the background. His face was covered, a precaution in case someone reported them to the soldiers. Still, he did not want him to hear his voice. Not yet anyway.

He thought ahead to how he'd feel about seeing the man who'd once been his childhood friend being whipped. He had known James all of his life since they were the same age and both had been born on the same plantation. When they were small they had played together and he remembered the good times they had together fishing. They had been very close. As he remembered it now, their separation had been gradual. As they grew up, James had to work more and had less time to play. One morning when he was ten years old he had told his father that he was going out to play with James, but his father had said that he could not because James was needed for work. This made Samuel feel like James was being treated more like an adult than he was. Then at twelve he began to go off to school, which he did not like, while James stayed working in the fields. He had envied James for not having to go to school and being able to stay and work in the fields, which seemed to him to be the more grownup thing to be doing. By the time he was fourteen he had come to understand the way of things and to realize that it was he who was the adult in the relationship. He became more accustomed to telling James what to do in the same way that his father had told him. As this transition developed, James and he became more detached. Then he put the thoughts of what had been out of his mind. There was no point to them now. He deserved to get what he was about to get. Even if he had once felt something for James, this was what had to be done. You couldn't let sentiments stand in the way.

They were tying James to a tree now and he watched them rip his torn shirt to expose the back. The first lash came down and he saw James's body shudder. Then the second came down and blood began to appear. With each lash he felt a strange liberation. He had crossed a line into territory that he had not known before. It made him tougher to watch that body writhing without feeling pity. By the thirty-ninth lash he was ready to take a crack himself. He dismounted and walked over and took the whip. "This one is for making my wife lose her baby," he said as he cracked the whip against the back with all the strength that he had.

22

Months later, after Bingham had become confident that James had learned his lesson and become trustable again, James left the Bingham house after delivering some firewood, crossed over the small hill beside it, and then started across the field to the woods under the blazing Texas sun, looking forward to the shade that the woods would offer. On the side of the field next to the woods he walked eastward until he found the sycamore tree that was his mark for the path that led through the woods to the other side. It was a path, he thought, that must have been made and used by Indians. He'd discovered it two years earlier while trapping for rabbits.

The shade of the woods offered some relief from the heat but not much. Mostly it offered relief to his eyes from the glare of the sun. He was sweating heavily; and the sweat on his back made the scars itch. He picked up a switch that lay on the ground and whacked it over his shoulder against his back to counter the itching that was driving him crazy. He thought of the irony of whipping himself to relieve the effects of the earlier whipping. Other times he found himself laying on the ground and moving his back around, like a dog with fleas, to relieve the itching. But that was only when it really got bad. Rachel kept telling him that the itching was a good sign. It meant that the wounds were healing and that he should resist the urge to scratch because that would only irritate them more. That was a fine thing to say, and maybe it was true, but even the strongest of men cannot resist the most fiendish of itches. It was of course, he realized, much better to be dealing with an itch now than with the searing pain of a whipping as it was happening. The itch was a mere physical annoyance. At the same time, though, it was a reminder of what had happened and that kept the pain from leaving his mind.

If the truth be told, as a boy he had always been curious of what a whipping felt like. He had then observed two whippings, and seen the men carried off to be tended by their women, or if they did not have women, by women who came to help. It had not been an accident that he had observed the whippings. Bingham's father had rounded up all the slave children to watch, and he remembered that Bingham the son had been there both times too. They were still playmates then, but they did not stand together watching the whipping. He remembered looking over at Bingham and catching his eye and noticing something different about the way he looked. It was not that he looked at him with hardness. It was rather that he was beginning to avoid acknowledging their friendship as he stood by his father watching the overseer bring down the lashes.

Men who had been whipped never seemed to complain or talk about it. About half the slave men had scars on their backs from whippings endured at some time in their lives. These he noticed when they worked outside without their shirts on.

As he thought now about those childhood memories, he could not help but put his adult thoughts into them. Had he actually wanted to directly experience a whipping because he had foolishly thought that the scars were the sign of manhood for slaves? Had he thought that being able to bear the pain silently marked a passage into manhood? Whatever curiosity he had about how a whipping would feel had been more than satisfied by this experience. This had been the first one. And now he knew that he hoped that it would be the last one. The only comparable image that he could think of was liquid fire. It had been like liquid fire invading his back. First there was the shock of it against which every feeling of life in him had rebelled. Then, and this is what was more frightening, the life seemed to dissipate and weakness descended upon him followed by disorientation and then darkness. And in the darkness he still felt the lashes against his back, but as if they were coming from some distant place and he was disembodied observing them.

For weeks the pain stayed with him. When he walked he had to be careful about shifting his back. When he worked—and Bingham made him complete the last of the harvest—he had to be careful how he carried sacks. They could go on the tops of his shoulders but not sag over onto the still fresh welts on his back. Sleeping was especially bothersome. He lay down on his stomach to start off to sleep. But he couldn't always go to sleep in that position. He could shift onto his side but he had to be careful. If in the course of slipping into sleep he forgot and rolled over onto his back, the needles of pain instantly awoke him.

Now, the physical memory of it remained as an irritant, an itch that came and went. What remained in his mind was something else and he thought about it as he walked. They wanted to punish him and they wanted to make an example out of him. It had not been an accident that they had made Ezekiel go to fetch him. But the effect on him personally had been strangely liberating. There was no question in his mind now that his destiny lay in escaping and making a new life somewhere else. It was time to start thinking about running so far south that he would be beyond the reach of the whites.

Up ahead he heard the sound of a horse. To be on the safe side, he quieted his steps. There could be Indians. Then he saw the familiar pinto and called out, "It's me."

"Ven," Pedro called back.

In the clearing now, he walked up to Pedro. They were not far from the place that they had first met. "Are you sure this is a good idea?" he said. "I don't trust soldiers."

"He gave me his word."

"And you believed him?"

"He is a sincere man."

"You think so? It's my back that will feel it if you're wrong."

"I know him. He thinks that the Anglos already have too much control. He also thinks it is wrong that slavery started here again."

"Maybe he was only telling you what he thought you'd want to hear so he could get information about slaves like me who might cause trouble. Maybe he wants to see slavery expand here and be very profitable so that the Mexican government can tax it."

"He is an honest man. He wants to end slavery completely."

"I never saw anyone in a uniform who was on the side of a slave."

"Maybe he is the first. If he is, then maybe what you tell him will make the end of slavery come more quickly. There is something else. He was one of the men who designed the Bustamante law. They also call it the April 6th law. It says that now no more Anglos or slaves can come into

Texas. Slavery still exists, but at least it will not expand. And children of slaves are free."

"That doesn't do me any good."

"It is one step closer to abolishing it."

"Why do you say that?"

"Because the Anglos can't keep the system going if they can't use the children of slaves as new slaves or bring in new slaves from other countries."

"They already did that back in the United States."

"Did what?"

"Stopped importing African slaves. My teacher told me that. They don't allow new slaves to be brought in. The old people I knew in Tennessee said that you used to see lots of Africans who couldn't speak English. Now you just see the children of Africans." Then James decided to change the topic to something else he had been thinking about. "But you don't want to just end slavery, you want to get rid of the whites too."

Pedro shrugged. "It is logical."

"Doesn't that mean getting rid of me too? You end slavery so that you can get rid of both the owners and slaves."

"I do not see you as an Anglo."

"What do you see me as?"

"Nothing."

"Nothing?"

"I mean you are my friend so I do not see you as a slave, an Anglo, an Americano."

"Or a Negro?"

"You are black, are you not? I am dark too."

Horse steps announced the approach of a rider and both men looked up. "It is him," Pedro said.

General Terán dismounted his horse and tied the reins to a low lying tree branch, walked up to the fire, shook hands with both men, and exchanged greetings in Spanish.

"You look different out of uniform," James said to him.

"We have met?" Terán responded.

"You asked me some questions once about a year ago."

"Oh yes," Terán said hesitantly. Then he looked James in the eyes and said, "I have heard from Pedro that you are treated badly by your owners. Is this true?"

"Yes, it is true. They have treated me badly."

"Do you have proof?"

"This will prove the point." James pulled his shirt up and over his head and then turned his back toward the general.

Terán took hold of his arm and drew him up close so that he could examine the welts and scars in a ray of sunlight that shined through the trees. "How many?"

"Forty I think."

"You cannot remember?"

"I passed out."

"Those are very deep, delivered with great cruelty."

"It has gotten worse since your government went back on abolishing slavery." James was putting his shirt back on. "Now the owners are running scared. They're afraid of what you're going to do and of what we might do, so they come down harder on us."

"How do you know this? Surely you are not able to go from plantation to plantation."

"The owners sometimes lend their slaves to each other when there's extra work to be done, and sometimes we get rented. So we pass the word around and hear about what they are doing."

Terán nodded his head. "I did not know this. So you have your own lines of communication."

"That's how I know that there have been a lot of whippings, much more than usual, since your false decree."

"I am very sorry," Terán said. "You know that this is the only place in the country where slavery was reinstated—"

"It does not do me any good to know that the slaves are still freed elsewhere in Mexico. Next time you abolish slavery, please do not change your mind about anywhere."

"I want to see slavery ended in the whole world. I cannot do much about that but I will do something to end it here in Texas, and this time forever."

"I hope I am alive to see it."

"You will be. I can assure you of that. Now, I have something important for you to do," Terán said to James. "If you really want to bring about its end, you will help me."

"Help you?"

"I want to know what the Anglo-Americans are doing. I want to know if they are bringing in more slaves. I want to know if they are importing slaves illegally from Cuba. I want you to gather as much information as you can and give it to Pedro. He will send it on to me."

"You want me to be a spy for you?"

"An informant," Terán corrected. "Pedro has told me about you. You are too intelligent to want to just escape. You would like to help to put an end to this abomination of human slavery."

James nodded slowly. He felt he had no other option but to nod. Then it slipped out of him again. "Your government didn't carry through—"

"The president was under pressure. He weakened. That will not happen again."

"And just when will that be?"

"Soon. We are bolstering our authority in Texas. When it is secure, slavery will be abolished for sure this time."

"Ha-mes would be able to get his own land then, if he stayed and helped us, would he not?" Pedro said.

"I will see to it personally," Terán said.

Then Terán stood up. "I must go now. One request. Do not tell anyone that I am here."

"Why not?" James asked.

"I have reasons that do not concern you."

Experience had taught James to not trust white men, and as far as he was concerned this man was white, in fact, much whiter than Pedro or his father. But for some reason, he agreed with Pedro and felt that the man was sincere. He did not look very happy, but he did look sincere.

He left the meeting in the woods with new thoughts. He had come looking for Pedro's support for an escape. He had not expected to be talked into staying on the Bingham farm. Much less had he expected to be enlisted as a spy. The more he thought of it, the more it made sense. If he escaped, he would only get back a little at Bingham for what he had done. Spying on him would be more satisfying.

23

Samuel Bingham had reason to be optimistic as he prepared to leave on a boat for New Orleans. He had had a double stroke of good fortune. Cotton prices were up and, fortuitously, he had received a small inheritance from a bachelor uncle he hardly knew. He could now afford to expand with more labor. He remembered that Holmes had said that a man was not really a planter until he had enough slaves to do the work so that his only job was to oversee them. That was not yet the case since he still had to put in a lot of backbreaking labor. He was still only a farmer who had one slave—one who had proved to be unreliable at that because he had run away once—and leased others. Now he could afford to purchase four more field slaves. There was only one problem: it was now illegal to import slaves because of the damned Bustamante April 6th law. This he treated as no more than an annoyance since there were, as always, ways to get around it.

"You be sure to bring me back a girl to help in the house," Sarah said to him as he was packing his bags.

"If we can afford it," Bingham replied.

"If you can afford more men to help in the field, you can afford a woman to help me in the house."

"The work in the field is more important—"

"My mother never had to do this type of nigger work." Sarah rammed a drawer shut. "Now you get a girl to help."

Bingham saw the anger rising and chose not to confront it. "Okay, I'll get a girl—"

"And don't you do any whorin'."

He wondered why she would care.

Ten days later after an uneventful crossing, he stood in the slave market of New Orleans. He had missed the auction but had been able to locate a dealer who also had arrived too late with his merchandise. His intention had been to buy four males and one female. The dealer did have a female, a girl who looked to be not much more than seventeen, but he only had three males—one short. That would have to do for now. The asking price was two hundred dollars each; he was prepared to pay one hundred dollars apiece for the males and try to get a girl for no more than seventy-five.

He began ridiculously low at fifty a piece and then worked up in increments of ten to ninety.

"You drive a hard bargain Mr. Bingham," the dealer said, "but if you give me three hundred for the men I will throw the girl in for nothing."

"Done," Bingham said.

"I believe that you have just bought three of the strongest young slaves to be found anywhere in the state of Louisiana."

"They will be ready tomorrow?"

"Tomorrow, so long as you leave a deposit."

"One-quarter now, the rest tomorrow." Bingham did not trust slave dealers but he had little choice.

"That will be quite satisfactory."

He returned to his hotel in the late afternoon feeling good. He had made a good buy. There was even something in it to make Sarah happy—maybe.

A Negro was lighting the lamps in the lobby of the hotel. The clerk had just finished sending two new guests up to their rooms when Bingham approached and announced, "I'm celebrating a business transaction. I wish to eat well."

"I can recommend a fine restaurant, the Colonial."

"Is it far?"

"Just a short walk."

"Very good." Then he hushed his voice and leaned over to the clerk. "I also wish to—"

"Enjoy the company of a woman," the clerk finished his sentence.

The insolence of the clerk was annoying, but he nodded his head.

"Black, white, or quadroon?" the clerk asked.

"Black."

The clerk took two handbills from out of the drawer. "I can recommend these establishments. They are also close by."

Bingham took the handbills and tucked them into his coat pocket and thanked the clerk with a coin. Then he walked up the staircase to the second floor and down the long narrow hallway to his room. He opened the door, surprising a cockroach that scurried across the floor and disappeared under a badly fitting baseboard. He walked across the room and around the bed to the shuttered window. He pushed out the shutters and stood for a few minutes, looking down at the cobblestone street below. With darkness descending, a vegetable stand was closing up. He could feel tiredness from the day's events. He took a step back and lay down on the bed and shut his eyes to get some rest before going out again.

An hour later he awoke, surprised that he had actually fallen asleep. For some time he felt uncomfortable. He always did when he slept during the day. The water from the basin on the corner dresser helped. He wasn't sure how he felt about being with a Negress that night. When he married he swore off of them and so far he had held to the promise. But it didn't help that Sarah was so cold. He once asked Holmes if he saw women when he went to New Orleans. Holmes had simply said that he wasn't a candidate for sainthood. Whatever second thoughts he had about the evening ahead, he had pushed them out of his mind by the time that he combed his hair and rebuttoned his shirt. He had earned this night. It wasn't easy to start a whole new farm on the other side of the frontier. And whatever happened here would be of no account to her since she would never know of it. He would, besides, return a better man by being more content with how things were going. The worst thing a wife should want, he reasoned, would be an unhappy husband.

By the time he exited through the lobby he had completely ceased to think of Sarah and simply saw himself as stepping out for a well-earned night of entertainment.

The Colonial was just two blocks from the hotel.

"Will you be dining alone, sir?" the tall, thin maitre 'd said.

"Yes. I'm here alone on business."

The maitre 'd led him back through a door and into a courtyard with a tiled fountain in the middle. There, he showed him to one of the tables gathered around the fountain.

Bingham thought about the night ahead as he sat waiting for what he presumed would be his first decently prepared dinner in a long time. He also thought about the men he had just bought. He and the dealer had agreed to make the exchange of money for merchandise the next morning on the dock. That way the men could be released directly onto the boat leaving for Texas, which made his task easier.

The waiter, another tall thin wisp of a man, now approached and Bingham realized that he had no idea what to order, so he looked at the next table where a man sat eating slowly from what looked to be a stew. "What is he having?" he asked the waiter.

"The court bouillon. It is a specialty we are very proud of."

"And just what is it?" Bingham asked, somewhat ashamed of his culinary ignorance.

"It is a stew made from red snapper, wine, and vegetables."

"It's very good," the man at the next table interjected. "I recommend it heartily."

"Then bring me a bowl," Bingham said.

After the maitre 'd left, Bingham turned to the other lone diner. "Thank you for your recommendation, sir."

"You are certainly welcome. If I may hazard a guess from your manner of speech, you must be here on business from Tennessee."

"Texas, actually. But you're right; I'm originally from Tennessee. And you?"

"Chattanooga. Will you join me? It is not good to eat alone."

"Certainly." Bingham stood up and moved over to the next table and sat down. "Samuel Bingham's my name."

"Wilfred Jones."

"And your business, Wilfred?"

"Importing. I buy goods here and sell them in Tennessee."

"What sort of goods?"

"A little bit of everything," Jones answered. "But woven cloth makes up the bulk of it. If you are from Texas, I assume that you must be in the farming business."

"Yes, I've been developing a farm there. But, tell me, what's become of Tennessee? You don't hear much where I am."

"The state remains pretty much the same. Sam Houston's still governor. Andrew Jackson went off to be President. And there are still problems with the Cherokee business."

"What Cherokee business?"

"It's all very complicated. They declared themselves an independent nation some time ago in Georgia and it affects us because it's not clear if the federal government recognizes them as such."

"What difference does that make?" Bingham asked, taking a forkful of the bouillon that had now arrived.

"If the Supreme Court recognizes them as an independent nation, then it'll complicate what Jackson wants to do. It's his policy to get all of the Indians out of the east."

"How?"

"Make them go west of the Mississippi."

"They are a nuisance, but they are peaceful. What's the need to get them out of there?"

"From what I hear," Jones said, "it has to do with gold."

"Not in Tennessee?"

"No. In Georgia."

"So there's gold on their land and they want them off it."

"Put bluntly, I believe that's at the root of it."

"I'm not so sure it is such a good policy," Bingham said. "It only delays solving the problems. If you push them west, it only causes problems for those of us who are trying to settle the west. There are already some Cherokees in Texas. I wouldn't like to see more."

"I didn't know that. How'd they get to Texas?"

"The way I understand it, the federal government—"

"Of the United States or Mexico?"

"Of the United States," Bingham answered. "The federal government about ten years ago began to urge them to move and settle west of Arkansas and some of them agreed. But then they didn't stay where they were supposed to and they began moving south into Texas. You know how Indians are."

"So, you're afraid that more of them will move into Texas?"

"In reality, I'm not really afraid of the Cherokees. They're peaceful. But you never know what could happen if they got influenced by the others."

"They're pretty fearsome out there, no?"

"They're savages," Bingham said. "The only thing that's going to get them under control is if there's enough settlement coming from here, and I mean people like us, not Indians."

"I can see then why you might not be in agreement with moving the Indians to the west."

"This stew is very good," Bingham said.

"Yes it is. It's one of my favorite dishes here."

"You come here often?"

"Whenever I'm in New Orleans."

"I haven't had a decent meal in a long time."

"There are no dining establishments in Texas?"

Bingham laughed. "There's hardly any food. It's all corn and pork with a little coffee to wash it down, day in and day out."

"I'm not sure then that I would like to live in such a place."

"Oh, that will change in time."

"As more people move in."

"Yes. That's the key. You tell people back in Tennessee that they should come to Texas."

"Then I'll lose my business," Jones said with a laugh.

"Well, if memory serves me correctly, there are still many people coming to Tennessee, and not all of them are going to be able to find the land they need. So you just send on the ones who won't have land and who you wouldn't want anyway."

"Along with the Indians?"

"That, I assume," Bingham said, "was a joke."

"Of course. You have a good point. It's not so easy for a hard working man to buy land at a reasonable price any more in Tennessee."

"It's much more reasonable in Mexico."

"That alone will ensure that you'll get all the settlers you want. But isn't it true that the Mexican government has stopped letting Americans come in?"

"That's true," Bingham said, "but they can't enforce it. It's very easy to cross the border. They haven't enough troops to stop you."

"But I imagine they could make it mighty hard for a man once he got there without legal permission."

"It'd be a problem. But if I were a man who was looking for land, I'd take the risk. Eventually the government will realize the stupidity of the policy and stop it."

The conversation was engaging but Bingham increasingly had something else of a more carnal nature on his mind and so he drew it to a close. "It has been a pleasure talking with you, Wilfred. If your trading ways ever take you to Texas, you must come and see me where you will be most welcome."

In the open air outside the restaurant he took a moment to consider his options. To the left took him back to the hotel, which he considered for a second since he still felt a twinge of ambivalence. Then he turned right and started walking toward the Post Office. The handbill said to take a right off of Canal Street at the Post Office. Three blocks back of it, according to the directions, he would find a three story blue house.

The dirt street off of Canal was unlit. Bingham checked his gun before venturing down it. One always took precautions in this port city at night. A five-minute walk, where he encountered no one, put him in front of the house. Its blue color could be seen from the light spilling out of the windows. He thought once again. He could just look at it and go back to the hotel. But then he chided himself for his hesitance and forthrightly walked up the steps of the porch to the entrance.

24

The next day, feeling good after his night on the town, he attended to one last task before returning to Texas. "I wish to emancipate my slaves," Samuel Bingham said to a notary public.

"You must be from Texas, sir," responded the official, a small man with a drooping mustache and an all-too-knowing and eager smile.

"That is right, but it is none of your affair."

"And you wish to then have them bounded over to you as contract labor for 99 years?"

"You are right again," Bingham said. He did not like the official's tone of voice.

"Very clever. Then you will not be importing slaves into Texas. Good insurance also in case the Mexicans abolish slavery, no?"

"Your impudent comments are causing me delay. Can you do this or not?"

"Don't worry. Of course I can do it. You are not the first."

Bingham proceeded to sign the necessary papers. When it was finished he paid the man his fee and put the papers into his satchel. Now that his principal business in New Orleans was accomplished, he proceeded back to the hotel to get ready to leave. A boat was leaving for Texas in the early afternoon and he intended to be on it with his new purchases. True, he did not have as many males as he wanted. He was lacking one. This one he would have to pick up in Texas, and for that he had a plan. The female would make Sarah happy. He wouldn't mind having her around either. She was certainly a fine looking young negress with an angular face and lithe body.

25

For the next months James found himself sharing his cabin with the three new slaves. It was crowded, very crowded, and Bingham had indicated that he was looking to buy still another, but there was hardly time to feel greatly put out by it. Bingham had them working fourteen-hour days to clear two new fields. By the time they got back at night they had barely enough energy to start a fire, heat the water in the iron pot, and then cook the corn mush for dinner. After that they collapsed to sleep onto the four piles of hay spread around the cabin, one in each corner. With the others not speaking English, communication was reduced to a series of gestures. After a while, James concluded that he might as well begin to teach them some words. The others understood that, of the four languages that had been brought into the cabin, his would be the most useful for the long term.

Once the crop had been harvested that fall and there was time to start building cabins for the others, James began to regain some of his privacy and life slowly returned to the rhythm to which he had been accustomed. He continued to do his usual field chores while the others worked on the newly cleared sections. For a while they continued to share meals, but then he broke off from the group most nights to eat by himself.

He was passing the Bingham house on an unusually warm winter morning when he saw the female Negro they called Elizabeth walking back from the garden.

"Where is the boss?" James said to her teasingly.

"You mean the master?"

"I mean the boss."

"He and his lady went to town," Elizabeth said. "Why you speak so disrespectfully about them?"

"I know them only too well. You can see for yourself what they're like."

"They don't seem to like each other very much."

"I'll tell them you said that."

A look of panic took over Elizabeth's face. "Don't—"

"I was just joking. I don't tell them anything I don't have to."

"You like to tease."

"I'm sorry."

"No, it's alright. You do it in a respectful way, not like some of them."

James looked at the high cheekbones in her face. "You don't look like most Negroes."

"That 'cause I'm part Indian. That what my mother told me."

"And I'm part white too."

Elizabeth laughed. "I part that, too."

"You're very pretty."

"Don't you get too forward."

"It's a compliment from here." James touched his forefingers over his heart.

From the distance both of them heard the sound of an approaching wagon.

"You better get out of here," Elizabeth said. "They coming back."

"When they leave again. Come and see me and we can talk some more."

"I'll think about it. Now, you get out of here."

Two days later James heard a knock on his door. It startled him because it was the first time someone had approached without him knowing it well ahead of time. He leaped to his feet and opened the door.

"You still want to talk?" Elizabeth said.

"Come in."

"You live in a mess," she said, eyeing his few possessions scattered about on the dirt floor.

"I was not expecting company," he said with a mock look of sheepishness.

"Well then, come. We take a walk outside. It is nice."

"You won't be missed?"

"They're gone for the afternoon."

That was all that needed to be said. She had come looking for him. This he immediately surmised from the situation and he took this to mean that there was interest.

They walked across the wide field with the tall grass with her walking a little in front of him until they came to the edge of the woods and found a nice spot to sit down in.

"How did you end up here?" James asked.

"The man who owned me, he run into some money problems and he sell me to a trader. He's the one who sold me to him." She pointed in the direction of the Bingham house.

"The Africans? Where'd they come from?"

"Africa," she said laughing at him.

"I know that," he said smiling. "What I meant is how'd you end up getting sold with some Africans? Besides, a teacher of mine told me that no more African slaves were supposed to be coming into the United States."

"I don't know since I couldn't ask them. They can't even speak to each other. All I know is that one night some men brought them and the trader he paid some cash."

"They must've smuggled them in. Where did this happen?"

"In New Orleans right before I was sold to Master Bingham."

"What do you think of him?"

"Who?"

"Bingham."

"I try not to think of him. He never been real cruel to me but I don't trust him. The lady, she is better. You've been with them a long time, haven't you?"

"Too long."

"How long?"

"As long as I can remember."

"You grow up around them?"

"Around him."

"So you born on his plantation back in Tennessee. When you first see her?"

"Just a few years ago. She's from someplace else in Tennessee. I first saw her when she come to the big house one afternoon all dressed up. It was a big occasion. Somebody else told me that he was getting ready to marry her."

"What do you think of her?" Elizabeth asked.

"She whines a lot. I wouldn't want to be married to a woman like her."

Elizabeth laughed. "You don't know much about white women, do you? That's how they control their husbands. They whine and whine and whine and then keep whining till the man he can't stand it no more and he give in on whatever it is she whining about."

"It looks like you got them all figured out."

"I see them every day up close. It give me something to think about."

"Do they know what you think?" James said.

"They don't know that I think." She laughed some more. "I try to keep that a secret."

"What do they say about me?"

"That you are a bad influence 'cause you think too much."

"They don't say it like that."

"No, of course not. They just say that you did something very wrong a while back that you had to be punished for."

"I walked away from here."

"You tried to escape?"

"They ended slavery here and then started it again."

"They did what?" she said.

"Just like I said. They ended slavery in this whole country but then the whites got them to let them keep it going here."

"And you? Where they catch you?"

"I was working for some Mexicans over there on the other side of the woods." James pointed over her shoulder. "That's when they whipped me."

Elizabeth lowered her voice. "Let me see."

"You don't want to see it. It's ugly."

"No, let me see."

"Alright." He took off his shirt and turned his back toward her.

"Ow," she said, cringing. "Your back look like the bottom of a dry creek bed. Does this hurt?" She was tracing her finger along a scar that ran from his shoulder blade diagonally across the back.

"No, it feels good."

Then he felt the kiss of her lips on his back.

"I am so sorry they did this to you," she said, now looking him in the face. "You are a fine man." She took a breath and looked at him in the eye and nodded her head slightly as if to say it was time and closed her eyes.

He leaned over and found her waiting lips and then they were in a very tight embrace for a long time.

When it was over, she stood up and brushed herself off. "This will be our secret. They don't like you very much in that house."

"They have reason."

They were walking back now and she said, "What you going to do? Run away again?"

"I won't have to."

"What do you mean you won't have to?"

"The Mexicans are going to end slavery soon. All the signs are there."

"Really?"

James nodded. "It's true."

"Then what are you going to do?"

"I have a good plan. I'll show you when there's a chance."

"When it is right." Elizabeth said. "Now you go." The Bingham house was in sight. "I don't want them to see us alone together."

He stopped and drew her to him and their lips met but she was in too much of a hurry and too worried to let the kiss deepen.

26

Samuel Bingham stopped his wagon by the edge of a beach north of Matagorda. He was with Adrian Johnson. The moon lit up the sand and the waters out into the bay. They climbed down from the wagon and headed for a small group of waiting men, some from Matagorda and others from other municipalities.

"Any sign of them yet?" Johnson asked when they reached the group.

"Not yet," one of the men said.

"They better hurry," Bingham said. "You never know when Bradburn and his damn Mexican soldiers will pass by. It's a damned inconvenience that Terán established that fort and customs house at Anahuac. And to command it by an ex-American."

"Don't worry," Johnson replied. "They're not going to venture out of their barracks at night."

"Bradburn is some pompous ass, isn't he?"

"Pompous does not do full justice to what emanates from that man. I've heard of men becoming Mexicanized before, but nothing like him."

"What would make a man turn his back on his own countrymen?"

"They say he fought in their independence revolution and then rose up through the military ranks. Wants to show his loyalty."

"It could be craziness too. Maybe a woman. Who knows? But that's his problem."

"Unfortunately, it's ours too."

"Maybe," Bingham said, "but let's not talk about him now. I'm still not so sure getting labor this way is such a good opportunity. The way that I figure it, they probably pick the best ones to stay in Cuba and then send the ones they don't want here."

"That's not the way they do it there, from what I've heard. They buy them in groups, not individually like we're used to. So, they'll send any extra groups over here, hoping to make a little more money on it. Besides, we don't have to buy if we don't like what we see."

After a long while of more standing around and talking, Bingham came to the conclusion that good opportunity or not, nothing was going to come out of that night sea for them, at least not on this night.

He was getting ready to suggest leaving when one of the men who had kept his eyes fixated on the gulf horizon, said, "I think I see a lantern out there."

Bingham swept his eyes across the horizon and thought he too detected a pinprick of light. "I do too. It must be them."

Someone picked up a lantern that sat on the beach and swung it back and forth. The pinprick of light coming from out at sea then moved similarly in recognition.

A half hour later three rowboats landed on the beach carrying the captain of the Cuban sloop, three sailors and a human cargo of fifteen African males.

Adrian Johnson, who spoke Spanish the best in the group, addressed the captain: "I trust your voyage was a safe one."

"We encountered no unforeseeable problems," the captain responded. "The sea was calm and we neither saw American nor Mexican vessels. Now, gentlemen, as you can understand, we do not wish to tarry here. So let us get down to business."

"Ask him how old they are," Bingham said.

Adrian Johnson translated the question and the captain responded that the ages varied, but almost all of them were around twenty years old.

"Surely he does not have proof of when they were born," someone said and some of the others laughed.

"That's alright," Johnson said. "We can tell by looking at them."

"Don't be so sure," Bingham said. "He could be lying. You can't always tell the age of an African."

"They look young enough to me. Let's get on with it," someone else said. "Ask him how much he wants for each of them."

After Adrian Johnson translated the question and heard the response, he said, "He says it's all or nothing. He won't sell them individually."

"So how are we going to work that?" Bingham said with irritation at the idea.

"We'll just have to pool our money if we want them," Johnson said.

"Then how do we decide who gets who?"

"We could either have our own auction, but that would be complicated, or we could just draw lots, which would be fairer or simpler."

"I say draw lots," Bingham said. "Everybody agreed?"

Most of the men were in agreement. Those who weren't said to go ahead with it but not to count them in. Then Johnson got down to the serious business of negotiating the group price. This took a long time. When the deal was finally struck, Johnson divided the group price by the number of men who were still in and collected the equal sums which he turned over to the captain.

The captain took the money and counted it. "Está bien," he said. He then motioned to his sailors to release the Africans, who were still seated in the rowboats. With that final act, he and his three sailors bid them farewell, and pushed their rowboats out into the Gulf waters, and began rowing back out to their sloop.

When they were sufficiently offshore to be out of earshot, Adrian Johnson began the lottery. He lined the fifteen Africans up. Then he tore a piece of parchment into fifteen pieces and numbered each one and scrambled the pieces in his hat. Each man in the deal took one, and then to avoid confusion, Johnson lined them all up opposite their purchases, including his own.

27

Pedro Gomez read the letter from General Terán for the third time. He had not heard from him for quite some time. Terán was now in Matamoros. He had taken up the post of Comandante of the Eastern Interior Provinces that covered, in addition to Coahuila y Tejas, Tamaulipas and Nuevo Leon. There had been no communication since the meeting with him and James in the forest. Pedro had continued to write to him with information he had about local conditions; and James had proved eager to supply him with what he discovered about his owners. Most of that information had to do with the purchase of new slaves. One of them had been bought illegally from a Cuban slave ship, and this information he had immediately forwarded to the general. But there had been no reply. He suspected that the general was simply too busy. Now he did have a letter. In it Terán told him that he thought that the new president, Anastasio Bustamante, was absolutely as opposed to slavery as had been Vicente Guerrero, despite having been instrumental in his overthrow. The immediate problem, though, was keeping Texas securely attached to the republic and to control its border area with the United States. Once that was accomplished, the central government would be a position to enforce an abolition of slavery. The letter ended with instructions to meet him at Anahuac. Terán would be visiting there for the opening of a new customs house and presidio and he wanted him to meet the military comandante, John Davis Bradburn.

Pedro already knew the name and some of the background of Bradburn from his time in Mexico City. Bradburn, American by birth, had come into contact with a company of Mexicans who had gone to fight with the North Americans against the British at the Battle of New Orleans during the War of 1812. From them he had learned of the ongoing war to rid Mexico of Spanish colonial control. There seemed to be in the mind of this North American no great difference between ousting the British and ousting the Spanish from the North American continent. By 1817 Bradburn was taking part in raids against Spanish military installations on the Tamaulipas coast to the south of Matamoros. Those raids ended unsuccessfully with the insurgent forces routed. Bradburn managed to escape. But instead of fleeing north back to his country, he chose instead to go inland westward and reached Guanajuato. There he made contact with Vicente Guerrero, then one of the insurgent generals. He and Guerrero carried on revolutionary activities together until 1820, when he purportedly defected to the side of Agustín Iturbide who was still commanding troops loyal to Spain. The story was that he had *purportedly* defected because it was widely believed afterwards that he had been acting as a spy for Guerrero.

At some point after Bradburn came into his ranks, Iturbide began to consider changing his loyalties in the war. What role Bradburn had, if any, in this change was not known. What was known was that Iturbide trusted Bradburn so much that he sought his counsel on how to approach Guerrero on combining their two military forces. Bradburn then became the intermediary in the negotiations to combine the two forces because both sides trusted him. This led credence to the widely held belief that Bradburn had been a spy for the revolutionary side all along. Why else would Guerrero have trusted a man who had on the surface just betrayed him? Once Mexico achieved independence and Iturbide made himself Emperor, he appointed Bradburn to go to Washington to seek diplomatic recognition; and this Bradburn did successfully. Bradburn then came back to Mexico City well positioned to parlay his post as an aide to Emperor Iturbide to his social as well as career advantage. Bradburn quickly was accepted by the leading families of Mexico City society. He was liked both for his military abilities and for the type of man that he was— discreet, charming, and yet modest. In an effortless way he slid into the routines of elite society—state dinners, dances, even family events. People found it to their social advantage to have him as a guest, for he added an international touch to the occasions. Bradburn's acceptance by elite society was so complete that he married into its highest level, taking for his wife María Josefa Hurtado de Mendoza y Caballero de los Olivos, the fifth Marquise de Ciria and fifteenth marshal of Castilla. Her family owned large amounts of land that surrounded the Zócolo, the very center of all that had been and was Mexico.

On the trip up from Mexico City three years earlier, Pedro had asked Terán if he knew Bradburn from those days and Terán had responded that he knew him well. He remembered Bradburn as having a very correct military air, yet with a certain softness to it that invited conversation. They had gotten along very well indeed at a state dinner the evening that they had been introduced to each other. His wife had also liked him very much, and they had later invited him to dinner with other guests at their home. It had been during that dinner that Bradburn had been introduced to his future wife.

If Bradburn had been adept at rising with Iturbide, Terán had told him, he proved himself equally adept at weathering his fall. It had been a winter night in 1823 when Bradburn had come to his house to announce the imminence of Iturbide abdicating the throne in the face of the approaching rebel troops led by Antonio Lopez de Santa Anna. After hearing all of the objective reasons for why the government, in Bradburn's estimation, would not be able to withstand the attacks, Terán had called for a pause in the report and poured a couple of glasses of rum. Then he asked Bradburn what he personally intended to do. Continue to serve his adopted nation to the best of his ability was the reply. That was his position also, Terán had replied to the younger officer. They would both survive so long as it was understood, especially then, that they were serving the nation and not a man. It was true that both leaned toward wanting a strong central government but not so much as to be completely distrusted or dismissed by those who wanted a more decentralized federated system. And so they had both survived the wide swings back and forth between centralist and federalist control of the government.

Pedro rode north up to Anahuac. He was looking forward to seeing General Terán again and he was curious to meet Colonel Bradburn, an American who he assumed had become as Mexican as it was possible for a foreigner to become. When he arrived he found both men consumed with a problem. Two months earlier, two Negroes had been picked up by one of Bradburn's patrols. Inasmuch as the soldiers could not speak the language of these Negroes and determine what they were doing there, they had brought them back to the stockade and notified Bradburn. Bradburn had talked to the Negroes and determined that they had been slaves in Louisiana and fled across the border. They had entered Mexico illegally, but he was under no obligation to return them as fugitive slaves to the United States. So he had decided to provide them sanctuary by allowing them to stay and work at the presidio.

As far as Bradburn could see, he was on firm legal ground to provide them sanctuary. Slavery might be semi-legal in the Department of Texas, but it was not in the country as a whole. And inasmuch as the men were not attached to any resident of Mexico, he did not have to return them to their owners. Furthermore, Mexico had no law that fugitive slaves be returned to other countries. Nevertheless, he knew that the Anglo Americans, once they learned that he was harboring them, would be furious and demand that they be returned. What would he do, he wondered, if a Texas slave heard about the fugitives and came asking equal protection? He was sure also that the Anglo-American slave holders would wonder the same thing.

Because the Anahuac presidio was the site of the soon-to-be opened Customs House, and because the Anglo-American colonists came to find out what awaited them in terms of customs, word quickly got out that two fugitive slaves from Louisiana were living there under the protection of Colonel Bradburn. The word went southward to Matagorda and inward and upriver as far as Brazoria and San Felipe de Austin, and it was causing Bradburn no end of complaints from the Anglo Americans. It also traveled by boat across the Gulf to New Orleans and to the owner of the runaways, who had hired lawyers to attempt to retrieve his slaves.

"They have nothing to complain about," Terán said to Bradburn shortly after Pedro arrived, "You are acting completely within the law."

"Unfortunately," Bradburn replied, "as you know, the law is one thing and the reality up here on the frontier another."

"You are the law, Juan. You must remember that. It is up to you to uphold it."

"I quite agree. The problem is that I don't have all the resources to uphold it."

Terán frowned. "What do you mean? You do not have enough arms and men?"

"Yes, those are quite lacking here. I'm not sure that we could withstand a well-coordinated attack from the colonists."

"The situation hasn't deteriorated that much, has it?"

"There are rumors."

"What would they hope to accomplish by grabbing the Negroes?"

"It would be an audacious act. But you have to remember that in their minds they have a right to practice slavery. They think that since they were originally allowed to bring slaves in, the government is obligated to let them continue with the practice. Now if you have the government protecting two escaped slaves, it in their minds gives the wrong impression."

"Yes," the general said, "but a military attack? That would be extreme."

"They are willing to take the law into their own hands, especially because their loyalty to Mexico is, I am afraid, nonexistent."

"That is your impression?"

"I'm certain of it. Whatever loyalty they profess will be discarded at any moment they consider propitious."

"That is serious," the general said, speaking more slowly and deliberately. "You must under no circumstances countenance any threats of violence. Those must be dealt with immediately and firmly."

"You have in mind how the revolt of Vicente Guerrero was handled?"

"No," Terán said, taken aback by the implied analogy with the execution by firing squad of Guerrero. "That was not my intention." Then he sighed. "I know that you were close to him. You must know that I in Matamoros could have had nothing to do with his execution."

"Of course not, I know that. It is a bitter reality of our military careers though. Don't you agree? I liked Vicente very much as a man when we fought together. But as you know politically I am closer to you and Bustamante. I understand why they shot him, though I'm glad that I didn't have to carry out the orders."

"I would not have wanted to have carried out those orders either."

"Or for that matter to have been party to the execution of Iturbide."

"That neither," the general agreed. "But a military man does not always have the liberty to act according to his own beliefs."

"Manuel, I understand, but I still have the problem of the Negroes," Bradburn said, returning to his immediate problem at hand. "What am I to do if the owners come searching for the slaves?"

"Should the former owners of these men appear to claim them," Terán said, "tell them that you as a military commander on the frontier have no authority to decide national matters. They can register a complaint through the American Minister in Mexico City."

The next day Pedro was walking with Terán and discussing his reports from James, when they found an Anglo American waiting impatiently for the general outside the main presidio office.

"General Terán," the man said, "I have important business with you."

"Wait," Terán said in exaggerated halting English, and he called for Bradburn to come out to interpret.

The man looked annoyed at the appearance of Bradburn but continued nevertheless. "I am William Logan from the state of Louisiana and I am the rightful owner of the two runaway slaves who this man is harboring." Logan motioned in the direction of Bradburn. "He has told me that I must direct my request through the proper channels in Mexico City. But I have documents here," he pointed to his satchel, "that prove my ownership. Surely you, sir, can intervene and make a decision."

Terán listened to Bradburn's Spanish rendition of Logan's request and then responded in Spanish, "Colonel Bradburn is absolutely correct in his interpretation of the law. There is nothing that I can do."

"General," Logan said, "I have spoken with the colonists here and they are all in agreement that I am completely in my rights to take the fugitives back. They will not be happy to hear of your decision. They had hoped that you would reverse the ill-advised actions of Colonel Bradburn. But I can see that you will not listen to reason and so I will go now to pursue my claim by other means."

After the frustrated Logan left, Bradburn exchanged a knowing look with Terán. It was a look that bespoke of a man who had just had an uncomfortable character removed from the group he was with, as having a thorn taken out of the tip of one's finger. The irritant gone, he could talk more freely and easily even if it was something serious which he was about to propose. He was a man no doubt, Pedro surmised, who had left his compatriots and found a new life among Mexicans and did not wish to look back. But when circumstances required that he not only look back but actively interact with one of them, especially when it would inevitably be conflictual, it was for him an excruciating experience that combined awkwardness with seeing in the eyes of the other the constant accusation of being a traitor.

"In all seriousness," Bradburn said to Terán, "I have a request."

"What is that, Juan?"

"You could help to defuse this whole crisis if you would escort the Negroes under your protection back to Matamoros."

"No," the general said immediately. "I cannot do that. Then I would be seen as abetting their escape. The government can passively allow slaves from the United States to escape here, but it cannot get involved in actively transporting them."

"Then what am I to do with them?"

"I am afraid that there is little you can do beyond what you already are."

"If they leave, they'll be captured by the colonists."

"Then let them keep working here. They are not complaining, are they?"

"No, but the colonists certainly are."

"It is a difficult situation, but you will have to wait it out. You are completely within your rights to employ the Negroes and the Anglo Americans will have to get used to that idea. In fact, it will be a good example for them."

"How would that be?"

"That Negroes who are no longer slaves can work in the Department of Texas as free men. In time the Anglo-Americans will get used to the idea and tire of their protests." Then he turned toward Pedro, "I have a communiqué that I wish for you to deliver to Colonel Piedras in Nacogdoches. I will tell you what is in it because you need to know. I am instructing him to help the Cherokees and their associated tribes legalize their land claims. This must be done as quickly as possible."

28

Weeks after Terán left without the Negroes, Samuel Bingham was riding into Anahuac with four others from Matagorda. He had known for a long time about the outrage of the traitorous Bradburn harboring fugitive slaves. Bradburn's actions set a dangerous precedent. What if, Bingham had wondered, his own slaves heard that they could run away and find refuge with the Mexican military? That could cause serious problems. James had already run away once. It was bad enough that the Mexican military could not be counted on to enforce the provisions of slavery. Now it was actively aiding and abetting runaways. This had to be stopped. If that were not bad enough, when William Travis, a lawyer from Brazoria, had tried to have Bradburn turn over the fugitives to him so they could be returned to their owner, Bradburn had thrown him in his stockade and there he had sat and looked like he would sit for a long time.

Bingham was answering an urgent call for help from other colonists who were as concerned as he was about Bradburn and his hostile actions. What made the actions of Bradburn all the more galling was that they were coming from a man who had betrayed his country. Bingham wondered why he—or anyone for that matter—would want to throw his lot with the Mexicans. Perhaps they had given him a lot of land. Maybe it was a woman as someone had said. Maybe he was just scared of them since they were officially in control. It didn't matter though what his reasons were. He was a traitor, and there was only one thing that you did with a traitor. Bingham was on his way to Anahuac because there looked like there might be an opportunity to rid themselves of Bradburn's tyranny. There was a new civil war in Mexico that looked like it was working in their favor. Ordinarily he had little interest in understanding the politics of these wars because they seldom reached as far north as Texas in their consequences. It had been enough for him to know that Mexico was a mightily unstable country. In some ways, that was to his and the other Anglo colonists' advantage. So long as the country was not unified to the south of them, it could not spare the resources to fully impose its will over Texas. That was what was allowing them to continue using slave labor to build up their farms when its use was prohibited in the rest of the country. This particular civil war, he understood, though, was reaching into Texas and to his and the other colonists' advantage. Santa Anna, the insurgent general, was on the verge of driving out the sitting president, Bustamante. This turn of events would work out very nicely. It was the Bustamante regime that had prohibited further immigration and importation of slaves from the United States. With him gone, there was a chance that they could win relief from Santa Anna, especially if they supported him in the civil war. The local angle to this was that Bradburn was in the Bustamante camp while a number of his soldiers supported Santa Anna. This presented an opportunity. They could join forces with the soldiers and topple Bradburn. Then, if all went well, they could oblige the soldiers to abandon the presidio, return south and return the fugitive slaves.

Bingham and the others cautiously rode through the dusty, empty Anahuac plaza. There were no soldiers nor colonists to be seen. They then proceeded out a dirt trail toward the presidio. From the distance they saw a crowd of colonists gathered there.

"What is going on?" Bingham demanded of the first person they reached.

"The soldiers are about to release Travis. Then they're abandoning the presidio and going back to Matamoros," he said.

The gate to the presidio opened slightly and a man edged himself out. Then the door quickly shut.

"It's him," someone shouted and the crowd cheered.

Travis looked like he was adjusting his eyes to the sunlight. Then he smiled broadly as men rushed up to pump his hand and slap his back. The crowd moved slowly away from the gate still cheering and shaking hands and slapping backs until they reached a waist high rock with a flat top a short distance away.

"Fellow Texians and neighbors," Travis said after climbing up on the rock, "It feels good to be back with you."

The crowd erupted with cheers again and Travis smiled and waited for them to die down. Then he continued. "I am deeply grateful for all that you did to make my freedom possible. But what is more important is that today we celebrate the end of Bradburn's tyranny."

The crowd erupted once again in cheers.

"But we must not stop here." Travis was now shouting. "We will not be able to work our farms and live our lives in peace until that symbol of Mexican oppression," Travis pointed back at the presidio and the soldiers who were now riding away from them, "is gone forever. Bradburn is gone but tyranny is not. I beg you, all of you, not to rest until the last Mexican soldier leaves our communities."

Travis stepped down to more cheers. They stayed there for a while longer talking excitedly and then, one by one, the crowd of mostly men began to break up.

"Where's Bradburn?" Bingham asked one of the men.

"Nobody knows."

"And the fugitive slaves?"

"They're gone too."

29

James knocked on the door of the Bingham house. He wasn't sure who of the three people attached to the house would answer. He had a feigned purpose for the knock if either one of the Binghams answered. If Elizabeth answered, he would say that he was there to talk to the Binghams about work, assuming that they were in earshot of the door. These different possibilities he had rehearsed.

Elizabeth answered. "Come in Mr. James," she said with a conspiratorial smile. Then she gave him a big kiss. "Don't worry. They're gone. Won't be back till tonight."

"Then we have the day to ourselves."

"I suppose so if I'm not too busy."

James had a mock look of surprise. "Are you too busy for me?"

"I suppose not. What do you have in mind?"

"Let's take a little trip. I want to introduce you to some friends of mine."

An hour and a half later they were crossing the top of the hill before Pedro's house and saw Pilar seated with her back against a red oak tree. "What are you doing here?" he asked, looking down at her.

"Oh, you startled me," she said in Spanish, jerking her head upward. "How are you, Ha-mes?"

"Good, really good," he said. "It's a wonderful day. This is my friend Elizabeth."

Pilar held her hand out and Elizabeth shook it.

"She does not understand Spanish?" Pilar said.

"No, just English," James answered in Spanish. Then he looked at Elizabeth.

"Go ahead and talk," she said. "You can tell me what you said later."

"Your back," Pilar said, "it still hurts?"

"No," he lied, "it feels alright now. Probably looks like a river map though."

Pilar shook her head slowly and she shuttered. "They are such beasts. How could they do that to another human being?"

"Oh, I don't think it bothered them at all. If anything it made them feel stronger."

"Stronger? How does it make you feel strong to whip a tied up man?"

"Exactly because I was tied up. They were in complete control and that's what they have to have. The thing they fear the most is losing control." He had not thought of it that way before. It had just come out. The whole slave system depended on control and if the slaves ever got out of control it would collapse. So he continued with the same thought. "When it looked like slavery was over with here and I walked away, they lost control. Then when they found out that slavery wasn't really over with, they had to reestablish the control. And that they did by signing my back with a whip."

"They feel very good and strong about hurting you," Pilar said. "That is horrible."

"It's the way it is in the world."

"I hope I never have to do horrible things to feel good," she said. "You? Do you want to get back at them?"

"Give them a good whipping myself?"

"Or some other way."

"I don't know." In fact he had more than once fantasized as he lay with the still-searing welts on his back of one day standing, whip in hand, before a tied-up Bingham, the shirt ripped off of his white back. But he didn't want to admit this to her. He changed the subject. "What were you thinking about before we came?"

"I was just thinking about a lot of things," Pilar said.

"What sort of things?"

"For one, about when I was a little girl. It was when my grandmother was still alive. She used to tell me so many stories and I loved her so much. But you? You have a family, no?"

"I have parents, of course, but I don't see them anymore since they brought me here."

"You miss them?"

"I don't think about it."

"Why not?"

"I just don't. Besides if you are a slave you can't really have a family. You know that man who owns me is my blood cousin but I don't consider him any family of mine."

She looked puzzled. "I do not understand...."

"His grandfather raped my grandmother." He had not been sure whether to say such a thing to a woman, but he just had. He expected her to look shocked. There was though no discernable change in the look on her face. She just nodded slightly. "You don't look surprised," he said.

"We have the same thing in this family."

"You do?"

"My grandfather—he is not my real grandfather—he sort of violated my grandmother, or that is what we all think. All my real grandparents were Indians and we don't look like full Indians. So we think that because my grandmother was a peon for a rich gachupin landowner—"

"Gachupin?"

"Spanish. He practiced what they call here the privilege of the first night. If a young couple gets married and they live on the estate of a landlord, they have to ask his permission. If he grants permission he has the right to sleep with the bride the first night. It is an old custom."

"It is an old custom of rape. Just like where I come from."

"So I am not so different than you. We both have blood in us we hate."

She said it so matter-of-factly that he was at first taken aback. Then he was fascinated. "I have never heard you speak so strongly before."

"I am sorry that I have misled you. I do not feel strongly about it. It just is."

"You used the word hate. That is a strong word."

"One can have a strong feeling that is a part of them without it—how do you say?—spilling over into how they feel all the time."

"You have the feeling in a box?"

"Maybe, if I know what you mean."

"The box is in you. You can't get rid of it. But it keeps the emotion locked up and safe."

"Yes, that is how I feel about it. It is the same with you?"

"No," he said. "My hate is not locked up in a box. I think about it all the time."

"That is not good."

"Why not?"

"It will make you into a bitter man."

"Do I look bitter to you?"

"Sometimes," she said.

"I must do a better job of hiding it."

"You should go to Mass."

"Go to where?"

"To church. It helps you to feel better about yourself."

"They tried to teach me religion in Tennessee and it didn't work. So I don't think it will work here."

"Maybe they teach you the wrong religion."

"It wasn't Catholic if that's what you mean. This is all Catholic here, isn't it?"

"Of course. There is no other religion."

"Not according to my so-called owners. They're all the time complaining about not being allowed to have Protestant churches. Me? I don't care."

"You should care."

"Why? So I won't burn in hell?"

"That is ugly. Where do you get that?"

"Oh, it's just something that they always used to say back in Tennessee. Far as I'm concerned, if there really is a hell, it couldn't be much worse than this."

She shook her head. "You are very bitter if you think that."

"Do you want to know what I really think?"

"Yes, tell me."

"I think that religion teaches you to not be bitter because it promises that it will be all better when you go to heaven. And I agree with some of that but in a very special way. I think that you have to have hope or life really is a hell. But it has to be hope in something good happening before—not after—you die."

"And you have hope?"

"Yes. I have hope. That's what keeps me from being completely bitter."

"I am glad that you came," Pedro said, coming up suddenly.

James stood up and introduced Elizabeth and the two men embraced. "Not so tight," James said, feeling the soreness come back.

"I am sorry," Pedro said, quickly dropping his arms. Then he drew James to the side. "The war is not going well."

"What have you heard?"

"I received a letter from Nacogdoches from one of our group, Dutokeh, a Cherokee. He says that the Anglos drove Colonel Piedras and the rest of the troops out of the presidio. He and some other Cherokees tried to help Colonel Piedras but they arrived too late. That means that both the presidios at Anahuac and Nacogdoches have been abandoned."

"Whose in control then?"

Pedro shrugged. "For now, anyone's guess."

"What are the Africans like that your owner brought in from Louisiana and Cuba?" Pilar asked when the two men came back.

"Well, they look like me," James answered.

"Are they different in the way they think and act?" Pedro asked.

James thought for a few seconds and then nodded his head. "Yeah, they are different. They have a lot of ideas about magic and spirits. I found a pile of bones and feathers in a corner of the shack where they sleep. They say that it is to ward off evil spirits."

Pilar looked at Pedro. "It is an altar."

"I guess you could call it that," James said.

"A lot of Indians have them in their houses. Not the ones you see around here, but the ones further south. My mother talks about it sometimes."

"But they are not Indians," James said.

"No," Pilar said. "But maybe they believe similar things. What do you believe?"

"Believe? Believe about what?"

"God," Pilar answered.

James laughed again. "If there is a God, he must be a white man."

"Why do you say that? That is nasty."

"Why else would he allow the white man to enslave Negroes?"

"Maybe he is testing them to see if they are worthy of entering heaven."

"Yeah, I heard that before. The meek shall inherit the earth. That's what they told me when I was little. I don't believe it."

"Why don't you believe it?" Pilar asked.

"Because I only believe in what I see with these two eyes of mine. What I see now is that if I want to have anything, I have to leave here—" James caught himself. "I mean there." He pointed northward."

"Have patience," Pedro said. "Just wait a little longer until they abolish slavery here altogether. Then you can work with us again."

"I thought you said that it was illegal for them to bring slaves in now. She," James pointed at Elizabeth, "is living proof that they're still bringing slaves in."

Pedro acknowledged with his face the obvious truth of what he had said. "It is the war. It is keeping us from getting enough control to stop the slave trade. I will send your information about the new slaves on to

General Terán. I am sure that when the war is over he will do something about it."

Later that afternoon as they walked back to the Bingham house, James summarized what had been said and he told her of his plan to get land from them when slavery ended.

"That's some plan, Mr. James," she responded.

"I want you to be a part of it too."

"I already am. You don't think I would stay in that house one day longer than I had to, do you?"

He did not tell her that he was an informant. She did not need to know that.

30

With five slaves working the fields now and one taking care of the house, it was still far from being a plantation, either in comparison to what existed back in Tennessee or to the actual plantations of Jared Groce and others in Texas that numbered more than twenty slaves. But it was well on its way and Samuel Bingham could foresee steady expansion so long as the Mexican authorities did not interfere. The Mexican soldiers had abandoned Anahuac and Nacogdoches so that was, at least for the time being, the reality. But there was still the issue of whether, once the civil war was over, the Mexicans would get around to enforcing the odious laws against immigration and bringing in new slaves.

On a fall afternoon he was driving the wagon alone down the road toward Santa Anna, a new community close by that had just been founded by several families from the United States and named in honor of the leader who the Anglo Americans now supported in the civil war. The back of the wagon was filled with freshly picked cotton and he was headed for the community's new gin that had been operating since

September. It would cost him to get the cotton ginned here rather than to send it raw to New Orleans as he had been doing. But it was worth it, he calculated. If he subtracted the ginning cost from the value of ginned cotton and compared it with the value of raw cotton, he would come out ahead by a lot.

He pulled into the yard and recognized Jonathan Holmes's wagon. This was a fortunate coincidence, he thought. They had both been so busy with the harvesting that there had been no time recently to talk. He would be able to catch up.

A slave directed the wagon around to the side of the gin house and then began to unload the sacks of raw cotton. Bingham saw Holmes standing across the room watching the operations of the machine and he waved.

Holmes motioned him to come over. "This is some machine, isn't it?" Holmes said. "You've seen these before, haven't you?"

"Of course, but not in Texas."

"Well they're in Texas now. We're moving up in the world, Samuel my boy."

Both men watched as two mules walked in a circle on the bottom floor of the house to rotate the power wheel, pushing the cottonseed grate. On the other side of the grate a toothed cylinder revolved, catching fibers and pulling them apart from the seeds. From the cylinder a revolving brush then took the fibers off.

After watching the gin for a while, Holmes said, "They've still got a ways to go. Let's go outside. It's noisy in here."

"One of the disadvantages of machines."

Outside in the yard, Holmes turned and said, "There's a lot going on politically now, Samuel."

"The business with that stupid war in Mexico?"

"That and some other things."

"Whose great idea was it to name this place after General Santa Anna?"

"Now Samuel, you have to remember that they're fighting to remove Bustamante, who caused us a lot of grief with the slave importation and immigration laws."

"He was also the one who had Guerrero, the president who tried to abolish slavery, shot."

"That is true—"

"So you can see why I don't think it makes a hoot in hell's difference who's President."

"I can see why you might think that," Holmes said, "but you must remember that politics is a game in which you get what you can when you can. Now I know that Santa Anna can't be counted on for more than five minutes to favor our interests. But for now our interests and his coincide and we must take advantage of that."

"You assume that he'll win the war."

"He will win. There's no question of that. Bustamante's last defenses are crumbling as we speak."

"So you think we can get something out of Santa Anna?"

"I know it. Once he or whoever he designates takes over, there will have to be a decisive move against all that Bustamante stood for. And that includes the laws against slave importation and immigration. This will also be a good time to move on separating from Coahuila."

"That would be a dream come true," Bingham said. "We're now the clear majority in Texas."

"But still a minority in all of Coahuila and Texas. And as long as we are a minority, our interests will not prevail."

"Why would Santa Anna listen to that?"

"Because he'll be looking for bold things to do. And if he thinks that will make us happy up here, then maybe he'll do it to win our loyalty."

Bingham shrugged. "That doesn't seem to me to be that obvious."

"No, you're right. It's not all that clear that our interests coincide on that question, but it's worth a try, so we're going to petition for it and see what happens. By the way," Holmes said, suddenly changing the subject, "I just met one of your former governors, a Mr. Sam Houston."

"What's he doing here? Last I heard he left Tennessee for Indian Territory to go live with the Cherokees."

"Good question, what he's doing here. Says he's here to stay."

Bingham returned home and walked up onto his porch and then into the front door. The house was empty except for Elizabeth who sat in the kitchen mending clothes. Sarah had told him earlier that she would be over visiting with Lily until the evening. He took out a bottle of rum from the liquor cabinet. He would have preferred whiskey but he had finished off his last bottle and none were expected in Matagorda until the next ship came in from New Orleans. Mexican rum was always around though even if it was not totally his drink.

The house was peaceful now with Sarah away. He sat and poured himself several drinks and mulled over what Holmes had said. After a while of that he lost interest and began to think about the sad state of his relationship with his wife. At best they tolerated each other and at that, only barely so. It seemed as if every small piece of conversation touched off a disagreement. It was true that she had had a hard time getting over the miscarriage. It had taken a while for her to get pregnant again, which she was somewhere in the middle of now, but that only seemed to make her irritability worse. He could not understand how she could fail to appreciate all of the work that he had done to get the farm built up. She always dismissed this as never being good enough and constantly compared their life here to what she missed in Tennessee. He always responded that she could go back if she wanted to, which he knew was not an option for her.

He was now on his fourth drink and realized that he was quite hungry. "Elizabeth, bring me something to eat."

Elizabeth looked up from her mending. "Right away, sir."

Bingham watched through the door her stand up and go over to the fire, where she heated up some bacon. She had not yet borne children, he thought, as he saw her hips from behind.

"Here it is, sir," she said, handing him a plate with two thick pieces of bacon on it and a slice of cornbread.

"Sit down Elizabeth," he said. She looked nervous at the command and he saw it in her eyes. She had never sat down at the table to eat with them. "Just sit down," he repeated less aggressively. "Better, get yourself something to eat and come and sit down here."

Elizabeth took a plate, put some bacon and corn bread on it and sat down at the corner of the table as if in a position that was not fully at the table.

"Don't you ever get lonely here all day?"

"No, sir."

"I do," he said. She looked puzzled at the comment and so he continued. "I'm going to tell you something that I don't want you to tell anyone. Is that clear?"

"Yes, sir."

"You can talk to me in more than two words, Elizabeth."

"Yes, sir."

"That's what I mean. Don't just say 'yes, sir.' Anyway, I get lonely because the lady of the house is not very good to me. She doesn't act much like a wife. Now, I've told you that and that is a secret between us." Bingham took another drink. "You're a fine looking woman and you'll make some man a good wife someday."

Elizabeth edged to the front of her seat.

"You can go back to your room now," he said.

Elizabeth picked up her plate and then went over to pick up his. As she lifted it, he placed his hand lightly on her arm. "Remember, what I told you is between the two of us. I like you and trust you." As he lifted his hand from her arm he felt a subtle nausea beginning in his stomach. Nothing would be able to go any further with her, at least not on this night. He would wait until the nausea went away.

But it did not go away and over the next few days he began to feel progressively more wretched. Nothing stayed down in his stomach. He was feverish. He had chills. He was too weak to get out of bed. Sarah, far along in the pregnancy, was suffering from her own miseries, but she could see that her husband's were more serious so she sent James to fetch Grayson Jones, a well known drunk but also a doctor of sorts.

"So tell me what has happened Mr. Bingham," the doctor said when he came at last and found Bingham writhing in bed.

"Can't you see?" Bingham cried. "I'm half dead with this thing."

"And this thing, what is it?"

"I can't keep anything down. I haven't eaten for two days because I keep throwing up and running out the other end. That's cholera, isn't it?"

"Anyone else here sick like that?"

"James says that two of the Africans are very sick," Sarah said to both her husband and Jones. Then she added for the benefit of the latter. "All three of them work for us."

"Then it could well be cholera. You better be careful, Ma'am." Jones looked at Sarah's stomach. "You look to be expecting a baby any time now and you don't want that baby to catch this. Some eighty people have already died from it around here."

"Am I going to die too?" Bingham said in exasperation.

"It's possible," Jones said slowly. Then he added in a tone that was not entirely convincing, "But not necessarily. Men do survive it and you might." He prescribed two shots of rum a day, equal doses of camphor and laudanum, and more bed rest. The last was unnecessary since Bingham was too weak to get out of bed anyway.

After the doctor left, Bingham was sure that he was going to die and slipped off into a feverish sleep. He did not die, though, much as he felt like he was going to. After ten days he was able to leave bed and wobble around the house. In two weeks he was well enough to receive visitors.

"Well Samuel," his first visitor, Jonathan Holmes, said, "you look like a man who almost met his Maker."

"I'll be okay."

"He looks a lot better now," Sarah said. "You should've seen him ten days ago. I thought he wasn't going to last the night."

"That's the way of cholera," Holmes said. "It takes you right up to the shadow of death and then it either covers you right up or backs off. Didn't back off of Adam Jones."

"He's dead?"

"Two days ago."

Bingham's head fell back on the pillow. "That could be me in two days. I feel like I don't have one ounce of strength left in me."

"No you'll be okay. Once you get over the worst of it, it doesn't come back."

"How can you be so sure of that?"

"I've heard about a lot of cholera cases and I always talk to the survivors—"

"You couldn't very well talk to the others," Sarah said.

Holmes laughed. "Good point, Sarah! No, the survivors always say the same. They got to that point when they thought they were going to die, even hoped they would die to put them out of their misery, then they slowly got better."

"You didn't hear about the ones where it returned because they're dead."

"Now, now Samuel, don't think the worst." Holmes changed the subject. "This will brighten your spirits. There are very good indications that Santa Anna's government is about to repeal the Bustamante immigration law. Stephen Austin did some nice work in convincing him, just like he did in getting our exemption from the 1829 decree abolishing slavery."

"What does that mean?"

"What do you think it means? There'll be nothing stopping more Americans from coming here now."

"Slaves can be imported too?"

"That's not so clear. But if more Americans come, it'll be more difficult for them to stop the economy that we're building."

"We'll still have to go through this charade of calling them contract labor though."

"Perhaps so, but that's not so bad."

"What else is going on?"

"I gave you the good news."

"And the bad news?"

"Santa Anna repealed the Constitution of 1824."

"He did that?"

"Yes indeed he did."

"And just like that?"

"Just like that."

"This country never fails to surprise me. You couldn't do that in the United States."

"It's a different system. More important, we're a different culture. We value stability more than these Mexicans do. It just takes one strong man to come along who they think has all the answers and they let him sweep away everything that they have built up to start all over again."

"What does that mean for us?"

"I don't think that it's good news. We do better when the laws and governance are all very clear. Now it isn't even clear how we're supposed to go to the government to support our legitimate interests."

"From now on if we want something done," Bingham said, "Austin will have to go straight to the top, to Santa Anna himself and forget everything in between."

"It's always been like that, but that's not good. We need a stable government that we can count on, not access to a mercurial personality. One day he can do something for us, but the next day he can just as easily take it away. The way I see it while we're fighting the Indians, the Mexicans are fighting themselves. They're obsessed with how the government ought to be organized. We're more interested in developing our farms. Our interest in governments is that they not interfere with our business affairs. The Mexicans seem to care more about their governments than their businesses. One more thing."

"What's that?" Bingham said weakly.

"They say Terán, the general who was here, was killed in the war. That's good news for us."

31

Pedro Gómez was approaching Victoria. He had two pigs leashed in the back of his wagon. He had decided not to market them in Matagorda because of the plague that had claimed many lives there. It would be better to go south to Victoria even if it was much further away. There he hoped the Anglos and their disease would not be present. He knew that it was not a uniquely Anglo sickness, but from everything he had heard it had so far been contained in their areas. He could not be certain, though, and he began to think of what the signs of the plague would be. He was also thinking about the end of the war that had gone badly for the centralists. Santa Anna was now in power. Personally bad was that according to a letter he received from Colonel Bradburn, who had escaped Anahuac and made his way back to Mexico City via New Orleans, an extraordinary tragedy had occurred. General Terán had taken his own life near Tampico. That was the official cause of death, though there were rumors that he may have been murdered. Pedro had always thought that there was something sad about the general's demeanor. But suicide? This was hard for him to fathom. Then again, the general was on the losing side of the war and in addition, so he had heard, his wife had just left him. It was probably logical, he thought, that Santa Anna seemed to be taking apart much of what Terán had put together to protect Texas from the Anglos. He was even letting them immigrate freely again.

He could see now in the far distance the low buildings of the town. Then he saw to his immediate right two men digging a fresh hole in what looked to be a new cemetery, different from the one that he knew was on the other side of the town.

He stopped the wagon and climbed off and walked up to the men.

The men saw him approach and put down their shovels.

"This is new," he said. "Why is there need for a new cemetery?"

"God has taken many people in the last weeks," one of the men said, sighing and wiping his brow.

"Plague?"

Both men nodded.

"So it has come here too. It hit very bad in Brazoria and Matagorda."

"It is everywhere," the second man said.

"Why aren't you burying them in the old cemetery."

"The wind blows from it toward the town and with it comes the disease," the first man said.

It was the news he had feared. He would just have to sell the pigs and leave as soon as possible. He said good-bye to the men and climbed back up into the wagon and drove on toward the town.

As he passed the first of the outlying buildings he saw that for which the men had been preparing. A procession marched somberly behind a raised cross down the center of the road. In the front six men carried, resting uncomfortably on their shoulders, a long box that could be none other than a coffin. The town priest followed. Behind him, fifteen villagers walked with looks of deep resignation on their faces.

Pedro stopped the wagon, took his hat off out of respect, and watched the procession go by. He also covered his mouth with his bandana until they were well past him and downwind. Then he proceeded on to the center where the market was always held.

The look of death was all about. Men walked hunched over, their faces drawn up as if in a final defensive pose before the invisible stalking killer. Black-garbed women carried the pain of the people, their faces drained of expression. Crows sat on rooftops staring down at the spectacle before diving to the road for spilled grains.

The market did not seem to be as active as he remembered. The sickness must be slowing it down too, he thought. He drew the wagon up alongside it and climbed down and went to the back and began to unleash the pigs.

"You cannot sell those here," a man said when he noticed what he was doing.

"I have sold many pigs here before." Pedro said. "They are good pigs. You can see for yourself."

"I do not doubt you, but no one can sell pigs in this market, so you best fasten them up again and take them away."

"I do not understand."

"It is by order of the ayuntamiento." The man pointed to a bill posted on a tree.

"I have made a long trip here. Why can I not sell these pigs?"

"I do not understand why myself but they say that pigs carry the sickness."

Pedro's heart sank. He had heard that before but he knew that his pigs could not be carrying the sickness. Nevertheless there was no way that he would be able to sell them now, so he did what the man said and tied them back up and turned his wagon around and headed back the way he had come. On the road back he passed the procession just entering the new cemetery. He cast a sidelong glance at it and hoped that he was not bringing something unexpected back with him to his ranch.

For weeks after the trip to Victoria, he monitored his physical condition for any symptoms of sickness. If he coughed, his heart almost stopped out of fear that he had it. When he defecated he hoped that it would not be loose, a sure sign that he had it. If his stomach felt queasy, he held his breath, anything to keep from vomiting, which would prove that he had it. Once he was so sure that he was coming down with it because his stool was loose that he asked his mother if she remembered anything from the curandera that she had once seen in Tamaulipas. She replied that none of the herbs for a bad stomach existed as far as she knew up here in Texas. But then the stool returned to its normal consistency and his mortal worries receded.

After several false alarms that only he knew about, he gradually allowed himself to believe that he had not gotten it. At the same time he urged his parents and sister not to go into any of the towns. Their isolation would be their defense.

32

"You've heard what happened to Stephen Austin, haven't you?" Holmes said after taking a long drink of water from the well bucket. He and Bingham had just finished fixing a broken axle. They were seated on the horseless wagon resting before going on to fix a pulley on the well.

"He's supposed to be back here soon. That's all I've heard." Bingham was feeling sufficiently well now after his brush with cholera to do this type of work. He had recovered quickly enough from it that Sarah had been able to give birth to a baby girl without having to tend to him at the same time. They named the girl Jessica. He would have preferred a son, but that would just have to come in time.

"He's been delayed to put it mildly. They've thrown him in jail."

"What on earth for?" Bingham said, genuinely surprised at the news.

"He was in Saltillo on the way back here when they arrested him. Seems that he'd written a letter to the Bexar ayuntamiento urging them to take the lead in trying to break Texas off from Coahuila."

"They must have intercepted the letter," Bingham said.

"Or more likely, someone in Bexar reported him. He has enemies there."

"Figures since they're all Mexicans there."

"That's not exactly true," Holmes said, annoyed. "But I think that he has really tried to get along with the Mexicans. This experience may change his mind."

"If I were Santa Anna," Bingham responded, "Stephen Austin is the last man I'd have arrested in Texas. That man has always bent over backwards to be loyal to Mexico and discourage what we really need here."

"What is ideal and what is possible," Holmes said slowly and patiently, "is not always the same thing. That's what politics is all about. I think that Stephen has been very diplomatic in how he has represented us."

"There are limits to him."

"Yes, there are limits to him, as there are to any man. The problem he faces now is that he feels bound by his original agreements with the Mexicans. In a way, you have to respect him for that. But the reality has changed—"

"We're no longer a minority here," Bingham cut in.

"That has been true for a long time," Holmes said slowly. "We are not going to be able to sustain this situation unchanged much longer."

"I don't know," Bingham responded as he stood up. "Nobody around here seems to care much anymore. They just go along with it. I doubt that people have even been much riled up by Austin's arrest."

"That's because everybody here is still burying the dead. A plague is a terrible thing. It'll take us a time to get over it. But we will eventually. Then we might see something develop."

Both men left it at that, but Bingham was growing impatient with the go-slow attitude of Holmes. He had lost two slaves to cholera and it wasn't at all clear how he would be able to replace them. Direct importation from the United States was still out of the question, and the Cubans had stopped their contraband trade. But he was not so impatient as to risk his friendship with Jonathan and Lily.

One of Holmes's sons was now coming across the yard from the house toward them. He was back from school in Louisiana. "Mama says that it's time to come in to eat," he said when he reached them.

Holmes let the bucket drop down into the well and then pulled it up directly. Both men then used the water in the bucket to wash the grime off of their hands and faces.

The Holmes house had grown with a new wing the past year and it was beginning to come up to the standards for nice houses that Bingham remembered from Tennessee. There was now a separate dining room with a proper table that Lily had imported from New Orleans.

Samuel took his seat across from the Holmes boys, Burt and Thomas. They were sixteen and fourteen years old. Burt, the older, had sandy-colored hair and blue eyes. He was eager to return home according to his father because he did not particularly take to schooling. His brother had the dark auburn hair of his mother and seemed to be more at ease with learning and studying away from home.

"You boys must see something different every time you return home," Bingham said.

"Oh yes, sir," Thomas said. "The house gets bigger and it has more furniture."

"And there is more land under cultivation because my father has new slaves," Burt added.

"Before you know it," Bingham said, "this will look just like a proper Louisiana plantation."

"It already does," Jonathan Holmes said, "just on a smaller scale."

"This must be a real shock for you boys," Bingham continued, "going from a civilized country into this. Doesn't it seem strange going back and forth like that?"

"Oh," Thomas said, "not so much any more."

"You're used to it?" Bingham said.

"No, not so much that. I think at first that there were a lot of sharp differences when we first started going away to school five years ago. But now it doesn't look so different here than it does in Louisiana."

"There's no New Orleans here, for sure," Lily said.

"No, there's no New Orleans," Thomas agreed with his mother. "But outside of New Orleans the countryside looks just like it is here. It just seems that now that there's more and more people here that it's not that different."

"Your boy has a good point," Bingham said to Holmes. "The mere fact of having a large population has made us more civilized."

"I would say that that's the biggest difference from when we first came," Lily said. "I would say that it's an even bigger difference than the buildup of farms."

"That buildup of the farms took a lot of work," Holmes said.

"Well, of course it did," Lily said. "I'm not denying that. But without all these people around now, I doubt that all this politics would have progressed much."

"What do you mean by that, mama?" Thomas asked.

"We could have had a bigger farm but still had no sense of life getting more normal. You know, there are more people in Matagorda now, and with more people there are more stores, and with more stores there are more goods coming in from the United States that are worth buying. That's what I mean. If there weren't more people here, there wouldn't be all of that now."

"No thanks to General Terán," Bingham said.

"Who is General Terán?" Burt asked.

"He tried to stop Americans from coming here a few years ago and got a law passed to that effect," Bingham said.

"Then he killed himself when his side lost the civil war," Holmes added.

"Please," Lily said, "let's not talk about such unpleasant things at the table."

"But that's no longer true, is it?" Thomas asked.

"No," his father responded. "They repealed the law and it's a good thing they did."

"People in Louisiana say that it's only a matter of time before Texas becomes a part of the United States," Thomas said.

"Hush," his father said in mock fear. "The Mexicans don't want to hear that."

"I have heard," Bingham said slowly as if he were about to reveal a great secret, "that Andrew Jackson has offered to buy Texas from Mexico."

"Oh," Holmes said nonchalantly, "That rumor has been around here for a long time. But for there to be a buyer, there has to be a seller and Mexico has no mind to sell."

"People in Louisiana say that the Mexicans don't know how to govern," Burt said, "and that anyway the United States would be right to take over Texas."

"I'm not so sure that the United States would have a right to take over Texas," Holmes said.

"But would you fight to stop them?" Bingham asked, just half seriously.

"That's not likely to happen."

"But would you fight to stop them, papa?" Burt asked.

"No, probably not," his father answered. "Actually though, when you consider that Santa Anna lifted the darned immigration law, it is hard not to be optimistic, the jailing of Austin notwithstanding. The legislature in Monclova has done a lot of good for us. If you look at the central complaints that we had—distant courts, having to adjudicate in a language for which most of us have little facility, and supposedly having to become Catholics—those have all been resolved. It's a lot different from when I first came here. It was greatly impressed upon us then that we were foreigners who only had the most tenuous of rights to be here. Now there's real progress."

Bingham would not be convinced so easily. "There is one problem with your scenario, Jonathan," Bingham said. "It presumes that there is enough stability in Mexico for us to be able to count on any accomplished reforms in our favor. But you should know that this country is so unstable that today's reform can dissolve tomorrow with one uprising or another."

"You exaggerate, Samuel. It may appear to be that way, but I have every confidence that these reforms are here to stay."

Now, Bingham realized, he had him. He was privy to information that would show who was really politically informed. "Are you aware Jonathan," he asked, "of the developments in Saltillo?"

"No, but Saltillo is irrelevant now. The capital is in Monclova."

"Saltillo never accepted the removal of the capital from them."

"That's understandable, but what's your point Samuel?"

"Saltillo has declared itself in support of Santa Anna and wants the capital back. More than that, it has declared the move to Monclova illegal with all laws passed there by the legislature to be void. There are now troops preparing to march on Monclova. Depending on what happens, all of our reforms may go up in smoke. And Santa Anna may have been good for us at first, but now he no longer is. He's just another dictator who wants to centralize all the power in him. Whatever autonomy we have will be short-lived."

33

"I will inform the Negroes," Colonel Juan Nepomuceno Almonte said to Pedro, "that President Santa Anna considers them to be free under the laws of Mexico."

Pedro heard the words incredulously. He was in the United States for the first time in his life. Colonel Bradburn had sent him a letter, delivered by military courier, with instructions to go to New Orleans to meet up with Colonel Almonte who was arriving by sea from Veracruz. He was to accompany Almonte overland from there to Texas for an inspection tour, the same assignment he had had six years before when he had accompanied General Terán through the department. The ostensible purpose of Almonte's trip was to inform the Texas colonists that the government, now that the turmoil caused by the civil war was over, would be able to consider and act on their complaints. These included the case of the incarcerated Stephen Austin. Almonte would assure them that he would be released soon. Unofficially Almonte would be assessing the danger of secessionist tendencies among the Anglo Americans. He would determine the distribution of the colonists and the military means at their disposal; and he would renew and expand the network of loyalist informants that Terán had set up. All this was to buy time. The government, still in a weakened condition from the civil war, hoped to delay the outbreak of an independence movement until it was better prepared to deal with it.

"I have a friend," Pedro responded, "a Negro slave actually. He was once before told that he was free. In fact it was I who told him because I believed it was true."

"I know," Almonte cut in. "I have heard the story from Colonel Bradburn. I really do not know what to tell you because it is true that they are only free in the legal sense of that term. In reality they remain in bondage."

"I think that it would be cruel to tell them that they were free when they were not."

"Not necessarily," Almonte countered. "If they know that the government considers them free, then it will give them hope. It will also win them over to the government when it reasserts its authority in the department."

"Perhaps," Pedro acknowledged.

"Now, there is an immediate project that I have for you along this same line. I want you to find some free Negroes here for a meeting. This will be your first assignment."

It took some time of asking around to get the name of a free Negro to talk to, but finally Pedro was directed to a David Walker who owned a small restaurant in the center of the city. He sent a letter to Walker requesting a meeting with him and other leaders of the free Negro community. Two days later he received a response directing him to come to Walker's house that Sunday.

At one o'clock on the appointed day he and Colonel Almonte arrived by carriage at Walker's modest frame house on the edge of the city. He knocked at the door and was met by a tall black man with balding hair and spectacles.

"Colonel Almonte, Señor Gomez," David Walker said, extending his hand, "I am most happy to make your acquaintance. I trust that you did not have too difficult a time finding this house."

"Mr. Walker, the pleasure is mine," Almonte said. "I see that you have a number of guests."

"I have invited four of the most respected members of this community as you requested." Walker introduced Erasmus Smith, a carpenter by trade; Josiah Hutchison, a merchant; John Porter, a farmer; and Peter Sanchez, who repaired wagons.

"I am happy that you are all here," Almonte said. "What I have to propose will be, I am sure, of great interest to all of you. It concerns land in Texas. My government is prepared to offer land to members of your community on the most favorable of terms."

"It was my understanding Colonel Almonte," David Walker said, looking incredulous, "that your government did not want more Americans moving into Texas."

"It is true that my government is concerned about the unauthorized movement of Anglo-Americans into Texas. But it would be different with you for we are extending an invitation."

"Now just why would you want free Negroes in Texas alongside of the slaves?" Peter Sanchez asked.

"Forgive me, Mr. Sanchez, but I must correct you. We do not have slaves in Mexico. That was abolished five years ago—"

"This is preposterous," David Walker interrupted. "Surely you are not denying the existence of slavery in Texas. If you are you are deeply ignorant of the true facts of your own country."

Almonte sat up straight and spoke slowly. "I am aware that slavery exists in Texas but it is entirely contrary to the laws of the republic. As you gentlemen may or may not be aware, my country has just suffered a grievous civil war and much sickness. During that time we have been unable to enforce the national law regarding slavery. But now, I can assure you, that will be attended to swiftly."

"I am happy to hear that, Colonel Almonte," Erasmus Smith said. "Are you intending on allowing the existing slaves to get land when they are effectively freed?"

"That would be my personal wish and my government is looking into it now. For now though, we are exploring the idea of distributing land to any free Negroes from the United States who are interested. What I should like to know from you is whether you think such an offer would appeal to free Negroes."

The four men looked at each other and then David Walker spoke for them. "It is not easy for a Negro to obtain land here now. It is even increasingly difficult for whites who are not wealthy to obtain land. So, I greatly suspect that any such offer by your government would be looked upon most favorably by members of this community."

Almonte looked like he had heard a response that he wanted.

Ten days later at three o'clock in the afternoon, he and Pedro were seated in a different room, this time at Fort Jessup, twenty-two miles southwest of Natchitoches and the last military outpost of the United States before the Sabine River and Mexico. The room exuded military austerity: a simple desk and two chairs, a kind of way station for a man more accustomed to being on his feet or horseback in the outdoors than behind a desk. Facing him was that man, General Henry Leavenworth, an imposing barrel-chested walrus of a man complete with a handlebar mustache.

"The border is quite well marked here," General Leavenworth said.

Apparently the North American general thought Almonte was with the Border Commission. That was not a bad impression for him to be under. Almonte did not to correct him about the true nature of his business this day.

"That is the beauty of rivers," Leavenworth continued, "They make it clear where one country ends and another begins, saving men the chore of putting up their own physical markers."

"Unless the river changes course over time."

"That indeed can be a problem," Leavenworth acknowledged. "But it usually takes so much time and it is so gradual that no one notices. Anyway," he said with a laugh now, "I won't be around for it to be my problem."

"You think that the Sabine will remain for a long time as the clear border between our countries?"

"Oh Lord yes. Why should it be changed? It's the obvious marker. Now some damn fool from your government or mine could probably make a case that here and there there was a reason that the river did not conform to the true border, whatever that is. But in all practicality it makes the most sense to accept the river as the border and be done with it."

If this high officer knew anything of preparations for an invasion of Mexico, Pedro thought, his remarks did not indicate it. He seemed to accept the present border as the long-term reality.

"You know General Leavenworth," Almonte said, "there are reports that your President Jackson wishes to buy Texas from my country."

"And I would buy the Taj Mahal if the price was right. It will not happen. For there to be a buyer there must be a seller and I don't suspect that your country has any interest in selling, now does it, Señor Almonte?"

This North American did not seem interested in moving against Mexico, Pedro thought. Could one trust that outward appearance though? It was one thing for a military officer to spout public policy and quite another for him to betray closely held secrets, especially to foreigners. He did not think that Almonte would be so gullible as to believe everything the general was saying. But he felt on an intuitive level that for now they would not invade to take Texas. Why would they have to when there were so many Anglos moving in?

The real question then shifted in his mind to what the attitude of the Anglos was. If they continued challenging Mexican authority, then one day it might spill over into a full-fledged insurrection. If that happened, would General Leavenworth and his government sit idly by or would they take advantage and invade at the behest of their compatriots? It was hard to know just what the Anglos had in mind when they challenged Mexican authority as they clearly had been. Were they simply aiming for more autonomy for the department like other federalists in the republic, or were they aiming ultimately to break away? Almonte indicated that he thought the former possibility was the more likely motivation of the Anglos and he had a certain sympathy for it, having been himself on the federalist side during the last civil war. Pedro was more convinced that the Anglos would never be satisfied until they had broken Texas away and made it a part of the United States.

From Natchitoches they rode west across the Sabine and into Nacogdoches, the first town in Texas and Mexico and where he had visited, coming from the other direction, with Terán five years earlier. Nacogdoches had been without a Mexican military presence for two years now. Almonte said that he found this odd. Even though he believed as a federalist in having local control, it seemed to him that any country had to have a military presence at its borders, even if only a token one. Certainly the United States had one on its side as they had just seen. But the Mexican one had been driven away by Anglo Americans with some Mexican support during the civil war and never replaced. Replacing it, as it would have to be, would lead to renewed conflict with the Anglo Americans if it was not done properly. There were only two possibilities that Almonte could think of here. It could be done with an overwhelming show of force so that the Anglo Americans would have no choice but to accept it. That would get the task accomplished but at the cost of alienating further the Anglo Americans. The preferred course would be to have the Anglo Americans welcome its reestablishment. That seemingly impossible goal could only be accomplished if the government won them over with a series of judicious policy changes to redress their most outstanding and legitimate grievances. Almonte thought that the latter course held the most promise, though the government could not go too far to accommodate the Anglo Americans or it would lose its authority.

Pedro thought of the irony that Almonte was covering ground covered by General Terán before him but in reverse order. He was entering Texas at what had been the general's destination point. He would look up and assess the same contacts here, as had the general, among Mexicans, Anglo Americans, Indians, and Negroes. Undoubtedly he would talk to many of the same persons.

Vicente Córdova—who Pedro knew from the first visit—was among the first to tell him about the general's stay. "He was quite an imposing figure." Córdova said, "Much more impressive than the comandante of the presidio, Colonel de las Piedras. There was something about him that carried authority. It is terrible that his life ended the way that it did."

Almonte acknowledged the concern with an obligatory grimace but one that covered his less than full homage. They had been on opposite sides in the civil war. "You have been the alcalde here and have seen much don Vicente. Are you worried about the Anglo Americans?"

"They are always a worry," Córdova said, leaning back in his seat. "Their numbers keep growing."

Almonte already knew this so he just nodded and moved on. "And the Indians? What is your impression of them now?"

"Their situation is very interesting. Most of them are migrants here like all of us."

"Really? Do they not come from outside the country like the Anglo Americans while you come from within?"

"Yes, that is certainly an important difference," Córdova acknowledged. "But everyone here is nevertheless new to the area. Nobody has family that goes back several generations here."

"What has that got to do with the Indians?"

"Like everyone else here they want secure title to the land they inhabit."

"And do you believe the supreme government should grant it?"

"That was the conclusion of General Terán."

"He is dead now. The question must be reexamined."

"I think it is rather simple," Córdova said. "The reason why General Terán was in favor of their claims was because they were loyal to the republic—more loyal, I might add, than the Anglo Americans. The Indians do not trust the Anglo Americans for obvious reasons, given their experience in the United States with being cheated out of their lands."

"And you believe that this is still true?"

"I know that it is true," Córdova said.

"And just how is that?"

"I know well the Cherokees and talk often with them. We have common worries about the Anglo-American majority."

Pedro listened and wondered whether Almonte was drawing the right conclusion that something had to be done to secure the loyalty of the Cherokees and their followers. That something could only be to legalize their lands. Terán had drawn that conclusion earlier but then died before being able to make sure that it was put into practice. Then it occurred to him why Bradburn had made him the aide to Almonte. It was precisely because he was taking Almonte through the same chain of contacts that Terán had visited and being exposed to the same worried points of view about the Anglos. He then thought ahead to make sure that Almonte would meet James.

This he did and Almonte seemed to be as impressed with hearing his story first-hand as had Terán. When he told James that he was instructed by President Santa Anna to tell him that he was legally free, James, unfortunately, laughed, which irritated Almonte. Pedro came to the rescue to smooth out the situation by explaining that the words were not as hollow as they sounded. They indicated that the government was committed to ending slavery as soon as it was able. You could not say the same for the government of the United States. James then apologized for laughing and he and Almonte parted on cordial terms.

By the time Almonte prepared to leave for Saltillo, he was overflowing with information. He said to Pedro that he would write two reports based upon it, a secret one for government consideration and one later on for public consumption. Vice President Valentin Gómez Farias had originally solicited the information. He was no longer Vice President though, having been ousted by Santa Anna in the spring. The secret report would have to go to the appropriate government ministries instead.

Texas was a veritable paradise in Almonte's mind and he was glad to have had the opportunity to discover it early in life. Its noble forests offered shade, verdant beauty, and a welcome relief from the aridity of much of the other parts of the Republic. Its rivers flowed with waters that were as navigable as they were refreshing. There was no question that Texas was brimming with resources waiting to be developed. There was also no question that Mexico had to treat it carefully to avoid losing it.

From what Almonte could tell, the fervor for independence of the Anglo Americans had subsided as a result of the plague and several judicious reforms, which had gone a long way toward calming their grievances. The Coahuila y Tejas legislature meeting in Monclova had, in his mind, acted wisely in passing reforms that met some of the colonists' most pressing grievances. They were taking the wind out of the sails of any movement toward wanting their own state government or, worse, independence. By creating the new Texas municipalities of Matagorda, San Augustine, Bastrop, and San Patricio, the legislature was giving the Texans more local autonomy. It gave Texas an additional representative to the state legislature, raising its number from two to three. Granted Coahuila still had the majority with nine representatives, but it was still a movement in the right direction that the Anglo Americans would not be able to fail to recognize. Most important for the Anglo Americans was that they would be able to use English in legal documents. They would also be entitled to their private religious opinions so long as they did not disturb the public order. They would no longer be required to convert to Catholicism, though he doubted that any actually had. That had been as truly an unenforceable a policy as it had been ill-advised. The legislature repealed the law that confined retail trade to native-born citizens, another law that had been unenforceable for the three years that it had been in existence. Finally, and very important, the Monclova legislature established appellate circuit courts and trial by jury for Texas. The Anglo Americans would no longer have to travel to Saltillo or Monclova for legal matters; trips that the colonel recognized presented an unfair burden on them. There was though one remaining issue for which Almonte could see no resolution in sight—what was to be done about slavery? It did not seem to be growing, but it was widespread. The colonists would not voluntarily give it up and the legislature was not going to give it permanent legal recognition. Given the irreconcilability of the two positions, he decided that he would leave mention of it out of his public report. He wanted the Anglo-American colonists, when they read it, to believe that the government was favorably disposed toward them and their endeavors. His favorable sounding words would add to the impression created by the repealing of Bustamante's April 6, 1830 law and the recently passed remedial legislation. Any talk of the disagreeable subject of slavery would be kept to the secret report for the moment.

34

In the spring of 1835, several months after Colonel Almonte left Texas carrying with him ambivalent opinions about its likely future, Captain Antonio Tenorio arrived at Anahuac with a detachment of soldiers intent upon reestablishing government authority at the Anahuac garrison and reopening the customs house that had been abandoned earlier. This did not sit well with the Anglo-American colonists; and as if to intentionally make history repeat itself, William Travis sounded the alarm and began agitating against this new imposition of Mexican authority. Travis, who had struggled against Bradburn when he had been in charge of Anahuac and had ended up in jail for it, led the struggle against Bradburn's replacement.

By the end of June, as a result of Travis's agitation and actions, shots broke the long plague-induced lull that had covered Texas. Travis unilaterally led a group of colonists against his old nemesis, the garrison protecting the customs house at Anahuac. The Mexican commander, seeing the superior force of the Americans, immediately surrendered and agreed to remove his troops southward all the way to Matamoros, just as had happened three years earlier.

Throughout the spring and summer undercurrents of more confrontation grew. Travis's action in driving out the Mexican troops from Anahuac cast a huge cloud of uncertainty over life in Texas. No one knew what the response of Santa Anna would be to the provocation. All that was known was that Santa Anna was brutally putting down an insurrection in Zacatecas. No one knew what would happen when he was fully finished with that and free to move on to other problems, including Texas. Many braced for the worst.

The mounting crisis split the colonists into two camps. The war party, which now included Samuel Bingham as one of its most fervent members, was ready to do all that was necessary to attain independence. The peace party, which included Jonathan Holmes, also wanted independence but not at the price of war.

As Colonel Almonte had promised, the government released Stephen Austin from jail and all eyes were on him when he returned to Texas to see what position he would take toward the crisis. The war party did not trust him. They had little patience for what they considered to be his go-slow attitude. Privately they accused him of being an accommodationalist for personal interests. The peace party continued to hold him in esteem and was especially eager to learn his views.

Austin was the pivotal figure, holding in his hands the destiny of the colonists. If he came back promoting independence, he could easily sway the majority peace party. By contrast, if he came back continuing to urge reformism, the colonists would remain divided and an opportunity, maybe even the last one, for independence would be lost.

What should be done with such a figure? Bingham wondered as he drank his morning coffee. Austin had too much power and he was unpredictable. All his past actions would lead one to believe that he would continue to urge accommodation. The one glimmer of hope, as far as he could see, was that he was coming back from sitting in a Mexican jail for a year and a half. That experience surely would not leave him with much of a good taste for continued Mexican rule. But maybe there was a nefarious reason for why the Mexicans were letting him out now—so he would go back and dissuade the colonists from the path of independence.

Then, suddenly, Bingham hit upon a bold solution to his quandary. If Austin had too much power and could not be trusted, the best thing would be to assassinate him and blame it on Santa Anna. If that could be arranged, it would solve all the problems. For people like Holmes in the peace party, it would be the last straw. They would be so enraged that they would join forces with the revolution.

As these ideas rushed through his mind, Bingham thought that there was brilliance to them in how quickly they would deal with the problem at hand. He congratulated himself. In times like these, reckless boldness, even ruthlessness, was needed. The alternatives of caution and timidity would only prolong the agony of uncertainty and foreclose any way out.

Bingham thought about the idea of an assassination for some time. He could justify it in his mind on the grounds that the cause of Texas independence was too important to allow its success to rest in the hands of a proven accommodationalist. An assassination, of course, could be botched. Its authors would have to plan it very carefully. There must be no possibility of error. The fate of Texas depended on this. This was truly a great idea, Bingham thought, and he was ready to enlist support. He pulled on his boots, told Sarah not to wait up for him, and rushed out of the house to ride as fast as the mare would take him to Zachariah Nettle's house.

"It's too dangerous," Nettles said after hearing him out. "It has more chance of succeeding than not, it is true. But there's still too much of a chance that it wouldn't and that'd be disastrous."

Bingham was annoyed but he did not show it. Instead, he sighed. "I don't think you're right. We could make it work."

"Maybe so, but you haven't convinced me."

"That the end is worthy or that it could succeed?"

"That it could succeed. Hell, I have no beef with getting rid of Austin. He's an obstacle now. We were better off with him in jail. You're right there. You're also right that the best gift he could give us now would be as a martyr."

"That indeed is the point, isn't it Zachariah? He'd be more useful dead than alive."

Nettles laughed. "Wisdom in your words, Samuel."

"Then we have to make this plan work."

"No. Like I said, it's too dangerous."

"How do you know that?" Bingham said, trying to revive the idea.

"I know it in my guts."

"That's not enough to prove anything," Bingham cried.

"No, but it's enough to stop your plan." Nettles leaned over and directly faced Bingham. "Look, Samuel, maybe you're right and I'm wrong, but if you can't convince me, then you're not going to convince anyone. More than any man here I hate Mexicans and being ruled over by a mongrel race that is morally, intellectually, and politically inferior."

Bingham sat back, deflated again. "Then the idea is dead."

"Not completely. I think there is something we can rescue from it. Sometimes the threat is as good as the action."

"I don't get you," Bingham said.

Nettles shrugged. "If Austin thinks that he might get killed for saying the wrong thing—"

"That's it!" Bingham jumped up and pounded a fist into an open hand. "We let him know the consequences of his actions. Brilliant." Then he calmed a bit. "Now, how do we do that?"

"He's supposed to speak in Brazoria at a public dinner next week. That's where everyone will be waiting to see how he views the situation. Whatever we do has to be done before then."

"I say then that we get several of the men together and pay him a visit. Tell him what he has to say and the consequences if he doesn't."

"Too blunt. He won't take kindly to an open threat like that."

"What does it matter?"

"We don't want him to stand up at that dinner in Brazoria and say that he's just been threatened by members of the War Party," Nettles said. "Then he'd get them riled up against us instead of the Mexicans. No, far better that we do it in a way that he can't blame us if he has a mind to."

Bingham was becoming impatient. "And? What would that be?"

"We send him an anonymous letter of concern expressing our deep worry for his health"—Nettles paused and smiled—"because passions are high and there are rumors about. We'll flower it up with all kinds of words about what a great leader and patriot he is and how much of a shame it would be to see him pass away prematurely."

"You think that'll be enough to do it?"

"He'll get the point."

Bingham rode home that night thinking that the plan had a better than even chance of succeeding. If it didn't, they'd have to come up with another one.

He rode into the yard of his house and dismounted. Sarah and Jessica, as he had known, were away at the Holmes house. After he prepared the horse for the night he walked first into the kitchen and poured himself a cup of rum. He drank it quickly. Then he went out the kitchen door to the small cabin where Elizabeth stayed.

He pushed the cabin door open and found it empty. "Elizabeth," he screamed.

"Coming, sir." The voice came from the other side of the trees.

"Where were you?" he demanded when she came up.

"Out looking at the stars."

"Oh," he said, calming considerably. Then he took her shoulders and pulled her up against him. She stiffened. "Relax, I won't hurt you. I just want to be with you for a while in your cabin."

As he walked unsteadily with his arm around her waist into the cabin he found his heart racing and himself tensing. She was doing nothing to make it easier. He had wanted her to submit willingly but she wasn't. She would submit, this he knew, but it would be with all of that implied resistance that he hated. There would not even be the easy docility that, while not as good as willingness, at least made it easier on him. She though seemed to know the line and did not resist enough to make him mad.

35

It was a hurried trip into Matagorda. From what James understood, Bingham was to meet someone there who he would then go with to the town of Gonzales. He was along so that he could take supplies back to the farm, something that Bingham's wife had insisted upon, now that she was there taking care of the baby with Elizabeth.

They had just finished getting the supplies and James had loaded them up in the wagon when three white men and a Negro came riding up.

"Samuel," the lead man said, "let's get a quick drink before we go."

"That's fine with me, William," Bingham said and he retreated with the three whites into the saloon leaving James and the Negro alone outside.

"Who are you?" the Negro said.

"James. And you?"

"Joe. Joe's my name."

"You going off with them?"

"That's where he's taking me."

"Who's your boss?"

"Colonel William Travis. He's a lawyerman and soldier."

It was indeed a quick drink because the men were now coming out.

"Well, watch yourself," James said.

Joe shrugged as he left to rejoin his owner.

James climbed back into the wagon and drove back to the Bingham farm.

Even though he didn't consider it his fight, James felt his interest peaked by the building war and he was all ears for any news he could get about it to relay to Pedro. The whites weren't going to tell him anything and so he didn't bother to ask. His sources were limited to what he could see directly with his own eyes and infer from the actions of the whites and to what he heard from other slaves who had seen things themselves. It was the beginning of cotton-picking time. Bingham had made arrangements before leaving to bring in leased slaves and James inquired casually from them what they had seen. It seemed that there had been a skirmish at Gonzales, something to do with the colonists not wanting to surrender the town cannon to Mexican troops who had come trying to get it. They had beaten off the troops and kept the cannon. After that, according to one of the slaves leased from Jared Groce, all kinds of men had converged on Gonzales, including a lot of volunteers from the United States. Then they had begun to march toward the main presidio, the Alamo, at Bexar.

James listened to the account and then in his mind drew the connection that that must be the reason why Bingham had left the farm a couple of weeks earlier. Bingham had told him that he was going to be right back but had acted mysterious about where he was going. And he hadn't come right back. He fantasized the possibility that Bingham had gotten himself killed. If that had happened, he wondered, what would happen to him? Would that scrawny wife of his take over? Not likely. He laughed at the idea of Sarah running the farm and telling him what to do. More likely, they would probably try to take him back to the Bingham plantation in Tennessee—unless of course he escaped first. That possibility began to come back in his mind though he feared that, with war going on, any attempt of his to take to the roads alone would be risky. Whites didn't like to see Negroes alone on the roads in peacetime. No telling what they would do if they saw them in wartime.

One thing that did occur to him was that with Bingham gone and his wife not being able to keep so closely on top of where he was and what he was doing, he could easily slip away for an afternoon and find out what Pedro knew.

When he arrived at Pedro's house one October afternoon, he found that the family was excitedly talking about what had just happened at Goliad. According to news from Santiago Alvarez, Anglo colonists had taken over the presidio there. Alvarez supported the action, saying that the Mexicans in Texas now had more common interests with the Anglos Americans than they did with those Mexicans far to the south of them in the country. It would be best to make common cause with them in the interests of Texas.

"It is very bad now," Alfredo said in Spanish to James. "The Anglos have tasted victory and they won't stop."

"It is not just the Anglos," Pedro said. "According to what don Santiago said, there were Mexicanos helping them."

"They were deceived into helping," his father said.

"Because they are federalists?"

"Yes, because they are federalists. They think that by helping the Anglos they will help the federalist cause. But they do not understand that the cause of the Anglos is not the federalist one. They adopt it now only because it is convenient."

"They want to take over in Texas."

"Yes."

"And then what happens to us?"

"Or to me for that matter," James added.

"God knows," Alfredo said.

36

Pedro and his father watched with apprehension as four riders approached their house. With Goliad under Anglo control, there had been attacks against Mexicans.

Pedro recognized the lead rider and gave a sigh of relief.

"Captain Savariego," he said when the men had dismounted, "I heard that you had been taken prisoner."

Savariego spat on the ground. "Not for long. I got away to Matamoros."

"Why are you back here now?" Pedro asked.

"We need to have men we can count on," Savariego replied. "Things are moving very fast now. The Anglo Americans control the presidio, but our troops are coming and will take it back."

"When will they come, Captain?" Alfredo asked.

Savariego shrugged. "It's difficult to tell. Maybe in a week, maybe a month. But they will come. And when they do, we will need information about who is loyal and who supports the rebels."

Alfredo nodded. "You want me to keep my ears open."

"Exactly," Savariego said.

"There is a lot of confusion now," Alfredo said. "Many don't know where they stand."

"Or if they will take any stand at all," Pedro added.

Savariego kicked the dirt. "I don't know which is worse—those who take a stand against us or those who refuse to take any stand at all when the country is being attacked."

"It is always this way in a war, is it not Captain?" Alfredo said.

"Perhaps," he replied. Then he turned toward Pedro. "Are you willing to take up arms to defend the republic?"

Pedro looked at his father who nodded slightly. Then he said, "I do not have a choice. It must be done."

"Good," Savariego said. "It will not be right away. But when our troops arrive, you will join them. Your knowledge of the area will be valuable. You will bring a mount and a rifle."

37

"In most armies you would not be so free to take leave for personal reasons," Jonathan Holmes said. Samuel Bingham had returned home on temporary leave from the colonist army camped outside Bexar. He and the others had been waiting for the right time to attack and take the Alamo. But the right time seemed to be ever distant in the future and he had grown increasingly worried about his cotton harvest. For all he knew it was rotting in the fields.

"There is nothing to worry about," Bingham said on the defensive. "The Mexicans can't break out of the encirclement."

An insistent knock at the door interrupted the response Holmes was about to make. He pulled open the door and saw Zachariah Nettles with blood and fresh bruises on his face. "Zachariah, what happened to you?"

"My slaves are loose." Nettles said. "They attacked me and are burning the house."

"That looks very bad, let me see it," Lily said, who had come rushing into the room. She examined the cuts on his forehead and chin.

"Got you with a stick?" Bingham said.

"Hoe," Nettles replied.

"Where's your wife?" Lily asked.

"In town, luckily. Someone has to tell her so she doesn't go back there."

"We'll take care of it," Holmes said.

"Rachel," Lily shouted at her house slave. "Heat some water. We have to take care of those wounds."

"It's lucky you made it here," Bingham said.

"I hope you have your slaves under control," Nettles said.

"Samuel," Holmes said, "you better get home fast in case this thing spreads. Bring Sarah and the little one over here."

"Be careful," Nettles said. "They might have gotten a gun of mine out of the house."

Samuel Bingham left the house. In the distance he could see flames reflected on the clouds. If he did not otherwise know, he would have taken them to be either a prairie fire caused by lightening or a bonfire. But this was no idle fire and all of his senses heightened. If they made it as far as his place, that would be the end of it. He shouldn't have left Sarah and Jessica alone.

Oh my God, Bingham thought, someone, a black, was coming toward him on the trail. He pulled his gun out and aimed it at the figure. "Stop and put your hands up," he shouted.

"Master Bingham, it's me, Ezekiel. What is the matter?" Ezekiel said.

"What are you doing out here?"

"Just enjoying the night air."

Bingham kept his gun aimed. "You get back to your cabin immediately."

"Why, Master Bingham?"

"Don't question me."

"If you say so, Master Bingham."

By the time he reached his house, his nerves steadied. Sarah and Jessica were asleep when he entered. He stood over her breathing heavily and then said in as calm a voice as he could manage, "Wake up. We're all going to spend the night at Jonathan and Lily's house."

"Why?" Sarah asked, sitting up immediately.

"There's troubles."

"Indians?"

"No. Zachariah Nettles' slaves just set fire to his house."

"You don't think that James and the others would—"

"I don't think nothing. We can't take chances."

"What about Elizabeth?"

"Leave her here."

Bingham took his rifle out from the cabinet by the fireplace and loaded it. Then he walked back to the door and stood staring out waiting for Sarah to get the girl up and ready. For some reason he found himself to be even more calm now. He had taken the trail to Holmes's house hundreds of times and knew every bend in it. But he had better be cautious nevertheless. He did not think that James was likely to attack him. The others, though, he did not know. They could barely speak English now and he had no sense of them. They just seemed to acknowledge that they knew him when he saw them in the field. For that reason he had had to rely on James a little more than he wanted to as the intermediary.

If he had calmed, though, Sarah was just beginning to feel fear when he drove the wagon out from the house. She grasped the girl tightly. "What is that glowing in the sky over to the left?" she asked.

"It's Zachariah's house. The slaves set it on fire."

Sarah let out a little shriek and began to tremble and grasped the girl more tightly.

Bingham immediately regretted having told her that. He should have said that it was a prairie fire. At least she would know the seriousness of the situation though. For the rest of the ride she trembled and wept softly.

When they reached the Holmes house they found Jonathan, Lily, and Nettles, waiting in a hitched up wagon in the yard.

"We're all going to stay in town tonight," Lily said.

"Let's go," Jonathan Holmes said, starting his wagon off.

The two wagons, Holmes's in the lead, lurched off onto the trail. To the left, in the distance, the low-lying clouds still glowed orange.

By the time they reached Matagorda the militia was already assembling. Men milled about talking and checking their guns. It reminded Bingham of the Indian troubles. His feelings now shifted from being on nerve to feeling good about being with these neighbors who were coming together. It would be a good rehearsal for things to come.

After getting Sarah, the girl, Lily, and Nettles housed for the night, he and Holmes unhitched the wagons and saddled the horses.

"What do you think we're going to find out there?" Bingham asked Holmes.

"A bunch of drunken slaves," Holmes answered back matter-of-factly.

"It's bad timing with so many men off fighting at Bexar. Don't you think we should send somebody over there to get help?"

Holmes shook his head. "It's not necessary. We should have no trouble rounding them up with the men we have. If I were one of those niggers, I'd take off running right now. We have many times more guns. They don't have a chance."

"By the way, I saw Ezekiel on the trail to my house. You don't have to worry about him being a part of it."

Holmes turned his head. "I never worried. You're the one who should be worrying."

"And just what do you mean by that?"

"You can never trust a slave who has tried to run away."

38

"I tell you," Elizabeth said, "they left in a mighty big hurry. They afraid that that them slaves over there are going to come here and attack them too."

James looked off at the glowing clouds. As far as he could tell there would be more white men than slaves and for sure the whites had all the guns. "This doesn't look good. They're going to be a lot of dead men before the sun comes up. You and me better lay low."

"I'm staying here with you. They won't be back tonight."

"Okay. Go on inside. I'll tell the others."

James did not know whether to tell the Africans to stay put for their own safety this dangerous night or to simply inform them that a revolt was underway and let them figure out what they wanted to do. After mulling it over as he walked to their cabins, he ended up telling them that the flames were from a revolt and that they should be careful.

Back at his cabin he lay down beside Elizabeth and waited and thought. Was he being a coward? He could join them and strike a blow at the whites. Probably he would die but he would die with the satisfaction of having fought back. But what would that get him beside an early trip to the grave? He was finally drifting off to sleep when shots began to ring out. "Oh my God," James said, sliding his arm out from under her head. He stood up and walked over to the door.

"Where you going?" Elizabeth said.

"Nowhere. Just worrying."

39

"Good thing Zachariah kept a lot of liquor on hand," Bingham said. He and the other militiamen were standing guard over forty slaves, some drunken, who they had herded into the corral. A burned out house smoldered off to the left.

"It's the first time it ever did him any good," Holmes said.

"What happens now?"

"They pay for their crime," Holmes said. "You want to do the honors?" He held up a rope. "Here, know how to tie a noose?"

"We're going to hang them all?"

"Just the leaders. Whipping will suffice for the rest. Don't want to kill off all the labor, not that they don't deserve it."

"Shouldn't we take them into town?" someone asked.

"Listen," Holmes responded with a weary irritableness, "this is not an ordinary legal matter. We are the law now and all of us better get used to it." Then he said to Bingham, "Samuel, hurry up with that noose or let me do it if you don't know how."

Bingham stared at the rope and then began twisting it into a knot.

"No," Holmes said, shaking his head. "Let me have it. It goes like this." He quickly made a loop and wrapped one end around the other several times and tied the knot. Then he slid the knot up and down to make sure that it would work. When he finished, he shouted, "It's ready, over here."

Four men were pulled out of the corral. Holmes pitched the rope over the branch of a tree.

With the butt of a rifle the first slave was pushed up onto the wagon where the noose was fitted over his neck. Once the knot was set, the man who had fitted it shouted, "Now," and the wagon lurched forward discharging part of its human cargo.

As the militiamen stared at the swinging body, the second slave in line bolted and took off running.

Samuel Bingham took steady aim with his rifle and with a single bullet dropped him.

"Good shot, Samuel," Holmes said. "Probably isn't dead though so we'll still have to hang him anyway unless you want to finish him off."

Bingham had never shot a man before and he was feeling good about the skill with which he had made the shot. It was one thing though to shoot from a distance and quite another to walk up to a downed man and coldly unload a bullet into his head. But this was not the time to hesitate and he knew it. So he walked up to the groaning man, pulled back the bolt, and with a single shot, ended the groaning.

After he had walked back to the men who were readying the third man on the wagon, Holmes leaned over to him and said, "I'm sorry you had to do that, it's never pleasant."

Bingham said nothing but did not take the comment well. After some time, he turned and said to Holmes, "We better be careful with this. It wouldn't do us any good to have to fight slaves at the same time we're fighting Mexicans."

"Stop saying that we're fighting Mexicans," Holmes angrily replied. "We're fighting for our rights." Then he took a deep breath to calm himself and said, once again taking on the tone of experience, "That's why we have to hang men now so that the others will think a thousand times before they decide to follow their example. You're right. It wouldn't do us any good to fight two enemies at the same time."

40

The next evening James walked over to Ezekiel's cabin. The night sky was clear with bright stars and there were no fires big enough to break through the darkness.

"I figured you'd come over," Ezekiel said when he arrived at the door.

"You must've heard what I heard."

"They made sure we all heard."

"Four hanged. Damn," Ezekiel said.

"We should've helped them," James responded.

"And what? Get ourselves stretched too? No way you can win. They too many of them."

"If they were smart, they would've just tried to escape instead of staying around."

"You still got a hankering to do that?" Ezekiel said.

"I still think about it."

"No way you can go north from here. You have to go south out of Texas."

"That's for sure." James responded. "But I can't go now."

"Why not?"

"I have a little matter of the heart to attend to."

"Who?"

"Elizabeth."

"For a minute I thought you was going to say that Mexican woman you sometimes talk about and I was going to say what makes you think them Mexicans would let a nigger marry one of their own?"

"I get along better with them then I ever did with the whites."

"That just because they don't like the whites either. That don't mean they let you join their family."

"Who knows? But it isn't an issue 'cause Elizabeth is where my heart has gone."

"What makes you think Bingham would let you marry his house slave even if she would be stupid enough to take you as husband? You still a slave case you ain't noticed. You can't just do what you want."

"We shall see. But even if he doesn't allow it, the Mexican government is going to abolish slavery soon enough."

"What makes you think that?"

"The whites are nervous. That's why they're going to war. But the Mexican army is going to come and whip them worse than the whites did those slaves last night. Then we'll be free."

41

As far as Samuel Bingham could tell, the war was going well. The colonist army had routed the last of the Mexican defenders of the Alamo and taken it over. He would have liked to have been there for the victory, but he couldn't because he needed to be at home making sure that the farm was running properly. This could not be entrusted entirely to Sarah who, even with the help of Elizabeth, was preoccupied with Jessica.

In addition to now having control of the Alamo, the most important presidio in Texas, they had control of the one at Goliad, the second most important. But those victories had been almost too easy. There were ominous signs that Mexican armies were coming up from the south. It would do no good, though, to hunker down and worry about what might occur militarily. It was absolutely necessary to keep the momentum of the revolution going and consolidate their military control of Texas with a formal declaration of independence. Up until now there was still the fiction that their only goal was restoration of the Constitution of 1824 that Santa Anna had abrogated. Restoration of that constitution, though, would still leave them as a part of Mexico.

It was thus logical that a formal declaration of independence would be the first order of business for a convention called by the Provisional Government of Texas for the beginning of March. If Bingham had missed the military victory at the Alamo, he did not want to miss this political one. He did his best to maneuver events so that he would be elected as a delegate, and that he was. So too was his neighbor, Jonathan Holmes. This disappointed him, because he believed that Holmes might still be harboring reservations about the wisdom of declaring independence.

When he arrived, he found the convention abuzz with rumors about the military situation at the Alamo. Santa Anna's troops were either approaching or already there, depending on the source of the rumor. The fifty-nine delegates had business to attend to, however foreboding the circumstances. The first was the declaration of independence, which passed with little debate.

"What do you think," Bingham asked Holmes after the vote in favor.

"Well, there's no turning back now. We can't expect any allies in Mexico."

"Or among Mexicans here either."

"Oh, some of them are on our side."

"Not many, just a few. Almost all of them are Tories."

"And just why do you suppose that is, Samuel?" Holmes said.

"I think it's obvious. We're superior to them and can't be in the same country. Listen to this from Sam Houston." Bingham took out a piece of paper.

"What's that?" Holmes asked.

"Something he wrote a few weeks back—'The vigor of the descendents of the north'—that's us—'will never mix with the phlegm of the indolent Mexicans, no matter how long we may live among them.'"

"That's putting it a little strong—"

"Oh, I don't know about that. I wish I could have thought of putting it that way."

"It doesn't matter now. We have business to get down to with all the work that putting together a constitution entails. We have less than three weeks, and that's if we're lucky. If Santa Anna and his indolent

Mexicans are moving at the speed they're reported to be, then Texas will be swimming in that so-called phlegm."

Three days later Bingham and Holmes were attending the final reading for the approval of the Constitution. By this time the votes were largely a formality, both because divisive issues had already been settled in committee meetings and because, with Santa Anna's army breathing down upon them, the fifty-nine delegates did not want to delay getting out of there any longer than absolutely necessary.

It was mid afternoon and Section Seven had just been approved. "General provisions of the Constitution of the Republic of Texas," the Chairman of the meeting read in a stentorian voice. "Section Eight: All persons who shall give aid or assistance to the present enemy shall forfeit all rights of citizenship and such lands as they may hold in the republic."

The reader stopped and then called for the vote. "All those in favor signify by saying Aye."

After the section was approved unanimously, Holmes leaned over and said to Bingham, "Looks like certain Mexicans we know are about to have some problems."

Bingham looked puzzled, "Which ones?"

"The ones who harbored your escaped slave back in '29."

"They say the son is fighting with the Mexican Army."

"What about the old man?"

"Who knows about what he's doing. But if the son's guilty, he's guilty too."

"Well, that's the least we can do to punish them. What's the next section?"

"The one on labor," Holmes responded. "Here it comes now."

"General provisions of the Constitution of the Republic of Texas," the Chairman read. "Section Nine: All persons of color who were slaves for life previous to their emigration to Texas, and who are now held in bondage, shall remain in the like state of servitude; provided, the said slave shall be the bona fide property of the person so holding said slave as aforesaid. Congress shall pass no laws to prohibit emigrants from bringing their slaves into the republic with them, and holding them by the same tenure by which such slaves were held in the United States; nor shall congress have power to emancipate slaves; nor shall any slave holder be allowed to emancipate his or her slave or slaves without the consent of congress, unless he or she shall send his or her slave or slaves without the limits of the republic. No free person of African descent, either in whole or in part, shall be permitted to reside permanently in the republic, without the consent of congress; and the importation or admission of Africans or Negroes into this republic, excepting from the United States of America, is forever prohibited, and declared to be piracy."

The Chairperson looked up and then said. "Are we ready to vote on Section Nine?"

"Mr. Chairman," Samuel Bingham said, "I rise with a concern."

"State your concern," the chairperson said.

"I support the substance of the section and congratulate the committee for making it absolutely clear that owners can now carry on their legitimate businesses with slave labor without all of the ruinous uncertainty on that question that has existed under the Mexican yoke of oppression."

That drew sustained applause and Bingham waited until it subsided before continuing. "However, I question the need for the last clause."

The Chairman looked down at the text. "The clause reading 'the importation or admission of Africans or Negroes into this republic, excepting from the United States of America, is forever prohibited, and declared to be piracy'?"

"Yes. What if more slaves are needed than can be supplied by the United States?"

"We discussed that issue in committee and the general feeling was that there would be an ample market of slaves coming from the United States. It was also the general feeling that whereas the importation of slaves from Africa has been prohibited for some time in the United States that it would behoove us to have our laws conform with those of our good neighbor on this matter."

"Mr. Chairman," a delegate shouted from the back of the room. "I wish to speak on this question."

The chairman nodded at him to speak.

"Yes indeed," the delegate from the back of the room said. "It would be better to have our laws regarding slavery conform with those of the United State then to conform with those of our neighbor to the south."

After the laughter died down, the chairman said. "Are you satisfied Mr. Bingham?"

Bingham nodded ascent and sat down.

"Then we are ready to vote on Section Nine."

After the section passed unanimously and the delegates were in recess, Bingham said to Holmes, "I'm very happy with the Constitution. Who would've believed a year ago that we'd have gotten this far?"

"The change is dramatic," Holmes acknowledged, "but it's going to be a Pyrrhic victory if this military situation doesn't turn around fast."

Bingham sighed and looked down toward his toes. "That's what we have to do as soon as we get out of here. I'm joining up with Houston. You?"

"Going to Louisiana to recruit men and raise money."

"That is the safer course, but you're probably better at it."

Holmes heard the implied insult and replied, "Takes more than brave words to run an army, Samuel."

42

Pedro Gómez was stationed two hundred yards out from the presidio at Goliad with his eyes constantly trained on the front gate. Other men were watching the sides and back, making sure that none of the rebel Colonel Fannin's men could break out. He had heard that the Alamo had been retaken by Santa Anna's troops. Now if all went well, this second most important presidio would be retaken from the Anglos as well.

His post was near a house and from time to time he saw the inhabitants come and go, mainly on trips toward the center of Goliad. He wondered what their position was on the fight. He knew that while most of the town was loyalist there had been a few who had helped the Anglos take the presidio.

The door of the house opened and he glanced back to see a woman approach him with a stack of tortillas and a bowl of beans.

"You are very kind, señora," he said in Spanish, taking the gift.

"It is nothing," she said.

"Where do you stand in this?" he asked as he dipped the first tortilla into the beans.

The woman shrugged.

"You have no position?" Pedro asked.

"I do not know what it is all about but you are a nice boy who looks like he needs something to eat."

"And them inside?" Pedro motioned back toward the presidio. "They are nice boys too?"

"They do not belong there."

This was the answer he had been hoping for. He relaxed a bit and shared a confidence. "They will not be there for long. Our troops are coming."

The woman nodded as if she knew this too.

Then Pedro saw the door of the presidio swing open and a lone rider come out. "Go inside, señora," he said quickly, glancing back and forth between the woman and the approaching rider.

The woman grabbed the bowl and cloth she had brought the tortillas in and hurried back toward the house.

Pedro now put his full attention to the rider and readied his Brown Bess musket. He had never shot a man before or for that matter even shot at a man. Much as he disliked the Anglos he felt uncomfortable at the prospect of killing one of them. At the same time if the rider made it past him, he would have to answer to Captain Savariego. There would be no excuse since he had all the advantage of an ambush with the rider not knowing that he was even there.

He steadied the musket. He mustn't shoot until he could make him out clearly. Otherwise the shot would fall short of its target and the element of surprise would be lost. The Anglos with their long rifles and Du Pont gunpowder could hit targets from a much greater distance. They had the advantage in that respect and this was now known to both sides and entered into each other's calculations.

The rider was coming quickly into range and he could make out the blond color of his hair. He was riding at a gallop, no doubt suspecting that snipers surrounded the presidio. Pedro aimed for the rider's chest and counted to five to make doubly sure that the he was within range. At the count of five he squeezed the trigger.

The rider jerked to his left, his shoulder bleeding, and pulled his horse up short and turned it. Then he beat a hasty retreat back to the presidio where the gate swung open again to receive him.

Pedro stood now and cupped his hand over his eyes against the late afternoon sun and looked at the closing of the presidio gate. Then a white puff of smoke and cracking sound of a long rifle sent him scurrying for cover. There he stayed until a moonless darkness fell over his position and allowed him to move around again.

At midnight he heard footsteps approaching from behind. He turned and trained his rifle on the figure and then let it down. It was Efraín Rodríguez, another loyalist ranchero, come to relieve him at the post so that he could get some sleep.

"Any more outriders?" Rodríguez asked. "We heard the shots this afternoon."

"No. None since then. Be careful though. We're within range of their rifles here." Pedro smiled and pointed to where the rifle shot had hit the wall to the side of them.

"Why don't we have those rifles?" Rodríguez said.

"Ask General Urrea if he ever gets here."

"He'll be here in the morning. That's the word in the camp. He's very close and making final preparations for the assault."

"Good," Pedro said. "I'm going now so I can be rested for the attack."

The next morning when he awoke he saw smoke rising from the area of the presidio. Nearby houses were fully ablaze. After downing some coffee and a few tortillas, he carefully made his way back to the sniper post.

"What's the fire all about?" he asked Efraín Rodríguez.

"They're getting ready to flee. They are burning everything in sight they cannot carry."

Pedro resumed his sniper post alongside Rodríguez and at eight o'clock saw the gate of the presidio open up. The Anglos were beginning to move out. This time though they were coming in force. It would not be wise to shoot from a short distance at them.

"They're going north," Rodríguez said to him. "We'll follow them."

"And General Urrea?" Pedro said. "Where is he?"

"He's moving to cut them off. They don't have a chance."

The two of them watched the last of Fannin's troops leave the presidio and then they rejoined their guerrilla unit. For most of the morning they kept track on Fannin's retreating troops, riding at a safe distance away beyond rifle range. In late morning they were in pinewoods on the edge of a wide prairie. They were watching the Anglo-American troops slowly beginning to make their way out onto the prairie when they encountered the advance guard of Urrea's troops coming from the east.

"You," the Mexican captain with the advance guard said, addressing Captain Savariego, "go to the other side ahead of them to cut them off from reaching the cover of woods. We will attack from here."

With that order they rode out into the prairie and made a wide arc beyond gun range around Fannin's slow-moving caravan. At the other side they found the beginning of more pinewoods and there took up position and waited. Fannin's troops were coming toward them but ever so slowly.

In the early afternoon, when the caravan was fully exposed in the prairie, the first Mexican gunfire exploded in the air. From where he stood watching, Pedro saw the wagons begin to circle up.

"Now we go, muchachos," Savariego said. "But don't get too close. We just want them to know we're here."

For the rest of the afternoon Pedro and the rest of the ranchero unit took pot shots from the north at the encircled wagons. From the south, the fire coming from Urrea's force was incessant.

At nightfall the gun and artillery fire died down and the rancheros withdrew back to the woods and made camp.

"Should we not have a closer guard," Efraín Rodríguez said, "so that they cannot slip out under the cover of darkness?"

"They will not be able to," someone else said. "If they do, they will not be able to take their wounded with them. They are stuck."

"I think they are finished," Pedro said.

"It will be over tomorrow morning," Rodríguez said. "Urrea has fresh troops coming. They will bring more cannons."

The rancheros ate well from provisions that they carried with them and then slept.

Heavy artillery fire coming from Urrea's side broke the dawn. Then it stopped as suddenly as it had started. Colonel Fannin was limping out into the open with a white flag.

43

James was walking from the barn toward his cabin that evening when Elizabeth came running up. "Wait," she called. "The lady, she moving completely away from here tomorrow in the morning and she taking me with her."

"Where does she say she's going?" he said slowly. He was used to Sarah Bingham's impetuous ways.

"Says she going to get out of the way of the fighting. Says that Mexican troops is coming and they don't respect womenfolk."

"That means I have to go too?"

"No. She say she don't want you or any of the other men with her. You to take care of the fields till she or the master get back."

James felt his heart sink. Then he said, "You don't have to go with her."

Elizabeth stared at him. "Oh, James, I do have to go. I raise that child and it ain't my choice anyway. I know what you thinking. I'll be back soon."

For the next few days he did nothing but sleep late and attend to his eating and other creature needs. He really didn't think that there was any great necessity to work on the farm. Who knew what was going to happen with the war on and the owners gone?

On the fourth day he was surprised to see Pedro Gómez brazenly ride up to his cabin.

"I rode past the house of your owners," Pedro said. "It looks completely abandoned."

"He's out fighting. She fled with her child."

Pedro then told him about the battle with Fannin's troops. James listened quietly and then asked, "What are they going to do with the prisoners?"

Pedro sighed and then raised his eyebrows. "There are no prisoners now. They're all dead."

"Dead? All of them?" James said incredulously. "How did that happen?"

"It was very bad. In war you have to win. Most of them were from the United States. I guess General Urrea wanted to discourage any more from coming."

James shook his head. "I don't know. That's pretty ruthless."

"Don't look at me. I'm just a soldier."

"You kill any of them?"

Pedro shook his head. "It was the regulars who did it. We just stood guard on the outside." Then he bowed his head and lowered his voice. "It was the worst thing I ever saw in my life. It was like a slaughter of animals."

"Would you have killed them?"

"If they gave me the order. That's what it means to be a soldier."

"I suppose," James said. "I'm glad I'm not a soldier. What do you think is going to happen now?"

"They're just about finished. General Santa Anna is closing in on the last of them. That's where I'm headed." He patted a leather bag he carried. "Got to deliver messages from General Urrea."

"What happens to me after this?"

"What do you mean?"

"Am I still a slave when this revolt gets put down?"

"Oh," Pedro said, realizing what was foremost in James's mind. "I did ask some of the officers from the south about that and they all think that they're here to liberate slaves."

"You kidding me?"

"No. You'll see once we completely put this revolt down. The government will end slavery in Texas."

"It would be about time."

Pedro smiled. "I knew you would say that. Now I've got to be going. I'll be back in three days though, maybe four."

"With messages from Santa Anna to your general."

"Yes."

"Okay," James said. "Be careful."

James watched him ride away from the cabin and then it began to sink in that maybe slavery was going to be over now that the Mexicans were reestablishing control over Texas. He began to wonder about what he would do. For sure he would not stay on the Bingham farm. He could probably go back to work with Pedro's father. Then again, maybe he should just strike out on his own and look for some way to get by that didn't require working the land anymore. Since he could speak Spanish, maybe he should head south and work in some city. He couldn't go back to the United States. He was sure that even if he became free in Mexico they wouldn't respect that there. So his options came down to staying in Texas as a free man or moving further south. That he would have to think about.

He continued doing just enough work to scrounge up enough food to keep him going. The crops could go to hell as far as he was concerned. He would've liked to go into Matagorda to find out what was going on with the war, but that seemed dangerous. The whites were running scared. No telling what they would do if they saw a Negro on the road by himself. The other slaves slowed down too. He didn't let them know what was on his mind because he didn't quite trust them. He didn't exactly distrust them either. It was rather that he thought that they might not be able to keep that kind of information to themselves. He assumed that Pedro was probably right that the Mexican Army would be soon in control again. But what if they weren't and the whites were back in control? Right now it looked like no one was in control. Whichever way it went, he had to be cautious and make preparations at the same time.

It all seemed now like he was living in a giant void. The whites were gone but the roads were too dangerous to travel on. He was free and trapped at the same time. It seemed like being in a prison where the jailors were gone and you were free to roam about but the inescapable fence still remained. But, if Pedro was right, in short time the Mexican troops would take charge. Then he would be free to do whatever he wanted.

44

It was a little after midnight and he was having trouble sleeping when he heard a lone rider coming across the field. He rose, pulled on his pants, and walked across the dirt floor to the door to look out. The rider was leaning over as if hurt and coming straight for the cabin. He pulled up in front and then James recognized him.

"Pedro, qué pasó?" he said, walking up and taking the reins of the horse."

Pedro slid off of the horse awkwardly. "I am shot, but not bad, just in the shoulder."

"Come in. I have some water we can heat up."

Inside the cabin, James held a candle up to the blood stained sleeve and then ripped it away to expose the wound.

"It don't look bad, just grazed you. We'll clean it up and then put something on top of it to stop the bleeding. Hold your arm up high for now." In the corner where he made his fires he put two rags in his one iron pot and then built up the fire under it.

"I have to hurry. They beat us badly. You remember when I told you that what happened to the Anglos in Goliad was the worst thing I had ever seen."

James nodded.

"It no longer is. What the Anglos just did to us at San Jacinto is. I saw them bayonet soldiers who were trying to surrender. They even killed their wives. Some of our men were trying to escape by swimming across a lake. The Anglos surrounded it and shot them till the water ran red."

Then Pedro leaned up against the wall. "I also saw the Anglos taking the scalps off of men they killed. I never saw so many men killed at one time in my life."

"You look terrible," James said. "You better rest here."

"No. That's not possible. If they find me—" Pedro took his finger and drew it across his throat. Then he looked up into James's face. "And if they find you hiding me—"

"They'd have a black scalp to add to their collection."

"The Anglos captured General Santa Anna. They also captured Colonel Almonte, who I was working with last year."

"He came back to Texas?"

"Yes. He commanded troops with Santa Anna at both the retaking of the Alamo and this terrible loss at San Jacinto."

James was dabbing the blood away with one of the heated rags. "I think it's all cleaned out now. I'm going to tie this around it to stop it from bleeding. But try to keep your arm up anyway."

James pulled the cloth around Pedro's arm tightly and began to make a knot.

Pedro grimaced. "Not so hard."

James loosened it a bit and then began to tie the knot again.

"You want to come with us?" Pedro said after James finished tying the rag.

"Come? Come where?"

"You always wanted your freedom. Now is your chance. You stay here and you will always be a slave. But we have to go now before the Anglos catch up."

James thought fast. The war had turned and the whites were suddenly winning. There was no point in waiting for slavery to end here. He thought about Elizabeth but she was gone. "You know what you're doing?" he said.

"We're going to Matamoros. You will be safe there. Come. What do you have to lose?"

Nothing really, James thought—except his life and Elizabeth. But Pedro was right. He had hoped that the Mexicans would regain control and punish the rebels by abolishing slavery. But it wasn't turning out that way. If anything, the rebels would be more determined than ever to keep slavery forever. About the only consolation he could see would be to take advantage of the chaos of the war to break free.

"Alright, I'll go. You feel okay?"

"It is nothing. We must go now. There are militiamen all over looking for us."

James mounted the horse behind Pedro and they started off toward Alfredo's house across the field and toward the woods. They were half way across the field when they saw four riders coming toward them at a gallop from the side. "Trouble coming," Pedro said.

"They're whites," James said.

The lead rider pulled his horse up in front of them. "You stop right there. Who are you?"

"A Tejano. I defend Texas," Pedro said in broken English.

James looked at the mens' faces and did not recognize any. They had to be volunteers from the United States.

"How do we know you're not one of Santa Anna's soldiers?" the leader said. "Maybe you're a spy. Why do you have a nigger with you?"

"I am the cook for our unit," James said.

"And just what unit is that?"

"The Tennessee unit."

"What's its name?"

It was no use, James realized. He poked Pedro and Pedro dug his spurs into the horse.

The suddenness of the break caught the Americans off guard. James heard two shots. Their best chance lay in getting to the woods. They wouldn't be stupid enough to follow them in.

He could hear their horse hoof beats now and heard the crack of a rifle and saw a puff of dirt fly into the air to his right, just as he had once before when men were trying to recapture him. Then the first branches of the trees hit his shoulder.

Pedro led the horse intentionally through uncut brush at the edge of the field and then guided it toward the main trail. After ten minutes he stopped and both men listened.

"You hear anything?" Pedro asked.

"No, we lost them."

An hour later they were at Pedro's house. Alfredo came to the door with Pilar behind him. "What happened, son?" he said when he saw the bloodstains.

"We are losing. I have a scratch."

"And Ha-mes? Why is he with you?"

"I am helping him escape."

"Did they give you permission?"

"The captain gave me permission. We will meet up with them south of here."

"Well, good thing for Ha-mes, but for us? What will happen when the Anglos have the power?"

"We don't know."

"Will you sleep here?"

"We can't. There are militia after us."

"Run then."

"We will take the mustang for Ha-mes."

"Yes. Take it."

On the third morning of a hard ride the waters of Copano Bay came into view and then the encampment of Mexican soldiers guarding the port. A few soldiers were standing around campfires sipping out of tin cups. They looked up, mostly at the novelty of seeing a black man in their midst, and then went back to their own conversations. But if James thought of himself as an anomaly here, he was about to discover another. Pedro shepherded him through the encampment to a wooden building that oversaw the small port, saluted the soldier who stood guard in front of it, and then entered.

Brigadier General Juan Davis Bradburn stood immediately and walked around the desk when he saw the soldier and black man enter. "You must be the Negro I have been hearing about," he said to James. "I am glad you made it. You know that you are no longer a slave now."

James said nothing at first at hearing the words of the American in Mexican uniform. Then he muttered a thank you.

"You need not thank me. It is the policy of my country. But I must tell you that it gives me a lot of personal pleasure to be able to say that to you. I have been waiting a long time for the opportunity."

"So have I," James said.

"I am sure that you have," Bradburn said. "You must find it ironic that it is a man originally from your own country who pronounces those words."

"I don't care who pronounces them so long as they are real this time. I thought I was free once before."

"I can assure you that you are free this time, but you must not stay here. The war is not going well for us. After you eat and rest, you must travel further south to Matamoros. No one will bother you there. Indeed you will find others like yourself there."

45

Samuel Bingham found Sarah, his daughter Jessica, and Elizabeth in a caravan of wagons headed northward toward Nacogdoches. What he did not know at the time was that she had decided to not just get out of the way of the fighting but to leave Texas completely and return to Tennessee. Thus when he came flush with the news of victory, he found a woman who had already made up her mind to leave him. They threw angry words at each other, but then in the end, bowing to inevitability, she relented and unenthusiastically agreed to go back. In return she won nothing beyond being able to avoid the hardships and uncertainties of returning to Tennessee as a mother without a husband. It was the small comfort of a predictable situation. That night she made a special point of sleeping with the girl under the wagon. When Bingham tried to get close to her, she told him there was no room. If she was going back, she was going back keeping him at a distance.

That was enough for him for now. He had other things on his mind, now that he had retrieved his wife and daughter. The crops, he assumed, were all planted. But he could not be too sure that the slaves would have carried on as he had directed them without him being there to personally make sure. Then there was the question of the house. There was the possibility that it would have been destroyed if Mexican troops had been in the area. These worries occupied him more now than did the difficulties with Sarah. He had learned to live with those difficulties. Even if she was not the loving wife that some men liked to claim in their diaries that they had, she at least marginally did her part in keeping up the house where he lived and in taking care of his daughter. Now would be the time to try to get a son out of her with it being clear sailing ahead for building up the property.

It took four days to get back to the farm, and to his relief, the house looked just as he had left it. The first thing that he did when he left Sarah, Jessica, and Elizabeth off at the house was to look for James to find out how the planting had gone. James was nowhere to be found, so he went to one of the Africans and asked him where he was. The African said that he had left. When he asked him how long ago, the African held up the fingers of both hands. Then he clenched them in a fist and held them up again and shrugged as if to say maybe less, maybe more.

So, he ran away again, Bingham thought. The bastard took advantage of the war to run away. The bad thing was that he would probably get away with it this time. In time Bingham resigned himself to the loss and tried to put it out of his mind. If that was the only loss from the war, he had come out way ahead. All the other slaves were still there. Loss of one slave was a small price to pay, he consoled himself, since everything would now be much more stable and predictable for the future.

The war had actually produced very little interruption. The other field slaves had gone about with the planting as if nothing had happened. Bingham could see the cotton plants beginning to push their ways up through the soil. He could find three other slaves to replace James and the two Africans who had died from cholera. The prices would be coming down since they could now be freely imported from the United States.

46

"Well, Jonathan, how was your stay in New Orleans?" Bingham said aggressively to his neighbor at their first get together since the end of the war. "I trust that the city is as beautiful as ever." Bingham saw the older man wince at the jab for not being present for the fighting and war-related hardships.

"It was a productive trip as you no doubt saw from all the men who joined you."

"Now, c'mon," Lily said, "you both did your parts. I'm going to propose a toast to Texas even though that's usually the job of a man."

She handed a new glass to each of the persons in the room. When she reached Sarah, she whispered, "Jonathan brought these back from New Orleans."

Holmes came round behind her pouring whiskey into the glasses.

When every glass was filled, Lily raised hers and boomed out, "To Texas."

"To Texas," the chorus came back.

"To Texas without Coahuila," Bingham said.

"Yes, without Coahuila," Holmes said.

"To Texas without Mexico," Sarah said. "That was the point, wasn't it?"

"Yes indeed," her husband said, taking advantage of a rare opportunity to occupy common ground.

"We've come a long way, everyone," Holmes said. "It wasn't too long ago that we were citizens of an entirely different country."

"Now," Bingham replied, "we'll have to see whether this republic is viable or whether we just become another state of the United States."

"I personally think the latter is inevitable," Holmes said.

"So why," Bingham said, "are we going through this whole charade of creating a new country if you think that?"

"That's all we can do now if we don't want to start off another confrontation with Mexico."

"You're still worried about them?"

"They could come back with a lot bigger army," Holmes said. "And anyway I'm still puzzled about why they gave up after San Jacinto."

"Because we beat the hell out of 'em, that's why. Captured their president, Santa Anna, to boot."

"Yes, but Santa Anna only had a small part of their troops with him and we got lucky."

"Luck had nothing to do with it."

"Okay, luck or no luck, we had an army of only eight hundred men by the time San Jacinto happened. The Mexicans still had a couple of thousand or more other troops that could've come after us."

Bingham noted Holmes's disingenuous use of 'us' since he was in New Orleans at the time but let it go and said instead, "They were just afraid of the fight after hearing what happened at San Jacinto."

"Perhaps," Holmes said. "But for whatever reason, it suits us that they withdrew and I would not like to see them return. The way I see it, they can begrudgingly accept Texas as an independent country between the United States and them. Then they don't have to worry about the United States trying to expand further westward. But if Texas goes immediately as a new state into the United States, then that directly threatens them. They'll send as big an army as they can up here to try to stop it."

Bingham listened intently to the reasoning of his former political mentor and then decided not to give him the satisfaction of clear agreement. "It's an interesting theory, but what I'm more interested in now is what's going to happen to Santa Anna. You probably think we should let him go, isn't that right Jonathan?"

Holmes took a resigned breath of air in reaction to Bingham's aggressive tone and then said, "Yes, we have to do it—"

"What about the massacres at the Alamo and Goliad?"

"No question about it, death would be too good of a punishment for him but—"

"If I had my way," Bingham said, "he'd be marched to Goliad and shot in the spot where Fannin and his men were."

"That would give me a lot of satisfaction too, Samuel, but it would do Texas harm. He's more valuable to us alive than dead. The longer we keep him alive, the more we can get him to get his compatriots to recognize our independence."

"You can't trust the bastard. He'll say anything you want while in captivity and then the opposite when he's out."

"Yes, you're no doubt right there. But if we keep him a good long time, it serves us. They're not going to attack so long as we have him, Almonte, and the others. They know that'd be their death sentence. So, what else are they going to do? They have to take their armies back south 'cause they can't afford the provisions to keep them up here doing nothing. The way I see it, after they get their armies completely out of here, we can begin to think about letting him go. And by that time, they'll have completely lost any momentum to rekindle the war. Then our independence will be, as the French say, a *fait accompli.*"

Bingham was becoming increasingly impatient and angry at the words of this man who had not even risked his life. "I say we hang or shoot him now and let'em attack us again. Then we can finish all them off."

Holmes shook his head. "We got lucky at San Jacinto. Santa Anna spectacularly blundered and we took advantage of it—"

"That is, those of us who actually did the fighting."

"Yes, Samuel, Texas owes a lot to your bravery." Holmes took an annoyed breath of air and then continued. "What I was saying is that you can't sell the Mexican Army short. They wouldn't make that mistake again and if there were a next fight, I'm not so sure that we'd come out on top again."

"You forget, Jonathan, that the United States now has an interest in our independence. They would not stand by idly and let Mexico reconquer us."

"I said not to sell the Mexican Army short."

"They wouldn't stand a chance against the U.S. Army."

"Don't be so sure. Let's look at the logistics of this. What are the advantages of the United States? It has about eleven million people to the eight million that Mexico has. It can muster a bigger army, maybe. But that is not that much of an advantage when you consider that the eleven million are spread out over a much bigger area than are the eight million in Mexico. Mexico is much more compact—"

"And we just made it a good deal more compact," Bingham cut in, smiling.

"Yes, we certainly did," Holmes acknowledged. "The point is that just like a well-proportioned fist fighter has advantages over a big fat one, Mexico would have certain advantages in such a war due to its compactness. Then you have to consider that the United States has a very important division between the southern and northern states."

"Over the slavery question."

"Yes, over the slavery question, among other points of dispute. Do you really think that that many Yankees would want to come down here to fight over what they would consider to be an extension of slavery? Compare that to Mexico where they have no problem getting Indians from Yucatan to fight and you'll see my point."

"Yes," Bingham admitted, "that could be a problem."

"And now, there's one thing more that you have to consider. Let's say that an all-out war between Mexico and the United States were touched off over the question of Texas. What would happen if the Mexican Army invaded the United States? It would consider itself a liberating army for the slaves, just like it tried to do during our war. You can only imagine what would happen in Louisiana where there are many more slaves than here. It would be a bloody mess. So, Samuel my boy, I don't think that they'd be too anxious in Washington to get involved in a big war here, at least not at this time."

Bingham found Holmes's paternalism irritating and his logic to be extreme, but the argument was nevertheless interesting. "So you once again advocate caution, as seems to be your wont."

"Absolutely. Our situation is fragile. We cannot afford impetuous action, no matter how personally satisfying. We have to play our cards cautiously. The main thing now is to keep the Mexican Army away from here. If that requires letting the bastard Santa Anna live, then let the sorry sonofabitch live."

"Even if he deserves to die."

"Even if he deserves to die," Homes repeated. "He's a bargaining chip. That's the only thing that's saved his sorry life so far. But what I was saying, Samuel, is that we have to be reasonably united in this government. When you look at our situation objectively, our army is not that big and Urrea's army is still out there undefeated. Other armies could come from Mexico. The last thing we would need would be not to be able to form a united government."

Bingham saw where Holmes was headed, so he beat him to the question. "Who are you backing for president? Stephen Austin?"

"Yes, of course. And you?"

"Don't know yet, but not Austin."

"Why not? There's not a man who goes all the way back to the beginning like him and who has done so much over the years."

"His day has past."

"What do you mean by that?"

"He was too slow to endorse the revolution," Bingham said, still wondering whether the plan he had hatched with Zachariah Nettles had made the difference in getting Austin to finally endorse independence for Texas. "It was only just a few months ago that he was still arguing that we belonged in Mexico."

"That's true, but it was for tactical reasons."

"It doesn't matter. People like Houston were more in tune with what we needed."

"Look," Holmes said, sensing the increasing tension in the air, "let's drop that subject. There will be a campaign. I will back Austin and you can back whoever you please."

"You are joining the militia, aren't you?" Bingham said in an accusatory tone.

"Of course I am. Everyone has to whose under fifty. It's a good idea to have a defensive citizen's army on the ready in case the Mexicans come back. We will both serve together."

47

Once he had crossed the Nueces River, just south of Copano Bay, James had been technically out of Texas and entered Tamaulipas. But Texas had been too close for him to feel any comfort. He had remembered how, earlier, when he had thought that slavery was over, he had never really felt safe because he was too close to the people who had been his owners. He would not make that mistake again. If he was to be truly free this time he had to put a lot of distance between himself and anyone who could enslave him again.

It had taken four more days from there on horseback to get to Matamoros. Then he had felt safe and the sense of freedom he had felt briefly once before in his life returned.

After the initial euphoria wore off, he turned his mind to thinking of how to support himself. Most of the escaped Negroes he met in Matamoros earned their keep working on farms outside of town. They stayed in town for a short while after arrival and then hooked up with a farmer. A number continued living in town, going out daily to work in the fields. For this they received food and a small amount of money. It would have been easy for him to follow their example, but farm work did not appeal to him now. Instead, he took the more time-consuming and frustrating route of looking for work in town. He had thought it all out and wanted to get into something that would lead to him being in complete control. In his previous dreams, he had wanted to have his own land to farm and be in control of that. But now, tired of field labor and associating it too much with slavery, he wanted to have his own workshop.

Matamoros was a lot larger than Matagorda and, as he walked the streets, he saw many men working and then selling what they had made. This appealed to him. After some time, one contact led to another and he hooked up with a shoemaker who agreed to take him on as an apprentice. He, the shoemaker, was already old and finding it more difficult to get up enough energy to take care of the repairs and orders for new boots and shoes that kept coming. The shoemaker had a stall in the city market across from a cloth merchant. In return for working, the shoemaker let James sleep in the stall. He also worked out a trade with a woman who cooked and sold food in the market so that James could take his meals there. In addition to the room and board, he gave him a few pesos each week for spending money.

James found the work to be agreeable enough even if the old shoemaker was not always pleasant to work with. The workday began around eight o'clock when the shoemaker arrived. He would be up by that time and have moved the two large wooden doors away from the front of the stall. They would work together until mid-afternoon and then close down for three hours for comida. At night they would be back for three more hours of work.

The day had a rhythm that James became accustomed to and liked. During the three hours for comida he ate at the woman's stand and then had some time to himself. Sometimes he walked the streets of Matamoros. Other times he went back to the stall and read.

One morning the old man did not come to work. This had not happened before. James thought that he must be sick. He went ahead with the work as usual, planning that he would go over to his house at the hour of comida to inquire. At mid afternoon, when all of the stalls except for the food stands were closing down, he closed up the stall and walked the five blocks south of the market to where the shoemaker and his wife lived. When he rounded the corner to the street where they lived, he saw a group of people standing around a long black box raised on a table in the middle of the alley outside of the house.

After he reached the group, a man who he had met on one of his earlier trips to the house pulled him aside.

"Don Aurelio died last night," the man said in Spanish, bowing his head.

James felt a twinge of hurt within himself. "What did he die, from?" he stammered.

The man sighed. "He was old."

In front of the house he saw the shoemaker's wife seated, her face frozen in resignation. He went up to her and said in Spanish, "I am so sorry. Don Aurelio was very good to me. I will miss him terribly."

The shoemaker's wife listened, or at least seemed to be listening, and then said, "The business is yours. He told me to give it to you last night. We have no sons to pass it on to, and you were like a son to him. He liked you very much."

James felt tears welling up within him. He had never known that the shoemaker had felt anything for him. Then he felt guilty because he had not had a similar depth of feeling for him.

He stayed at the wake for the rest of the afternoon and shared food with the other mourners.

"Who will take care of the widow?" James asked one of the men who stood alone eating.

"She is old and will go to live with her daughter." The man pointed to a middle-aged woman who was serving food.

After expressing his regrets to the shoemaker's widow once again and introducing himself to the daughter and telling her all the good that her father had done for him, he returned to the stall in the marketplace to sleep.

He kept the stall closed out of respect for three days, during which time he attended the shoemaker's burial, and then he opened it on the fourth. By now he knew enough of the trade to handle it himself and most of the old customers kept coming.

He kept in frequent contact with the other Negroes in Matamoros, who now numbered over a hundred. The ex-slave community was growing larger, people thought, because there were more slaves coming into Texas and that led to more runaways. While he and the other Negroes had no formal organization, they did maintain a network so that whenever a new runaway arrived, he, and an occasional she, could count upon support until getting work. Most, but not all, of the Negroes participated in this. The ones who didn't were just looking out for themselves, James thought. He understood this though he did not agree with it. Maybe, he thought, no one had ever helped them and that was why they figured that they didn't owe anything to anyone. But he had had help—first from Joseph Robinson, then from Pedro and his family, and then the shoemaker.

170

Whatever the general principle at stake, it was something to which he felt bound.

Word got around among the Mexicans that there was a Negro in the market so that when they encountered a new runaway they would direct him there. It was on an April morning, almost exactly one year from the time that he left Texas, when a vaguely familiar face came by his stall looking for help.

James thought and then remembered. "You're Joe, aren't you?"

"Yeah, I'm Joe," the man said. "But who are you?"

"James."

"Where do I know you from?"

"Matagorda"

"Oh yeah, you worked way outside of Matagorda, didn't you?"

"That's me alright. If I remember right, you were on your way to Gonzalez with your owner. He was going to fight."

"Oh yes, that was Master William Travis."

James took a special liking to Joe and decided to let him stay at the stall and work until he found something better. It was a kind of special honor to have living with him the former slave of one of the leaders of the Texian Revolution. And word got around town about that and sometimes Mexicans would come by just to meet the former slave who had been spared at the Alamo. Joe wasn't the only slave of a Texian hero to escape. A short time later Sam Houston himself lost two slaves, Tom and Esau, and they turned up in Matamoros.

From Joe he learned that after the battle of San Jacinto most of the whites who were fleeing had returned. From this he surmised that Elizabeth must now be back at the Bingham farm.

He thought that his business was going well. A lot of people brought their shoes to him. He thought they did that because they wanted to show support for him and Joe. Every once in a while one of them would make a negative remark about slavery in the breakaway region. He would nod his agreement and then they would go on to attack Anglo Americans in general and the United States and he would nod some more.

The business was going so well that he was able to start saving some money. At first he thought that he would use the savings to finance a move to a room to live in away from the stall. But then he did some hard thinking about his situation. He was free and he was doing well in his work. But there was one thing that was so missing in his life that it hurt him to think about it. He'd left Elizabeth behind and he wanted her there with him, and so he began to make plans.

"You're crazy if you think you can just go back into Texas and get that girl," Joe said to him when he told him his intentions. "They'll hang you higher than a hawk."

"Yeah, I'm probably crazy, but I'm gonna do it."

"Well then, watch yourself. Just remember that where Texas start ain't so clear. It ain't supposed to start until north of the Nueces but they claim that it starts right here at the river. So you can get yo'rself grabbed anywhere north of heah. And watch out for the Indians too."

"I know."

That evening James closed up his stall and announced to the neighboring stall dwellers that he would be away temporarily for a couple of weeks. He also bought a gun.

He crossed the Rio Bravo early the next morning on a borrowed horse and rode northward toward the Nueces. This was no man's land now, claimed both by Mexico and the Republic of Texas with neither side being strong enough though to prevail.

Late in the afternoon he came across a lone Mexican riding toward him. The two men stopped their horses and exchanged greetings.

"Are there Anglo Americans up the road?" James asked him in Spanish.

The man shook his head. "Not today. I saw some Rangers yesterday though."

"Rangers? Who are they?"

"The army of the Republic of Texas."

"Must be what used to be the militia. A thousand thanks for the information"

"You're welcome. Be careful. They will stop any Negro they see. You also better watch out for Comanches. They killed some people a while back."

It was well after dark three days later when he reached the Nueces. He approached the river and then turned back into a grove of trees to make camp for the rest of the night. It had been a hard day's ride and he felt exhausted by the time he spread his bedroll out by the fire. Within moments he was fast asleep.

He awoke in the dampness of the early morning dew. He rekindled the fire and heated up some tortillas and beans that he had carried with him. There he would have to stay until darkness fell if he was to avoid traveling the roads of Texas in daylight. After a while he walked down to the bank of the river and looked across. There was no turning back now, but all the same he felt an intense anxiety. He wanted Elizabeth badly. It had been a year since he had seen her and he knew that she was the one he had to be with. When he left the year before, he felt for her but he had thought that it would go away in time. It did not. Was it just loneliness? It was partly that but it had to be more. He had been with two women in Matamoros for short periods of time and one of them could have lasted if he had wanted it to. But every time he was with her he kept thinking back to Elizabeth. It was then that he realized that he had to get her back.

He was skipping rocks now on the muddy surface of the water and it became clear to him that he was afraid. If he got caught this time, he would not be facing a whip. He would be good and dead after having been so free. He shook his head and thought, what a man will do for a woman!

At dusk he saddled the mare and broke camp. His plan was to make it to the house of Pedro's parents in the night and stay there the next day. Then the next night he would get Elizabeth and then make the run back to Matamoros.

Three nights later he was in the woods that lay between Bingham's farm and the Gómez house. He was now on familiar ground. These were woods that he knew well and knew exactly where he wanted to make camp—beside a small brook where he had gone many times to bathe. Once again he would stay out of sight during the day and then make contact during the night hours.

After a couple of hours of darkness he rode up to the house of his friends. He looked around the yard. It looked like they had made some changes. He tied up the mare to one of the posts of the corral and walked up to the door and knocked.

The door opened and a red-haired man peered out, "What are you doing knockin' at our door at this hour of the night, boy?"

"I'm looking for Señor Gómez. This is his house."

"Ain't his house no more." The man showed the barrel of a rifle that he had in his other hand. "Now you get outta heah."

James's heart was pounding. "Sorry to have bothered you, sir," he said, backing away from the door.

The door closed and he walked in a hurried step to his horse and mounted. His plan was now speeded up. No point in waiting till the next evening. He would go to get her now.

Shortly past midnight he rode up to the small cabin on the Holmes property and noticed that several others had gone up alongside it.

"Ezekiel, it's me, James," he called out as he rapped on the door.

"What are you doing here?" Ezekiel said, opening the door. "Come in. Rachel, look who done showed up."

Rachel smiled and gave him a hug. "Let me guess. You come back 'cause you miss bein' a slave."

"No, course not. I come for Elizabeth. But I might as well come for you too." The truth was that he had not thought of asking them before, but now he needed them and the idea was not a bad one.

Ezekiel stopped smiling. "No, I is settled here as ever."

"Be serious, Ezekiel," Rachel said. Then she turned to James. "You got a place to live in Mexico?"

"Yes, I've got a roof over my head."

"How you eat?" Ezekiel asked.

"I make and fix shoes."

"You a shoemaker now?"

"I haven't touched a plow in so long that I don't think I know what one looks like anymore."

"Mastah Holmes," Ezekiel said, "he work me much harder ever since they get the Mexicans outta here. Got him some more slaves too."

"The other cabins," James said, motioning with his hand.

"Yeah," Ezekiel said, "that what they for. He even workin' my son." He pointed to the side of the cabin where a boy lay sleeping on the ground. "And he just nine years old."

"How long would it take us to get there?" Rachel asked seriously.

"Three nights's ride gets us to the Nueces. Then we are mostly out of Texas but we ain't in the clear yet. We are clear, clear, clear when we get across the Rio Bravo. That's three more days later."

"And we have a way to live when we get there?"

"There are escaped slaves that arrive in Matamoros all the time and I've never seen one of them decide to go back."

"'Cept for you," Ezekiel said.

"I just came back for something I left. Now, Elizabeth, she hasn't taken up with another man, has she?"

Ezekiel and Rachel looked at each other.

"No," Rachel said. "She ain't with no other man. But she has a child."

James felt his heart heave. "From who?"

"Her mastah," Rachel said. "Who else?"

James took a deep breath and then after a pause said, "Think she would still want to go?"

"She still talks about you," Rachel answered.

"And you?" James asked the two of them. "I'm leaving tomorrow night. I'll hide in the woods 'cause a white man saw me at what used to be my friends' house."

"Yeah," Ezekiel said. "You better hide 'cause he sure to report a strange nigger comin' to his door in the middle of the night. Dem Rangers will be all over heah investigatin'."

"We ain't sayin' yes," Rachel said in answer to his question, "and we ain't sayin' no."

"I can't come back here tomorrow in the day to find out. It's too dangerous."

"Look," Ezekiel said, "you look out from dem woods tomorrow mornin' and if you see the wagon by the door, it mean we gettin' ready to go with you and you come back at night to get us. Otherwise don't come back."

"Well then, I will say good-bye now just in case."

"You take this with you." Rachel handed James a half of a round loaf of bread. "You look like you could use somethin' to eat."

That night he made camp in the nearby woods. He awoke the next morning wondering what he would see across the field. When he did peer out from the trees, the wagon was there in front of the cabin as he had hoped. The rest of the day, before crossing over the field to the cabin to meet them, he thought through the plan to extract Elizabeth from the Bingham house. Rachel would go over to the house, talk to Elizabeth, and then claim that her baby was very sick. They would say that she and the baby would stay with her and Ezekiel for a while so as to not endanger the Bingham child.

That evening after he had joined up with Ezekiel, Rachel, and their son, explained the plan, and sent them on their way to the Bingham house to execute it, he waited in the woods beside the trail leading south. He waited for a long time and began to worry that something had gone wrong. But then he saw their familiar wagon coming down the trail. He waited for it to cross a small creek before coming out from the woods and riding up to it. Elizabeth was in the back with her baby asleep, his head resting against her thigh. The son of Ezekiel and Rachel lay dozing on the floorboards with a sack over him.

Ezekiel nodded at James and then looked over his shoulder and said to Elizabeth, "Look familiar?"

"Damned if he don't," Elizabeth said. "James, what you doin' heah?"

James dismounted and put his hand on the sideboard of the wagon. "Came back to ask you to marry me."

"Marry you? Then you just gonna disappear again."

"That's right. But this time you come with me."

"Come with you? Come where?"

"To Matamoros. I got a business there."

"You crazy. I can't just go like that."

"Why not?" He looked toward Ezekiel and Rachel. "They are."

"When?"

"Right now," Ezekiel said.

"With the baby too?"

James placed both of his hands on the sideboard and looked straight into her brown eyes and nodded. "With the baby. Of course."

"Hold on," Ezekiel said, cutting in. The sudden sound of hoof beats made everyone hush and listen.

"It's him, the mastah," Elizabeth said

James looked over his shoulder at the figure on horseback approaching. "We got trouble," he said.

Bingham pulled his horse up alongside them. Then he slowly walked it around the wagon and when he saw James, he said, "Well, well, James.

You came back after all. Life must not be what you thought it would be in Mexico."

"I came for my fiancée."

"You're fiancée?" Bingham let out a laugh. "Who? Her?" He looked in the direction of Elizabeth who looked terrified. "She's not yours to marry. You forget that you're no longer in Mexico. You're now in the Republic of Texas."

"That won't be for long," James said. "The Mexican Army is on their way now."

"I don't know where you heard that but you don't argue with me. You are still my slave."

"You don't own me anymore. I'm a free man in Mexico." James was reaching now under his shirt.

Ezekiel looked at Rachel and then at the ground in dread. Elizabeth pulled her baby tightly against her. The boy pretended he was still asleep.

"Didn't you hear me?" Bingham shouted. "This isn't Mexico anymore and you're in a heap of trouble." He lifted up his rifle and aimed it at James. "Now you come out from the other side of that wagon."

James slowly walked down the side of the wagon. Then he suddenly turned, lifted the pistol out from under his shirt and shot.

The rifle dropped from Bingham's hands and his mouth hung open for an instant before he toppled from the horse, landing side first on the ground.

Ezekiel, Rachel, and Elizabeth looked in disbelief first at Bingham lying on the ground and then at James. The boy jumped off of the wagon to see closer.

James himself felt momentarily paralyzed. Then he snapped to and said, "Help me get him out of the road."

"Is he dead?" Ezekiel asked when he reached Bingham.

"I don't think so," James said, putting his hand over Bingham's mouth to feel for breath.

He and Ezekiel dragged Bingham to the side of the road.

"You can't just leave him lying there," Rachel said.

"We have no choice," James said. "What are we going to do, take him to Matagorda? We'd all be hanged."

"Leave him to die," Elizabeth said. "He deserve it."

"Let's get moving fast," James said. Then he turned to Elizabeth. "You coming?"

"Do I have a choice?" she said. "You sure got some way of convincin'."

The wagon with Ezekiel driving, the women and children in back, and James on horseback alongside it, moved out.

James knew that he was either going to get them away and free or all killed. If they made it to the Nueces and Mexico, they were free; if not, dead. Sooner or later someone would come looking for Bingham and figure out what had happened and then come after them. Whether they made it or got killed all depended on how much of a head start they had. Men on horseback could cover ground faster than they could with the wagon. With at least a night's head start, he figured, they could stay far enough ahead of the men who would be coming after them to make it to the Nueces.

They pushed hard for three nights traveling under the cover of darkness. Days they spent hiding and sleeping in woods along the way. They had been fortunate in that the wagon axles had held up. James dreaded one of them breaking. He was not sure what they would do if that happened except to abandon the wagon and strike out on foot. There were too many of them to ride on the two horses. He grew accustomed to looking back over his shoulder for pursuers. Surely someone had found out about what happened to Bingham. It would take a day at most for that to happen. Then they would start out after them. That meant that they probably started out a day behind them and would be closing fast. If only he and the others had not had to use a wagon. That forced them to follow the main road. If only they had more horses they could stay off of it.

At the end of the fourth night, they reached the Nueces River. Once they crossed the river they would be at least out of Texas but not totally safe yet. He guided his horse down the bank and into the river at the fording spot. Then he watched as the wagon followed. Off to the east he could see the first glow of the morning sun. Everyone was exhausted after the all-night drive but he would push them to keep going all day. Now that they were out of Texas they could keep going during the day without having to hide. It would be best to get as far out as possible before resting. If Rangers were chasing them, they might cross over the

Nueces, but they would not go too far beyond it for fear of running into Mexican troops.

He turned to watch as Ezekiel pulled up on the reins to keep the wagon from going too fast as it descended down the bank. In the distance behind them he thought he detected clouds of dust. He cupped his hands over his eyes and focused on the road they had been traveling. There in the distance he now saw riders, a large group of them, coming up fast. "Get moving fast," he shouted to Ezekiel. "Rangers coming."

The wagon was now down in the river with the water coming half way up the wheels and the horse was having a hard time pulling it. Ezekiel whipped the horse from the back and James used his reins to whip it from the side. Finally the horse made the side and stumbled up the bank. But then it stopped suddenly. The left front wagon wheel was stuck.

"Everybody out of the back," James shouted. Then he jumped down from his horse into the water and got on his hands and knees beside the wheel. It was wedged between two rocks. He looked over his shoulders and saw the Rangers riding at a gallop toward them. Then he pulled as hard as he could at one of the rocks as Ezekiel kept whipping the horse and suddenly the wagon lurched forward with the wheel catching and skinning one of his knuckles.

"What are we going to do?" Elizabeth cried. "They're almost here."

Ezekiel pulled at the bit of the horse and James pushed the wagon from behind to get it the rest of the way up the bank. The women and children stood on the bank.

"They're coming!" Rachel said.

James turned around and saw them as the wagon lurched forward and began to roll up the bank.

"Let's go, back in the wagon," Ezekiel shouted. Then he turned to James. "Are we safe now?"

"No, they'll cross the river."

"Ain't no way we gonna outrun them," Ezekiel said as the first of the rifle shots began hitting the ground around them. Then he turned to the women and children in the back. "Everybody lie down, far as you can."

"You go as fast as you can," James said to Ezekiel. "I'm going to double back and hold them off with my gun."

James pulled the reins of his horse and split off from the wagon at a gallop heading toward a rocky hill on the side of the road. Then he took cover and waited.

The Rangers pulled up at the northern bank of the river momentarily. There were at least fifteen and he saw a familiar face, that of Holmes, with them. Then they started to cross. The wagon had vanished around a bend. He took careful aim with his pistol at the lead Ranger and squeezed the trigger. The sound echoed off of the hills and the horse reared up, throwing its rider off and into the water. He wasn't sure whether he had hit the horse or the man but it was enough to send all of them scattering for cover.

He then climbed up the rocks to the hilltop and ran along it out of sight of the road until he was at the side of the Rangers and looking down at them. From there he took aim and fired again. A Ranger grabbed his arm. The rest turned and started firing back. He took one more shot at them. Then he ran back toward his former vantage point. He could hold them down a little while going back and forth and firing shots like this. It was only a matter of time though before they got him or got past.

Amidst the shots a military bugle sounded. This astonished him. He saw the Rangers look up too. He turned and looked down and to his left and saw from around the bend to the south a cavalry unit riding toward the river. If he had been more religious, he would have thought that a prayer was being answered.

The Rangers, seeing that they were heavily outnumbered, retreated back across the river.

James stood up and dusted himself off. A minute before he had been preparing for imminent death. Now he was free once again. He climbed down from the rocks to retrieve his horse. The soldiers looked at him and grinned. One of them patted his rifle and then made a sweeping motion with his hand as if he has swept the pursuers away.

A captain came over and said, "You are safe now. Your friends are up ahead."

"Thank you."

"It is nothing."

James mounted his horse and caught up with the wagon that was stopped and waiting a half mile up ahead. Then he saw that something was terribly wrong. Elizabeth lay in the back of the wagon with Rachel kneeling beside her. The baby was crying.

"She's been shot," Ezekiel said.

He felt his heart sink as he climbed up onto the wagon. She lay there gasping, with blood staining the top part of her dress. Rachel was stroking her forehead.

He felt helpless now. There was nothing that he could do for her but look into her face at her very distant eyes. Then the eyes closed and her body stopped moving. Rachel looked quickly at him and then began to sob. The baby sensed that something terrible had happened and crawled from the corner of the wagon and pushed up against his mother's side. He felt himself trembling as he took another look at her face. And then he kissed her forehead.

"She has passed." Ezekiel said softly from the side of the wagon.

He was too choked to speak and so he just nodded his head. It would have been better if he had just died fighting the Rangers without having to know this.

Rachel picked up the baby, came down off of the wagon, and began walking up and down the road, singing softly.

"What do you want to do?" Ezekiel said to James. "Bury Liza here?"

He shook his head. "No. We'll carry her with us to Matamoros."

48

For the next few months he found that recovering from grief was much more difficult than recovering from any physical ailment, even the scars from being whipped. He would awake in the morning as if everything was all right and then the memory of what had happened would come rushing back and bring him down. He had really not been that close to her for that long when they had been together in Texas; and he had not even gotten a chance to get close to her again after the escape. But he had thought about her so much during the months in Matamoros after he had escaped that he had been sure that she would make his life complete. And now she was gone.

They had come into Matamoros with her body and gone straight to a priest he knew. The priest then directed them with what to do with the body and the next day she was buried. A few people he knew from the market attended the burial. A few days later a newspaper, *El Mercurio del Puerto de Matamoros*, found out what had happened and published a story under the headline, "Slave Murdered Trying to Escape Texas."

Ezekiel and Rachel took the baby with them. James was in no position to raise a child—the child of the woman who he had loved most in the world and the man who he hated the most. They were headed south of Matamoros, down further into Tamaulipas where the government promised land to them. Rachel had insisted that they not stay in Matamoros. It was a little too close for her comfort to Texas.

Because he had no money, he immediately had to get back to work cobbling alongside Joe, who had kept the business going while he had been away. After a few months his life returned to its former routine. His old customers returned, and occasionally escaped slaves from Texas turned up and he let them sleep there until they found work.

On an afternoon when Joe was away from the stall on errands, James was tapping nails into a boot when he looked up and saw a white face, but one that looked somehow familiar.

"You don't remember me?" the white man said in English. "We met at Copano Bay when you were in a big hurry to get away from Texas."

James suddenly realized who was standing before him. "You are Bradburn, aren't you? What are you doing in Matamoros?"

"I live here with my family."

"Really? I guess I never think of army officers as living anywhere but in forts."

Bradburn smiled. "No, I do have a home like other men. It's a farm down on the other side of the river."

"Are you still with the army?"

"Do I look like an army officer?" Bradburn swept his hand at his civilian clothing. "I'm in temporary retirement."

"What does temporary retirement mean?

"It means that I might go back if there is a need."

"Like going back to fight in Texas?"

Bradburn winced. "I hope not. But when you're in an army, you don't have the luxury of choosing your assignments. A shoemaker like you is freer. You can turn down an order. I can't turn down one."

James appreciated the irony. "So you're saying that I'm more free than you are?"

"In a manner of speaking. No one is going to tell you that you have to leave your home—"

"Such as it is," James said, motioning to his cot in the back of the stall.

"Such as it is, humble though it may be" Bradburn acknowledged. "I, on the other hand, can get an order any day to leave my home to fight hundreds of leagues away."

"So," James said, "surely you have not come here to debate which of us is more free. What can I do for you?"

"To begin with, you can make me a new pair of boots. This pair," Bradburn motioned at the heavily worn boots he was wearing, "took a lot of punishment in Texas and are due for retirement from active duty." He paused and then smiled. "That is if you don't decide to exercise your newfound freedom and turn me down."

"It would be a pleasure, sir. That is, a pleasure to make you some boots, not to turn you down. Just take your old boots off so that I can take your measure."

Bradburn sat down on a bench outside the stall and pulled off his boots one by one. Then he stood up and placed his right foot on a piece of paper. James took a stick and dipped in a can of ashes and then traced the outline of the foot.

"You're the slave General Terán met, aren't you?," Bradburn said, as he placed his left foot on another piece of paper.

James looked up from his tracing. "How did you know that?"

"I just guessed it from what I know about where you came from and that you were with Pedro Gómez Quintero. At first when you came to Copano, I didn't make the connection. But then long after you left, I began to suspect it. By that time it was too late to confirm it since you and he were gone. But it's been riding in my head ever since. I knew that you would be most likely here. After returning and getting settled, I made some inquiries and that's how I found you."

"Then General Terán talked to you about me?"

"A little. Actually more than a little."

"It's too bad that he died. I never heard of a man killing himself. But then again, he did look kind of sad if I remember."

"It was a real tragedy for all of us. He was a very good man and he was very moved by the scars left by the whiplashes on your back. Do they still hurt you?"

James shook his head. "No the back doesn't hurt any more. It just hurts me here." He pointed to his head.

"Te da cólera," Bradburn said.

"Yes," James responded. "Mucho."

"Sometimes Spanish works better."

James nodded. "Sometimes. The anger in me will never burn out."

"You have a right to be angry and I as a white man, especially one originally from the United States, can't tell you not to be. But I can tell you that the anger will hurt you more than the man who laid that whip on you."

James furrowed his brows and stared back at Bradburn. "What are you talking about?"

"As long as you carry that anger around with you, the man who did it to you is still in your head oppressing you."

"How can you say that? You've never been a slave."

"No, but I've been a military man and I've seen all kinds of barbarities that could make me angry for a thousand lifetimes. If I let anger run my life, I couldn't go on being an effective officer."

"Surely you're angry at what they did in Texas," James said.

"Not at the men who rebelled, only at their cause."

"So I should forgive my ex-owner and only be angry at slavery?" James said sarcastically. "Is that what you're saying?"

"No, I wouldn't go that far. Don't forgive evil. Just don't let it get the best of you." Bradburn stepped back and smiled to break the tension. "Look, I'm no preacher man and here I sound like one now."

At that moment Joe appeared, back from his errands and James introduced the two men.

"You ever been at Anahuac, sir?" Joe asked.

Bradburn seemed surprised at the question and then said, "Yes, I was stationed there several years ago. Why do you ask?"

"My master talked about a man named Bradburn who he had a run-in with before he buy me."

"Who was your master?"

"Colonel William Travis."

Bradburn gave a start. "So he called himself colonel?"

"He was Colonel for a few months before he got himself kilt at the Alamo in Béxar. Die with all the rest of the Texians."

Bradburn tightened his face. "I heard he was with them. Were you the slave who was with him there?"

"That was me. Mexicans let me go. Say they have nothin' against the slaves. So I go back and tell the Texians what happened."

"That should have made you some kind of hero to them," James said.

"I wasn't no hero to them," Joe said. "They keep saying that it such a tragedy that such a fine man as Colonel Travis had to die and such a worthless slave as me survive. Then they put me back to work as a slave again and I get tired of that."

"The hell with 'em," James said. "You are here now."

"That's how I see it. The Mexicans didn't kill me and they didn't make me no slave. So I think one day that this is where I should be and here I am."

Bradburn seemed speechless upon hearing who Joe was. And then, as if he had resolved everything in his mind about it, he suddenly changed the subject and said to James, "Can you deliver those boots to my home two Sundays from now? If you can, I'd like to have a little dinner for both of you so that you can meet my family and some friends."

James smiled at hearing the sudden invitation. "I shall have your boots ready and we shall come with big appetites."

James went back to working after Bradburn left and thought about what he had said. There was only one other white man who could have made comments like those to him and that was Joseph Robinson. Being a Quaker, it was predictable that Joseph Robinson would say something about learning to live at peace with the past. But a military man?

On the appointed Sunday with borrowed horses he and Joe made their way out of town and up the road along the Rio Bravo to the Bradburn farm. Tied together and dangling from James's saddle horn were two newly made boots.

Bradburn met them at the front door. "Very good, I'm glad you've come. And I see you've brought my new boots." Bradburn took them and held them up in the mid afternoon light to inspect. "A very good job indeed." Then he discretely handed James several peso bills.

"Vicente," Bradburn called over to a man dressed in an officer's uniform. Then he said in Spanish, "Let me present to you Mr. James —" Bradburn hesitated, realizing that he did not know the ex-slave's last name or if he had one.

James noticed the hesitation and came to his rescue. "Robinson. James Robinson," he said forthrightly. He had been ready for this moment and had thought about what last name he would use when it became necessary. For sure it wasn't going to be Bingham, despite it being the usual practice of freed slaves to choose the name of the plantation they came from.

"James Robinson," Bradburn repeated. "He has come with a fine pair of boots for me, as you can see. I highly recommend his services. And this is his assistant, Joe—? I'm sorry," Bradburn said to Joe, "I do not know your last name."

Joe shrugged.

"Well, Joe it is."

"I am General Vicente Filisola at your service." The general stepped forward as if on a parade ground and shook James and Joe's hands.

"General Filisola knows something about Texas," Bradburn said.

Joe, who did not understand the Spanish that was now being spoken, took a step back and just watched the interaction between the other men.

"You were helped by our troops, is that not true? In fact, both of you were helped by our troops," Filisola said.

"Yes," James responded in Spanish, "that is true and I am grateful. You were there in Texas?"

"Yes, indeed. I commanded a number of troops that unfortunately were forced to withdraw temporarily."

"You are going back? I thought the war was all over."

Filisola looked at Bradburn and then both men looked back at James. "Of course," Filisola said. "The war is not over until we bring Texas back into the republic."

James furrowed his brow and looked at the general. There was something about him that struck him as unusual. "You do not seem Mexican."

Filisola looked at Bradburn who raised his eyebrows. Then he said to James, "You are very observant. I am Italian by birth but Mexico is my adopted land. Like my compatriot," he nodded in the direction of Bradburn, "and I suspect you now, I have chosen to become Mexican."

"We are all expatriates here," Bradburn said.

There was a knock at the door and James was beginning to realize that Bradburn had planned a far more involved affair than he had expected. This was not a simple meeting of the family.

At the door stood a tall Indian dressed in buckskins with drawn black hair.

"Dutokeh, come in," Bradburn said in English.

The Indian exchanged greetings with Bradburn and Filisola, who he already knew. Then Bradburn introduced him to James and Joe.

"You are from Texas," Joe said, "because you speak English."

"It is a tongue I speak reluctantly."

"And you speak Spanish?"

"I speak Cherokee."

Bradburn's wife was now motioning them into a room where a table had been set with bowls of rice, beans, and pork strips, along with stacks of tortillas.

Filisola was the first to speak after they had sat down and begun to eat, and he addressed himself directly to James in Spanish. "I asked our host to arrange this dinner because we need your help."

"My help?"

"Yes, your help. The war goes on for Texas. The manner in which we see it, to reestablish control we are going to need help. That is where he comes in." Filisola nodded in the direction of Dutokeh, who kept on eating, apparently not noticing that he was being talked about. "We have proposed an alliance with his people and we are working on alliances with other tribes. When we move our troops back in, they will support us."

"I am not a soldier," James said "but from everything I know from living there, the Indians do not like Mexicans any more than they do whites."

Filisola looked annoyed at the response and then turned to Bradburn who spoke in English.

"Any alliance involves agreements," Bradburn said. "What the general is saying is that we have proposed to Dutokeh that if we prevail in reestablishing control over Texas, we will immediately grant his nation complete control over the part of the territory that they now inhabit. The Texians had promised them ownership of their land, but their Senate has now formally nullified that agreement."

Dutokeh looked up now and followed what was being said.

"Control over the whites too?" Joe said.

The Indian smiled.

"Control means control," Bradburn said. "It will be their land."

"Separate from Mexico?"

"Perhaps."

"We have no treaty," Dutokeh said.

"Yes," Bradburn acknowledged, "we are only exploring possibilities now."

"So why are we here?" James asked.

"Because we also want to explore the possibility of having a general slave uprising to coincide with the military campaign. The slaves would all receive their freedom when we reestablished control."

James contorted his face. "We can't negotiate for the slaves."

"We know that," Bradburn responded. "We just want to hear your opinion of whether it would be realistic and how we could go about organizing it. Do you know slaves, for example, who we could contact?"

"Contact? How would you contact them?"

"There are still loyalist Mexicans in Texas."

"Well," James said, leaning back in his chair, "if you ask me, I don't think that it is a very good idea."

"And just why not?"

"In the first place, the slaves are all isolated from each other. In the second, they have no guns. They're not like the Indians who are off by themselves together with guns and horses."

"Those are indeed elementary points to be considered," Bradburn said. "The general has considered them and he thinks that they could be overcome. If the slaves were to know ahead of time that our army was coming to liberate them, they could do a lot to cause trouble for the Anglo Americans."

While Bradburn vigorously put forth the arguments of Filisola, James thought he could detect that he did not seem to be fully convinced of them himself.

"What do you think of this?" Joe said to Dutokeh.

Dutokeh looked up from his plate. "I am in favor of it because I trust the Mexicans more than the Americans. But not all of my people will go along."

"What don't they like?" James said.

"That we must be on your side or their side."

"The Cherokees can try to stay out of the conflict," Bradburn said, "but I can guarantee you that if the Anglo Americans keep the power, they will take away your land, just like what is happening in the United States with your people."

"And you Mexicans?" Dutokeh said. "What is to guarantee that you would not do the same?"

Bradburn was on confident ground now and he warmed up to the subject. "It goes back to General Terán. You met him back in 1828 or 1829."

Dutokeh acknowledged that he had.

"He always considered that the key to our security was to have Texas populated by Mexicans and immigrants who weren't Anglo Americans. That's where you come in. You're immigrants, actually refugees from the United States since they're driving you away from Georgia, the Carolinas, and Tennessee. That's how your part of the nation came to Texas in the first place. There's no guarantee that the Anglo Americans won't drive you away from Texas too."

"It is true," Dutokeh said. "Our experience has been very bad with the whites, but I do not see your country being any better with red people."

"What is he saying?" Filisola asked Bradburn in Spanish.

"He thinks we're just as bad with Indians as the Anglo Americans are," Bradburn said back in Spanish.

"Tell him," Filisola said, "that we make a distinction between Indians who are peaceful and work the soil, like he and his people are, and the ones who are savage. There are Indians like his people living peacefully all over the republic."

Bradburn translated and explained the point. Dutokeh did not seem impressed. He just nodded with a slight look of annoyance on his face at the paternalism.

An impasse of sorts had been reached and Filisola retreated from his arguments to maintain cordiality.

When the dinner ended, Bradburn walked James and Joe outside to their horses. "You have to understand," he said, "General Filisola has only the most sketchy understanding of the slave situation. It is logical to him that they would rise up to support our troops. But I tend to agree with you more. There would be too much to prevent that from occurring. It is not something that can be counted upon."

"What more do you want of us?"

"Nothing, really. Just your opinions. I was trying to dampen his enthusiasm for trying to foment a slave rebellion."

"What about the Indians?"

"Oh," Bradburn said, "that will probably go ahead. I'm not so sure that Dutokeh and the Cherokees will be a part of it and the Comanches are unpredictable, but at the least we will keep exploring an active alliance with someone for when we retake Texas."

"And if the slaves don't help?" Joe said.

"If you mean, would they still be slaves? No, of course not. It would be in our interest to free them whatever they did since that would ensure their loyalty."

"And the whites? What would happen to them?" James asked.

Bradburn kicked the dirt. "A lot of them would probably have to leave, especially the ones that took part in the rebellion. But not all of them."

On the way back into town James thought about all the talk at the dinner. What they saw in him and who he was were not the same. He did not really have that much interest now in looking back at Texas.

He resumed the normal routines at his stall in the market. Occasionally he thought about what had been said at Bradburn's house and he thought about himself. Maybe his dismissal of what they had said was too quick.

He was free but incomplete. He had found his freedom but then they had killed Elizabeth, as if to exact one last punishment on him, a punishment that he would carry deeper within himself than the scars on his back from the whipping. The pain from the whipping had gone away, but the pain from her loss would never go away.

He was cobbling boots alone one afternoon when he looked up and saw Pedro Gómez Quintero standing and looking at him.

"I thought you would never look up," Pedro said. "You are so engaged in your work."

"I almost did not recognize you. You have changed."

"We have all changed."

"We are still friends," James said. "I have thought of you often."

"I heard what happened to your friend."

"She was more than a friend."

Pedro nodded his head sadly. "I know."

"How did you hear?"

"The story traveled far of the black cobbler who went back to Texas to rescue his love. I have even heard a song written about it. It is such a sad story."

"There is a song?"

"Well, it is also a romantic story." Pedro shrugged. "We are a romantic people."

"You are still with the army?"

"Sort of."

"Sort of?"

"I'm no longer with the regular troops. But I am still attached." Pedro waved his hand in a circle as if to try to clear up the confusion of his words. "I am on a special mission and I want to talk to you about it."

"Then you came here looking for me on purpose. You did not just happen to be in the market and discover me."

"That is right. I went looking for the black cobbler because I knew who he was, and everyone in Matamoros knows where to find the black cobbler."

"I think I know what you want to talk to me about, but before we talk about it, let's get something to eat."

"That is right. We are old friends. We must share food together before getting down to business."

James put down his tools and closed the door to his stall. Then the two of them walked to the far corner of the market and out the door to where a small cafe stood. James greeted the woman who served the food and then they sat down at a table. The cafe had not filled up yet for the mid-afternoon comida. The woman placed bowls of tortilla soup in front of them and they began to eat.

"I was at your house," James said. "There are now whites living there. What happened to your folks?"

"Driven out. Shortly after you and I left there Anglo men came and said that they were not safe."

"Because of you?"

"Yes. They knew about me. My father—you know how he is—he told them that he was proud of me. They did not like that. They said that he was a traitor to Texas, that all traitors' land would be confiscated, and that even if it was not, he would have more to worry about for his safety from them than from the Comanches."

"So they threatened him and he left."

"Yes. He came back to Tamaulipas."

"Where are they now?"

"South of here."

"You have seen them?"

"Yes. They are all right. They knew about you from the stories and songs. They send their greetings. But that is not what I want to talk to you about. I am going back into Texas next week and I want you to come with me."

He guessed what was coming. The city was filled with men plotting the reconquest of Texas, the reality he had first become aware of at Bradburn's house.

"You spoke once," Pedro continued, "with General Filisola and General Bradburn."

He acknowledged with a nod that he had.

"There is a mission related to that that I would like for you to be a part of."

"Into Texas?"

"Yes. In a very little time the army will reenter Texas and assume control again. For right now the strategic purpose is to gather information about conditions there. Find out where the Anglo-Americans are vulnerable. Keep them off-guard and nervous with hit and run attacks. Keep contact with our allies among the Indians. And, very important, forge alliances with the Negroes. That is where you come in."

"You want me to talk to slaves along the way."

"Yes," Pedro said. "That is part of the plan. We already know Indians who are friendly to us. They will introduce us to other Indians. It is the same with you. We will scout an area where there are Negroes working in fields. Then, when it is safe, you will go out and talk to them and tell them that the Army is coming to liberate them and that when it comes they should rise up against their owners. If the Anglos have to be fighting against the Indians and their own slaves, our army will be able to defeat them quickly and regain control of the territory."

"Land for the Indians and freedom for the slaves. That's what the army promises."

"Yes, in brief."

He leaned back in his chair and sighed. It was logical and it was a job that he could do. He wasn't so sure about the fighting part of it, but that could be learned. He certainly could talk with slaves. They would find him someone interesting to talk with since just shortly before he had been like them, a slave. Now he was free. He had succeeded at the fantasy held by most slaves of actually escaping to freedom. He could also tell them about what it was like in Matamoros. That would be interesting to them. But the Mexicans would not want him to encourage them to escape. They wanted them to stay where they were so that they could cause problems for the masters when the army came. What would he say if a slave asked him for advice on how to escape? Though he did not consider it to be of overwhelming importance in his decision, he felt that he did owe the Mexicans something since they had helped him to escape. He could repay that debt now. It would probably put him in good stead with them for the long run. More important, what little he could do to avenge the Elizabeth's murder, he could do now. "I will go with you," he said at last.

Pedro looked relieved. "I knew you would."

"I don't know why. I would not have gone for that reason six months ago."

"You are a different man now," Pedro said. "Six months ago you were content with being free. Now you want to do something with your freedom."

"You're crazy," Joe said when he heard about the plan. "You almost got yourself kilt the last time. Now you want to push your luck again."

"I have to. This is personal."

"Nothin' you do gonna bring that woman back."

"I know that," James said. "But I can at least strike back."

"Far as I'm concerned, I never want to go back there. It's too dangerous. I just want to stay good and escaped here."

"I've got to go back for personal reasons," James repeated. "But I also want to do something for this country that has been good to me."

"Hah," Joe laughed. "This country is too divided to call itself a country. You just got some friends here. That's all."

"No. It's more than that."

"I don't know what more it can be," Joe said. "But it look like you fixin' to go back to Texas. Well, that your decision. Maybe you become more of a hero in the eyes of these Mexicans and they write another song about you."

49

It took months for everything to get more or less back in order for Samuel Bingham. He had regained consciousness in the kitchen of the Holmes house just in time to see Dr. Grayson Jones pushing a red-hot knife toward the wound on his chest. They had then put a cup of rum to his lips and he had felt the liquor slither and burn its way down his throat till it merged with the pain from the chest wound. Then, although he had felt himself slipping again into darkness, he had been aware of what was being done to him. Jones had dug the lead out of his chest without the pain actually hurting. It was a strange sensation to be aware of bodily pain without feeling it. It would feel much worse when he woke up because it was so sore. The soreness would come and go in the months ahead, a constant reminder of what James had done to him; and Holmes would return with the further bad news that they had all gotten away, including his own slaves.

It could not have come at a worse time in the planting cycle. Bingham had to lend one of his slaves to Holmes, and he found himself short-handed. The women, Lily and Sarah, at first willingly took over the chores formerly done by Rachel and Elizabeth. In time they tired of the extra work and clamored for replacements.

Bingham's farm and household had been damaged, but his pride had been damaged more. Other men knew that his own slave had shot him. He kept seeing James's face in the instant that he fired, completely catching him off guard and, worse, humiliating him. A thousand times he thought of how he could possibly get even with him. That could not happen though, however much he wished it to. James was gone forever down into Mexico where he would never be found.

The damage to the farms proved to be temporary. With the Mexicans gone it was much easier to buy slaves, and both he and Holmes had found the needed replacements within a few months of the escapes. The costs had been high but both men had felt that, with cotton prices rising and the danger of a Mexican invasion receding, these were costs that would soon be recovered. Everything was back in order for Bingham except for his wounded pride and knowing that James had gotten away with escaping not just once but twice; and if you counted the escape a number of years back, it had been three times. The last time he had not just left, but left with other slaves and had shot him. Worst of all, Bingham knew that other men now considered him to be weak and unable to control his slaves.

"You are not going to believe what I have just heard," Holmes said one morning. He had walked in the door and caught Bingham just finishing breakfast. "James has been spotted back in Texas."

"What?" Bingham jumped to his feet. "That black sonofabitch is back in Texas!"

"That's right, or so they tell me. According to Fred Davis, James approached some of his slaves about starting a bloody revolution. One of the more sensible ones immediately reported it to him."

"How do you know it was James?"

"He said he had worked for a no good master named Bingham. That's you, I presume," Holmes said with a sardonic smile.

Bingham ignored the attempted humor and said seriously, "Where is he now?"

Holmes shrugged. "Who knows? For sure, he's not around Fred Davis's property."

"When did this happen?"

"Last week."

So, he's back, Bingham thought. Would he show up here? Or, for that matter, maybe he had already been here and he had not known it. He began to think of his slaves and wondered whether any of them were as loyal as one of Davis's had been. After picturing each one of the now twelve in his mind, he had to admit that probably none of them would tell him if James had been by. This was one of his failings. He was not able to inspire trust in the men who worked for him. He really had not cared much about them beyond the work they did, and he was quite sure that they did not have a care for him. He was not like his father, who had seemed to know his slaves much better. He had never really wanted to be like his father though. He preferred to have a strictly business relationship with the slaves. In part that came out of the experience with James, whom he had trusted and then experienced betrayal. You could not trust a Negro. This he had learned.

In the weeks that followed a good many rumors circulated from farm to farm and plantation to plantation between the Brazos and Colorado rivers. James was not the only unauthorized Negro to be spotted. Mexicans from Matamoros were in the area too, and they were stirring up Indians. Others said that there was a combined army of as many as a thousand Mexicans and Indians either on the way to the area or hidden somewhere within it. All of this caused the militia to be activated, and both Bingham and Holmes took their parts.

"I don't believe it," Holmes said upon hearing the latest rumor from Bingham. They were riding together to meet with other militia members. "It doesn't make sense."

"What doesn't make sense?"

"That the Mexicans would risk so many men when they have so many problems on their side of the Rio Grande."

"You mean the rebellion?"

"Yes, or course. There's always one revolution or another going on in that country. And they've got problems with France too."

"What's that up there?" Bingham said, pulling up the reins of his horse.

Holmes stopped and cupped his hand over his eyes. "Looks like a herd of horses being driven somewhere."

"No. There are men on all those horses. Let's catch up and see who they are."

Holmes sighed. "Could be dangerous. I wouldn't want to stumble across that Mexican Army, just the two of us."

"Me neither. We'll keep our distance. But we need to find out who they are. Come on." Bingham spurred the flanks of his horse and took off in a gallop."

When they had caught up enough, they could see that there were men indeed who had been riding the horses and that some wore sombreros. Others from the distance appeared to be Indians and Negroes. All of them were stopped now, resting by a spring.

"Let's get a closer look," Bingham said.

"You're crazy. What more do we need to know?"

"We can get an exact count and survey their arms."

"I'm not getting any closer," Holmes said.

"Then wait here," Bingham said impatiently as he turned his horse off the road so that he could circle up around to get a closer look.

A couple of hundred yards to the side of where the men were milling about the spring, he dismounted and tied his horse to a tree. Then he crept through the pinewoods as quietly as he could till he could see clearly. There were forty men—equal numbers of Mexicans and Indians. There looked to be three or four Negroes. Then he looked really closely at one of them.

He could not tell for sure, but if one of them was James, this one had to be the one. The others were either too tall or too fat. But the one that looked like he might be James was crouching down with his back to him. He thought about circling around to the other side to get a look at the face but then decided that would be too risky. Forty to one odds against him were not good if he was discovered making noise trying to get around; and he wouldn't be able to take his horse. He would just have to wait to see if the Negro turned around.

Bingham trained his rifle on the Negro just in case and waited. In a couple of minutes Bingham saw that the Negro was standing up and stretching and beginning to walk toward the horses. He followed his progress with his eye sighted down the barrel of the rifle. Then he saw the very familiar face of James as he turned to answer someone. It was risky to take a shot but he might not get a chance to shoot the man who had shot him, to return the favor so to speak. He knew that the rifle was a little off to the right so he first trained it between the eyes of James and then moved it slightly to the left. There would be time to get one shot off and then he would have to beat it out of there as fast as possible. Bingham let out a breath of air to steady his aim and pulled the trigger.

50

James heard the loud crack and saw a puff of dirt shoot up to the right of him.

"Get down," Pedro shouted at him. "Someone's shooting."

Several of the Cherokees rushed out of the temporary encampment and circled toward where the shot had come from. The rest of the men stayed behind trees and rocks until they came back, waiting to see if there would be more shots. But there were none and eventually the Cherokees returned empty-handed.

"He got away," Dutokeh said.

"Time to get moving," General Savariego said.

James assumed that someone had taken a pot shot at the camp as a whole and that he had had the bad luck of being the one it came closest to. They had been away from Matamoros for over a month now. They were on the move every day, never camping in one place for more than a night. That was just the way it had to be, Pedro explained. It was inevitable that lone Anglo Americans would see them, like the one who had just fired the shot, and they would tell the authorities who, in turn, would send out militia. But by always being on the move, there was less chance of being overtaken by these larger militia forces. The only exceptions came when they met up with allied Indians. Then they would spend a few days in their villages. The Indians had their own ways of discouraging Anglo Americans from wandering too close.

He had seen all manner of Indians in the last month. There were Indians who didn't seem to have any fixed place to live and Indians who lived in their own villages hidden far away from the roads. He was amazed to find that there was a village not so far from the Bingham property. He had never known about it in all of the time that he had lived there. They had known about him though. This he found out when one of the chiefs said through a translator that he recognized him and had wondered why he was no longer with the whites. To a one the Indians all complained that the whites were moving in and taking the lands on which they either hunted or planted. Savariego always promised that as soon as the army arrived, their claims to the land would be recognized and honored. But not all of the Indians were in agreement. The Texas Rangers seemed to enjoy the support of some Indians. The Comanches were not aligned with anyone and quite capable of attacking either one of the sides.

Pedro recounted to him that there were some differences among the loyalist Mexicans whom he had visited. They welcomed the idea of Mexico reasserting control over Texas, but had ambivalent feelings over who would actually be in control of the country. They wondered whether the army that came would be federalist or centralist. It would then come down to a question of whether they preferred to be under a

Mexican faction other than their own, or continue to be under the Anglo Americans.

They broke camp, rode all the rest of the day, and camped the next night in low-lying hills. The next morning they were riding again. The general destination now was to reach the Cherokee lands near Nacogdoches. They had supplies with them that included guns and ammunition. Some would be left for the coming battles, but the most would be distributed to badly armed warriors who would be joining them there to bolster their strength.

It was ten o'clock that morning when one of the Indian scouts came back to say that there were Negroes working in a field up ahead. This was James's work, so he rode ahead with the scout on a deer trail through woods. Up ahead he could see the woods ending and a field beginning. The scout stopped his horse and jumped to the ground, motioning for James to do the same. They crept to the edge of the field and kept hidden behind trees.

There were a half dozen Negroes working in the field all right. But there was also a white overseer there on horseback. It was hard to know what to do. James looked at the Indian, who did not speak English or Spanish. The Indian understood the problem and drew his knife and then with his finger traced a line across his throat.

James shook his head. The overseer carried a rifle and would see them coming. Besides, any action like that would terrify the slaves and no telling what they would do. He and the Indian would just have to wait to see if the overseer was going to leave. He would give it an hour and if he did not leave, then they would have to give up and leave.

Twenty minutes later the overseer said something and turned his horse and rode in the other direction. He had probably just been there checking on the slaves, James thought.

As the scout kept watch he walked out from the woods. The Negroes saw him coming and stopped what they were doing.

"Good day," James said.

"Good day to you," one of them replied. "Who are you?"

"James Robinson."

"You're not from around these parts, are you?"

"No, from Matamoros."

One of the slaves took off his hat and wiped his brow. "Now that ain't in Texas. It's way down south from here. What are you doing up heah?"

"I'm up here to help slaves like you. I used to be just like you but now I'm free in Mexico."

"That right. They don't allow no slavery there. You like it there?"

"Lot better than when I was a slave here."

"How'd you do it?"

"Escaped during the war." James answered.

"Then why you back heah now?"

"I'm with some army troops."

"Whose army?"

"Mexican."

"They're here?"

"Over there," James said, motioning toward the woods across the field. "I'm with a small scouting group setting things up for when the whole army comes to liberate Texas and you. You know that under the laws of Mexico there is no slavery."

"But this ain't Mexico."

"It still is according to the Mexican Army. These whites who are in charge here are in violation of the law. It'll only be a matter of time before they're all in jail or dead."

"So this Mexican army is coming back to take over. When's this going to happen?"

"In a month or two."

"And why are you telling us all this?"

"'Cause we need your help. The liberation will go a lot faster if Negroes help out."

"How we supposed to help if we ain't got no guns?"

"We can get guns to you when the time comes," James said.

"Ooo-ey. You are talking about something dangerous. You sure you know what you are talking about?"

"I'm as certain as I can be," James said. "Now I got to move on. You can tell all the Negroes you see that the Mexican Army is coming to liberate them and that they have nothing to fear from it. And when you see it coming, if you want to help, just present yourselves. They'll give you guns."

With that parting instruction, he left them. It was hard to tell what they thought. But in part it really didn't matter since it was enough to spread the word among them to welcome the army when it came. There would be enough of them who would help to make the plan work. It would only work, though, if the army was visibly there and quickly reestablishing its authority. Then the Negroes would be able to see that their masters had no one to back them up. Then they would have the encouragement to join the revolt.

The days and weeks ahead proved to be troublesome. They reached the Cherokee villages near Nacogdoches expecting to find warriors ready to join up with them. Instead they found a wait-and-see attitude on their part despite accepting the weapons that they had brought. With that turn of events there had been no alternative but to head back toward Matamoros, but more circuitously than they had come. The Anglo-American militia and Rangers knew the route that they had come up from Matamoros. The route back had to be different and more indirect. Now it was clear that they were on their trail. It was turning out that it was far easier to get into Texas than to get back out. Whatever they got into here, they would have to get out of themselves.

They were west of Brazoria now and headed south for Matamoros. They unpacked their horses and set up camp for the evening high on the side of a hill that overlooked a river. They could also see the trail in to where they were, but someone traveling on the trail would not be able to see them. It was a good spot that could easily be defended if need be. Unrolling the stiff heavy woolen blanket that he had brought with him from Matamoros, James smelled the smoke from many campfires embedded in it. There was also the rank smell of dampness and dirt. He carefully spread it out a few paces back from the fire where one of the Mexicans was heating up tortillas. That would the extent of their meal tonight. There had been no time for hunting. They were on the run.

"It does not look good," Pedro said. He had just returned from patrolling. "They are catching up to us and they are well armed."

"How many?" Vicente Córdova asked.

"At least fifty."

James heard this and he began to feel fear for the first time.

"They will not be stupid enough to attack us tonight up here," Córdova said.

"I think not," Pedro replied. "We are safe for the night. They know we are in these hills, but they do not know just where. They would be very foolish to come looking in the dark. They will wait until dawn."

"Then we must move before dawn."

James heard all that he needed to know and crawled under the blanket. There would be little time for sleep this night and he had best get as much of it as possible. But sleep did not come right away. He thought about other times when men had been after him. Before it had been when he had been trying to escape from slavery. Now it was because he had voluntarily gone into enemy territory. He had come back to the very danger he had escaped from as if drawn to it by some compulsion that he had allowed to take over. He had allowed Pedro to talk him into it so easily. Perhaps it was because there was something within him that had said that he would not be able to live with himself if he did not strike back at least once. Now, though, he felt less like an avenger than a hunted animal whose time was running out.

51

Samuel Bingham looked across the pine desk at Merle Sharp, the new land surveyor in Brazoria. What had been granted to him by Mexican authorities ten years earlier now had to be legalized in the new Republic of Texas system. It was all only a formality but a very necessary one. The land was his and no one doubted the claim. But with all of the new people pouring in from the United States and nearly all of them looking for land, it was important to protect his land legally. Aside from taking care of these legal formalities, he was also in town to find out what he could about James and the band of renegades he was with. It had been a couple of months since he had stumbled across them and then they had disappeared.

"What do you hear about the Mexican and Indian invaders?" he asked Sharp after signing the final document.

"Man came in earlier this morning and said they've been tracking them from Nacogdoches. He thinks they've got 'em surrounded over near Waterloo."

"I hope he's right," Bingham said, barely suppressing the excitement that he felt at hearing this news.

Sharp cocked his head. "Me too."

Bingham put the legal papers in his satchel and left the office looking for more information about this new rumor. This he was able to find at the militia headquarters on the other side of town.

"We're getting up a group to go there now," Zachariah Nettles said. "Want to come, Samuel? We could sure use all the help we can get. No telling how many Indians and Mexicans there are."

"Runaways too," Bingham said.

"Yeah, them too. Come outta their hiding places."

Bingham thought that he really should get back to the farm but then again had a personal stake in this if James was with them. "You've got one more volunteer," he said, patting the side of his carbine.

52

A morning mist covered the grove of trees where they had taken cover the night before. It was cool when he rolled out from under the damp woolen blanket and pulled on his boots. Off to his left James saw the morning campfire with an open pot for coffee warming. Most of the other men were still sleeping, their bodies like lumps under the blankets. The cawing of a crow broke through the mist. From his bag he took out the tin cup he had carried from Matamoros and dipped it into the open coffee pot. They had not eaten the night before and his stomach welcomed what little sustenance the coffee provided. As far as he could tell, they had finally lost their pursuers two days before and were now in the clear. If it kept this way they would be back in Matamoros in a week.

Here and there the sun was beginning to burn off the mist and men all around him were pulling themselves out from under their blankets when in the distance a shot rang out followed by many more.

"Nos están attacando," someone shouted out. "¡Apúranse!"

James grabbed his rifle and was starting to load it but it was far too late for that. Horsemen were riding and firing into the camp. They had taken them completely off guard.

"Run!" Pedro shouted at him.

Then he saw Pedro crumple with blood spurting out of his forehead. He dropped the rifle and began to run. The clearing was filled with men shooting. He made for woods on the left side, running now as as he could. A piercing pain shot through from the back of his thigh and he felt his leg crumple and then he fell. Running men and horses were passing him now. More shots and groans surrounded him.

He lay as still as he could now. Best that they think that he was dead. And he waited for a shot in the head as the shooting was still continuing. Then the shooting died down and stopped and he stayed still till he dared to open an eye.

"This one's still live," the man standing over him with a pointed rifle shouted.

"Where's he hit?"

"Looks like in the leg."

"Okay, get him over with the others."

"Okay nigger," the man with the gun pointing over him said. "Get up and start walking over there."

As he lifted himself up he felt the pain in his leg intensify. Then he shifted all of his weight to his good leg and slowly looked around. Bodies lay everywhere. There must have been twelve altogether.

"Get moving, nigger," the man with the rifle said.

"Can't, my leg's shot."

"Then hop dammit or I'll shoot the other one."

He hopped till he was back in the clearing. In the center the Texians were tying the arms of two of the Shawnees who had been taken prisoner. With one last hop he reached them and collapsed onto the ground. Someone was now tying his arms behind him. Then he felt another rope being slipped through the knots on the one holding him so that they were all tied together with their backs to each other.

Across the clearing he saw two men picking up one leg each of Pedro's body and then drag it over to where the other bodies were piled on top of a hastily built structure of logs. They were piling brush over the tops of the bodies. The only thing good was that there were less bodies and prisoners than men in his group. At least some had gotten away. Then he saw the torch placed on the brush that began to crackle and then roar as the fire picked up.

This he could not bear to see so he closed his eyes and he felt his body begin to shudder. The pain from the leg wound was coming and between the two types of pain he felt an overwhelming urge to die quickly. The trees ahead of him began to swirl and he felt himself sink into oblivion. There was the Bingham plantation in Tennessee and the first days that he had taken notice of his color and now it had come to this.

The pointed toe of a boot kicked against his wounded leg brought him back to consciousness. "Get up, boy," he heard the kicker say. He felt himself being untied from the two Shawnees. They pulled him up and half-dragged him across the clearing where a tall thin man, older than the rest, stood.

"Who are you?" the thin man said.

"James Robinson."

"From around here?"

"No. Matamoros."

"Runaway then?"

James said nothing in response till one of the men who had dragged him over shouted, "Answer! He asked you a question."

"I am a free man."

"Well then," the tall thin man said, "if you are so free, you must have gotten yourself in trouble with these Mexicans and savages of your own free will. You're smart enough to know that you're in a heap of trouble here in the Republic of Texas."

"There is no Republic of Texas," James said. "This is Mexico. When the Army comes back, you will be in a heap of trouble."

The thin man looked down at him. "You realize what you're saying boy?"

James looked up at him. "I know what I'm saying."

"You just sealed your fate." Then the thin man said to the other white men. "Take him back to the Indians and get up a firing squad."

53

Samuel Bingham had been riding hard from Brazoria toward Waterloo with the eight other militia volunteers when he had heard the shooting in the far distance. They had quickened their pace till they had come across a militia member riding out of the woods toward Waterloo. He pointed them toward where the battle had taken place.

"Any runaways with 'em?" Bingham asked.

"There's one nigger."

"Know his name or what he looks like?"

The militiaman shook his head.

"Might be my runaway," Bingham said. "He joined up with a renegade group. Let's go take a look."

"Better hurry," the militiaman said. "They're fixin' to shoot'em now."

Bingham spurred his horse forward.

"What are you in such a big hurry for?" Zachariah Nettles said when he caught up with him. "You don't want to see them shoot those men, do you?"

"It's personal," Bingham replied. He could not be sure whether James was among the condemned and he was not sure of what he could do at this late hour. But he had to try. He spurred his horse on as hard as he could and was far ahead of the men. This was one of those times when you had to be on time. Once it was over, it really was over. He kept expecting to hear the shots announcing that he was too late to do anything. Finally he reached the clearing and jumped off of his horse in time to see James and the two Indians being tied to trees. Across from them four men were loading their rifles.

"Hold up," Bingham shouted.

"Who are you?" the thin man who was organizing the execution said.

"Samuel Bingham. Militia from Matagorda."

"What's your business?"

"That nigger's mine. Ran away some time ago."

"He ain't no simple runaway, Bingham. He's taken up arms against Texas. Two of my men been kilt fighting them. No way you can take him away with you."

"That's not what I came for," Bingham said. "He shot me when he ran away and I wish to return the favor."

The thin man looked at the men who had finished loading their rifles and were standing listening and waiting. "This is a strange request, Bingham, but I don't suppose there's anything wrong with it if one of these boys over there wants to give you his place. But I don't suppose they will want to after all the trouble we went through."

"I'll offer any one of you five dollars to take your place," Bingham said.

The firing squad members looked at each other and then one of them said, "I'll oblige you," and handed his rifle to Bingham.

"I'll use my own," Bingham said, handing the rifle back.

"All right, now that that's settled," the thin man said. "We'll proceed."

Bingham sighted his gun and looked straight into the face of James. It had gone on for far too long, like a lingering illness. But now it was finally being resolved in a way that he never would have imagined ten years earlier when they first came to Texas. It was better this way, though. There would be finality and the demons of his humiliation vanquished. Then he heard the order to fire and squeezed with all the determination that he had in him.

Afterword

Escape from Texas is a historical novel. As such it blends fiction with the realities of the period depicted. Its protagonists and antagonists—James Robinson, Pedro Gómez Quintero, and Samuel Bingham—are fictional. A number of the other figures who they interacted with, including General Terán, William Travis, Joe, and John Davis Bradburn, were real historical personages. There are completely made-up events as well as others that closely follow what is believed to have actually happened, including the concluding scene.

More important, though, is that the main themes of the novel are patterned on the historical significance of the period and place depicted. To understand that significance, we must jump forward historically and then look back in hindsight.

The twentieth century was the "American Century," as Henry Luce dubbed it in 1941. By then the Americans (as people in this country imperiously appropriated the hemispheric name for themselves) had eclipsed the British Empire that had been the undisputed imperial power of the previous century.

But no one knew that in Texas back in 1828—the beginning year of the novel. East Texas, as it is known now, was a backward frontier area of the Mexican federation, the northeastern corner of the state of Coahuila y Tejas. Three groups warily and sometimes violently confronted each other over who was to prevail: Indians, the original inhabitants, who, along with migrant Indians being pushed out of the United States, sought to preserve their hunting areas; Mexicans, who wished to farm and ranch; and Anglo Americans, who also wished to farm and ranch, and who, most importantly, carried with them the slave system of the South.

Unbeknownst to them at the time it was in the struggle between these three groups that the roots of the American Century began to take shape. In short order, the Anglo Americans would triumph—first in the 1836 Texas War of Independence and then in the 1846–1848 war with Mexico. In 1848, with their troops occupying Mexico City, the Americans would force Mexico to cede over half its national territory for some twenty million dollars. The sold area included what would later become the western half of Texas, New Mexico, Arizona, California, Nevada, Colorado, Utah, and part of Oklahoma—in short, the contemporary Southwest of the United States.

Out of the Southwest in the second half of the nineteenth century would come half of the United States' total mineral wealth, including gold and copper, oil, the ranching industry, and California, which includes what is perhaps the richest agricultural area in the world. It is doubtful that without this windfall bonanza of wealth the United States would have been propelled in fifty short years to the first rank of world powers. It is also doubtful that if the area had remained a part of Mexico that the severe first world/third world inequality that exists between the two most populated countries of North America would be nearly as severe as it is today.

Even in hindsight, after the facts, there are different perceptions and interpretations of the events. Controversy continues to surround the motive forces of the Texas War of Independence. On one side, American folklore has traditionally celebrated the war as a heroic attempt by frontier pioneers to break out from under the yoke of cruel Mexican oppression. The view from south of the Rio Grande (called the Rio Bravo there) is distinct, seeing the war as the first step in American expansionism which would shortly cost Mexico over half of its national territory.

Connected to these opposite claims is the interpretation of the role of slavery as a motive force. Mexico abolished slavery on September 16, 1829, the ninth anniversary of its own independence from Spain. Two months later, after a windstorm of protest from slave-owning Texas colonists, the central government allowed slavery to remain in Texas under restrictions. On April 6 the next year, the Mexican government issued the Bustamante Decree, which forbade the importation of new slaves and severely restricted new immigration from the United States.

Though President Santa Anna rescinded the Bustamante Decree (or April 6th law, as it was popularly known) in 1833 after special pleading from Stephen Austin, it and the issues surrounding it contributed to the causes of the Texas War of Independence. Even before their victory in the war, the Anglo-American colonists made one of their intentions completely clear in their prospective constitution: they explicitly legalized slavery and slave importation—quoted word for word in the novel.

The Mexican government never recognized the independence of Texas. Throughout the rest of the 1830s and the 1840s it planned to retake the breakaway department, even sending troops to briefly occupy Bexar, which later became better known as San Antonio. Numbers of loyalist Mexicans, Indians, and Negroes supported the Mexican efforts to retake Texas, engaging in guerrilla skirmishes that lasted throughout the years of the Republic of Texas. On July 16, 1839, as a result of their rumored collaboration with Mexico, the Cherokees under Duwali were massacred at the Battle of the Neches and their survivors driven out of Texas, some into Mexico.

Slavery accelerated in size and density in Texas. Between 1836, the year of independence, and 1840, the slave population doubled; it doubled again by 1845; and it doubled still again by 1850. In 1836 there was one black for every six whites; by 1847 it was one black for every three whites.

As more slaves came into Texas, more escaped to Mexico. Matamoros in the 1840s had a large and flourishing colony of ex-slaves from the United States. Though exact numbers do not exist, it is possible that as many slaves escaped to Mexico as escaped to Canada. The Mexican government, for its part, encouraged the slave runaways, often with offers of land as well as freedom. This became a continuing issue of tension between the United States and Mexico, with the former continually lodging diplomatic protests against the latter down to the onset of the Civil War.

East Texas then, in the 1820s and 1830s was the location of a world-historical nodal point, or crucial turning point in the development of what was to follow. It is in such nodal points of history that men and women struggle with and resolve the problems of their personal and public lives with varying degrees of consciousness of the historical issues at stake.